"So we pretend to kiss, go on a fake date to the dance and your ex finally moves on. What do I get?"

Camden drew her bottom lip between her teeth. "I'll suggest to my grandfather that selling you those forty acres might not be a terrible idea."

Levi held out his hand, and when Camden took it, he pulled her closer. "But you haven't asked me to the dance," he said. It was fun watching those golden flecks in her eyes sparkle to life in annoyance.

"Levi, will you go with me to the Christmas dance tonight?" she asked, and turned on her heel without waiting for his answer. Levi held fast to her hand, and Camden turned to look at him again.

"Yes, I'll go with you. Do I get a corsage?" She pursed her full lips, and Levi couldn't hold back the grin any longer. "You're cute when you're annoyed."

"You're annoying when you speak," she retorted. "Are we doing this or not?"

"Yes, we're doing this."

"Good." Camden pulled away from him and said, "I'll see you tonight." Then she was gone.

When Levi got to the pasture, he was still thinking about kissing Camden. What kind of man cheated when he had a beautiful woman like Camden already in his bed? What kind of man pretended to date a woman like Camden, not to get her into bed, but to enter into a real estate deal with her grandfather?

Dear Reader,

I adore Christmas! From the music to the lights to the anticipation as gifts pile up under the tree, Christmas is by far my favorite holiday. I especially love small towns that go all out with one special event after another until everyone falls into a holiday stupor after the last sip of eggnog.

Levi and Camden are positive of one thing this holiday season: they won't be falling in love. But when Camden's sleazy ex comes to town, suddenly they're knee-deep in a pretend affair that is feeling all too real...and if they aren't careful, love is exactly what they'll find under their tree this year!

Christmas in a Small Town is all about the small-town celebration of Christmas and, of course, the greatest gift we can give one another: love.

I love hearing from readers. You can catch up with me through my website and newsletter at www.kristinaknightauthor.com or on Facebook, www.Facebook.com/kristinaknightromanceauthor, and if you're a visual reader like me, follow my books on my Pinterest boards—you'll get some behind-the-scenes information and lots of yummy pictures.

Happy reading!

Kristina

KRISTINA KNIGHT

Christmas in a Small Town

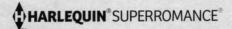

HARLEQUIN®SUPERROMANCE®

Recycling programs
for this product may
not exist in your area.

ISBN-13: 978-0-373-64054-6

Christmas in a Small Town

Printed in U.S.A.

www.Harlequin.com

Kristina Knight decided she wanted to be a writer like her favorite soap-opera heroine, Felicia Gallant, one cold day when she was home sick from school. She took a detour into radio and television journalism but never forgot her first love of romance novels, or her favorite character from her favorite soap. In 2012 she got The Call from an editor who wanted to buy her book. Kristina lives in Ohio with her handsome husband, incredibly cute daughter and two dogs.

Books by Kristina Knight

HARLEQUIN SUPERROMANCE

A Slippery Rock Novel

Breakup in a Small Town
Rebel in a Small Town
Famous in a Small Town

Protecting the Quarterback
First Love Again
The Daughter He Wanted

For everyone who loves the holiday season!

A heartfelt thank you goes out to Lyle and Lois at the Serendipity Stockdog School. I am awed by not only what you teach the animals in your care, but the way you teach them. The next time I'm in town, I want to see that herding ducks thing live and in person instead of on video!

CHAPTER ONE

SHE SHOULD HAVE changed before she got on the highway. Or off the highway onto the two-lane road leading into town. Or at any of the rest areas between Kansas City and Slippery Rock County line—she had to have passed at least twenty during the trip south.

Camden Harris eyed the stained parking lot and the layers of bodily fluids, oil, gasoline and whatever else that covered the pavement. She swiped a hand over the miles of tulle covering her hips, creating what her mother had described as "bridal perfection" in the dress shop a few weeks earlier. She eyed the stained parking lot once again. Nothing about this gas station was bridal perfection, but then, what small-town gas station ever promised perfection? Gas stations were about utility. Getting to the next stop on whatever journey a person was taking. Camden sighed.

She could chance that whatever gas was left in the tank of her car would get her where she was going—although the red needle was pre-cariously close to the E marker—or she could get out.

Knuckles rapped sharply against the window beside her, causing Camden to jump in her seat. An older man wearing a faded Slippery Rock Sailors ball cap and an old gray hoodie with grease-stained jeans stood beside her car.

"Fill it up?" he asked. His voice held the gentle twang of the Ozarks that she remembered from childhood summers spent at her grandparents' dog school just outside Slippery Rock. "I'm guessing you want the high-octane stuff," he said, not waiting for her to answer as he grabbed the nozzle from the machine at his back.

Camden rolled down her window. "Thank you. I didn't realize gas stations still offered full service fill-ups."

"Most people do it themselves. You had the look of a desperate woman, though, and I'm guessing that dress and my concrete wouldn't mix well."

The older man pulled a squeegee and a bottle of window washer fluid from a receptacle on the side of the gas pump and began washing her windows. In the stark lighting from the overhead bulbs, she realized she'd hit about a million insects on the drive down, and that the light rain storm she'd passed through around Springfield had left a thin coating of dust and spots on her windshield.

"Thanks, again," she said, and opened her phone. She'd gotten this far on her own, but now that she was in town, she would need help finding the old farm. She knew it was vaguely west of town, but other than that, she had no clue how to get to her grandparents' place. How ridiculous was that?

She was a twenty-seven-year-old woman, had been successfully navigating the Kansas City streets since she was sixteen, had managed to find her way around both Chicago and Atlanta on her own. But she had no idea how to get to her grandparents' farm in a town tinier than the neighborhood surrounding her parents' Mission Hills mansion.

Camden entered the address from her phone into the car's navigation system and waited.

"We don't get many cars like this one around Slippery Rock. Not even in the summer when the tourists come to town," the older man was saying as he finished cleaning the windshield. The gas pump clicked off, and he plopped the squeegee and bottle of cleaning fluid back into the side bin. "Passing through?"

Camden handed the man her credit card and shook her head. "Visiting for a while."

"I'll be right back," he said and hurried inside to ring up her purchase.

"Address not found," said the voice of the Australian man she'd chosen for her car's navigation system. Usually she liked the voice she'd dubbed Thor, but this time she didn't like what he had to say.

Camden entered the address again, and while she waited, looked up her grandparents using one of those online address finders. The same address she had in her phone popped up on her screen just as Thor told her, again, that the address didn't exist.

"You're just messing with me now, aren't you?" she said.

"Nope, it really is thirty bucks on the nose," the gas station attendant replied, passing her card and the receipt slip through the window.

Camden cringed. "Sorry. I was just talking to Th—uh, my navigation system. It says my destination is an unknown address."

The older man shook his head. "Happens all the time down here. Those computer maps focus a lot on the big cities, but you get into the rural routes and they don't know whether they're coming or going. Where are you?"

Camden blinked. "Where am I what?" She was in her car. At the gas station. Unless she'd fallen asleep at the wheel and was dreaming all of this while in some weird comatose state in a hospital. She pinched the back of her hand. Nope, that hurt. She was awake, all right. Awake and wearing her wedding dress at what was probably the last full-service gas station in the entire world.

"Where you going?"

"Oh, of course. Harris Farms." Camden began reciting the address from her phone, but the older man cut her off.

"Sure, Calvin and Bonita's place. You're gonna continue on this road till you hit the grocery store. At the light you'll turn south for a couple of blocks before taking Double A Highway West out of town. You'll turn back north a few miles out when you see the county road sign, then follow 251 until you get to their lane. Can't miss it. Bonita bought Calvin one of them big mailboxes a few years ago, in the shape of a collie. I swear you could fit a small child in that thing." He tapped the roof of her car. "Nope, we don't see many cars like this one around town. You have a nice evening, ma'am."

Camden's mind swirled with the information the older man had offered up. Straight to the grocery store, follow that road to the highway, follow the highway to the county road that would lead to the farm. She could handle this. Camden put the Porsche in Drive and waved to the older man as she pulled back onto the road that led through Slippery Rock.

Just as he'd said, a few blocks on, the grocery store stood on the corner with a flashing red light. Camden flicked her blinker on and turned toward what she vaguely remembered as Slippery Rock's downtown. The old brick buildings looked familiar, but the large grandstand area was new. Several of the buildings appeared to have recently constructed roofs or walls, probably cleanup from the tornado that had nearly ripped the little town apart last spring. She came to a stop sign, and hanging on the pole was a sign for the highway the older man had mentioned. With an arrow pointing to the right. The only problem was the other sign, the one that read One-Way Street, with an arrow pointing the opposite direction. Maybe there was an outlet.

Camden followed the one-way street down a few blocks, until another arrow directed her to turn left to meet back up with the highway that would lead to her grandparents' farm. She continued to follow the arrows and the highway markers until she wound up exactly where she'd been before—the same corner with the same arrow indicating the one-way street, going the opposite direction of the highway she needed to take out of town. Maybe she'd missed a sign somewhere.

Camden pulled the Porsche through the intersection and followed the signs, paying close attention to each intersection she passed. And wound up back at the first, with the arrows pointing in different directions, and Thor's voice echoing in her mind, telling her that the address she wanted did not exist.

There had to be another gas station or some business where she could ask for directions to get out of the endless loop she'd found herself in. Camden began following the signs again, this time focusing on the businesses—all with closed signs in their windows—along the route. The only place that appeared to be open at—she checked her watch—eight o'clock on a Wednesday evening was what appeared to be a bar. The Slippery Slope.

Camden blew out a breath, contemplating her options. Go into a bar in what would have been her wedding dress. Keep driving around in circles until the other businesses opened the next day. She'd already decided that she wouldn't call her grandparents, for two reasons. First, they didn't know she was coming. And second, as sleepy as this part of the state was, it was still dangerous at night. She didn't hunt, but she knew it was deer season. She wouldn't risk her grandparents trying to drive into town at night when deer would be out.

Yet driving in circles seemed pointless.

Decided, Camden parked the Porsche outside the bar and stepped out, shivering at the chill in the air. Camden gathered as much of the skirt of the dress in her hands as she could. This street seemed marginally cleaner than the gas station lot, but neither could be confused with the clean flooring of a church. She had no intention of wearing this dress again, no intention of getting married at all, but she didn't want to ruin it.

Until five hours ago, she'd been ready to become Mrs. Grant Wentworth, the debutante, beauty-queen wife of the next partner of Wentworth, Carlson and Wentworth, the best law firm in Kansas City, Missouri. Grant, a future mayor of Kansas City, would become governor one day, and probably president of the United States eventually. But instead of marrying him, she was running away because while she'd been prepared to marry a man she didn't quite love, she wasn't prepared to marry a man who'd had so little regard for Camden that he'd been banging her maid of honor. Yep, in the closet just down the hall from the room where her mother and several friends waited for the society wedding of the season to begin. She'd wanted Heather's opinion on the dress and hair combination before walking down the aisle, and thank God she had. If she hadn't gone looking for her maid of honor, if she hadn't heard the noises in the closet, she might have married that stupid son of a bitch. Might have truly thrown her life away.

When she saw Grant bent over Heather in the closet, though, it was as if a Camden she barely remembered had woken up. That Camden didn't scream or yell—she simply turned around, grabbed her bag from the chaise in the dressing room and walked out. She'd walked out of the historic mansion where the wedding was to be held, gotten into her car, driven to her mother's house and thrown some clothes into a suitcase, and driven out of their suburb, out of Kansas City. Out of a life she'd never wanted to live, and away from the rut her life had been in since joining the Junior League after that last pageant five years ago.

Camden caught a glimpse of herself in a picture window. Not a single lock of hair out of place, but there was a crease where the seat belt had lain across the bodice of the dress. She smoothed her hand over her hip and felt a few errant threads along the tulle roses. She should have left it at her mother's house, where it could have been returned and become some other bride's perfect dress, but she had been afraid if she took the time to change, someone might have found her. Convinced her to go back.

Now this dress would never see the inside of a church. Camden sighed. It wasn't her choice for a dress but it was pretty. And she'd ruined it. After an hours-long car ride in the cramped front seat of a Porsche, it would never be the same; she might as well stop pretending she could box it up and send it back.

Camden released the skirt of the designer gown, letting it trail along the pavement as she continued toward the bar.

If she were to consider marriage one day, it would be on her terms. No formal society wedding. No fiancé her parents liked more than she did. And no wedding that would seal a partnership or a merger, like the one she'd barely escaped a few hours before.

Her life had suddenly become an adult version of the game Clue. Only instead of the groom murdering the bride in the study with a candlestick, he was doing the maid of honor in the closet of the historic Kansas City mansion.

It wasn't that she'd expected Grant to vow his undying love, but she'd assumed—at the very least—those vows would have included fidelity. And that his fidelity would have been in effect since his proposal over the Fourth of July weekend.

Camden sighed. Obviously, she'd been wrong. On so very many levels.

And now, wearing what would have been her wedding dress, she had to face however many strangers were in this small-town bar and ask directions to the only place she'd ever felt was home.

LEVI WALTERS TOSSED a dart toward the board on the wall, liking the sound the sharp tip made as it sank into the rubber bull's-eye area. "That's three. You're toast," he said as Collin Tyler, his best friend, picked up three darts from the booth the two of them shared with Aiden Buchanan, another of their group.

It was Wednesday night, and usually there would be five of them here. Shooting darts, drinking a few beers. But James had his hands full with Collin's sister, Mara, and their two-year-old, Zeke. Adam was spending more time with his wife, Jenny, and while Aiden had been doing a good impression of a man about to propose ever since Julia Colson blew into Slippery Rock, he was here at the bar while Julia was going over lighting and dress options with Savannah, Levi's sister and Collin's fiancée. Julia ran a dress shop and was opening a destination-wedding business in a Victorian home that overlooked Slippery Rock Lake. Tonight, she and Savannah were testing out lighting options for Savannah's upcoming wedding to Collin. Since the two of them were also trying on wedding gowns, Collin was banned from the area. He didn't seem to mind.

For that matter, Aiden didn't seem to mind being away from Julia, and that was just weird. For the past couple of weeks, the two of them had been inseparable. Maybe Aiden was getting itchy feet again. He'd only been in Slippery Rock for a couple of months, but that was several weeks longer than any visit he'd made since leaving town after high school.

And why did Levi care what was going on

in Aiden's love life? Or, for that matter, the love lives of any of the guys he'd grown up with? It wasn't like he wanted what they had. Maybe someday, but not right now. He had enough going on in his life without dealing with a woman, too. This winter, he wanted to work on new organic lines for the dairy. They had milk and cream and cheeses, but he wanted to add ice cream and other dairy products. That would take time to develop.

He still had to figure out what to do with the older dairy cows, those his father had used before the dairy went organic. Right now, the cows were on land rented from a neighbor, but that wasn't a permanent solution.

And his parents weren't getting any younger. Sooner or later, they were going to have to downsize, and that would mean moving them into town from the farmhouse where they'd lived for the past thirty-five years of their marriage. That would also take time, not just with the move, but with the convincing. He didn't want Bennett and Mama Hazel to be overwhelmed with a big house, like their neighbors Calvin and Bonita Harris.

No, he had too much going on to be worried about a relationship, too. So why was he getting all maudlin when he should just be shooting darts?

Collin wrote down his scores on the little sheet of paper on the table, and Aiden grabbed the third set of darts to begin throwing. No bull's-eyes for Collin, but he was still hanging in. Aiden would drop out after this round, no matter what he shot. He had no chance of catching Collin, much less Levi.

"What's going on with you?" Collin asked and then finished off his bottle of beer. He signaled Juanita, the bar's waitress, and she started in their direction.

"Shooting darts," Levi said and finished his own beer. Maybe he had a brain tumor, pressing on whatever part of the brain that was in charge of impulse control. Because the idea of starting up a relationship, just because every person he knew was now coupled off, was definitely impulsive, illogical. Maybe the fog was some kind of early-onset seasonal affective disorder. Not that the changing weather had ever affected him before. He considered the empty bottle in his hand. Maybe it was just time to switch to water. It wasn't even nine, but it was a Wednesday, and he had work tomorrow.

"Anything else?" Aiden asked.

Levi rolled his shoulders. Would his two friends back off? He was fine. Nothing was wrong. He wasn't jealous; he didn't want what his friends had. Not right this second, at any rate. "Would the two of you just shoot darts? Since when is darts night also psychoanalysis night, anyway?"

Collin and Aiden exchanged a look. "Since its inception?" Collin asked. "Since you blew out your knee? Since Adam got messed up in the tornado?"

Okay, so he'd led a few interventions–slash–drinking nights. That didn't mean he was in need of one himself. "No therapy needed, just the check. Unless you guys want another?" he asked, indicating the empty bottles on the table.

"Another round, boys?" Juanita arrived at the table, and began clearing the empty bottles.

"Nah, I'm headed back to the orchard soon," Collin said.

Aiden tossed his last dart at the board and hit ten. "Nothing here." He pulled the darts from the board and put them into the holder to the side. "Julia should be finished up with Savannah by now, and I promised I'd measure for the new cabinets out at the Point."

The Point was what locals called the Victorian home, set on a low cliff, overlooking Slippery Rock Lake. It was one of the oldest structures to have survived the building of the lake fifty or so years before and had been vacant until Julia came to town in September and bought it, and partnered with Shanna's, the original owner of the dress shop. Her plan was to turn the old house into a destination wedding venue, although Levi couldn't see many people intentionally choosing Slippery Rock as their wedding event location. He loved his small town, but it wasn't touristy like Branson or Lake of the Ozarks. The first wedding set at the old place would be Collin and Savannah's, on New Year's Eve.

"Same, just the bill, and a water if you've got time," Levi added.

"If I've got time." Juanita chuckled and looked around the nearly empty bar. "Nope, just can't fit the water into my busy night."

"So what's up?" Collin asked again after Juanita had left. Aiden gathered the other darts, putting them in the holder on the wall. He joined them at the table.

"Where were we?" Aiden asked.

"Headed back to the orchard as soon as Levi here spills on whatever it is that's eating him."

"Nothing's bothering me." He had a new

product line to develop—that meant new vendors to contact and new contracts. Aging parents. A sister getting married in a few more weeks. He didn't have time for a relationship. And he wasn't jealous of the relationships his friends were building with their women. Nothing was wrong.

"Sure, you *always* try to kill the dartboard when you throw."

"And you *always* get that look in your eye when you're taking aim," Aiden added.

"What look?"

"The look like we're on the fifteen, fourth down, and need one more touchdown to win state," Collin offered.

"The look like you're about to unload on the running back across the line, hoping for a first down," Aiden offered.

"You guys didn't play with me when I went to defense. How would you know what I looked like?"

Collin blinked. "High-definition TV. Replay shows. And, you know, we did play with you all through junior high and high school. Doesn't matter if you're quarterbacking or playing the defensive line, like you did in college and the pros—the Levi Walters focus is the same."

"Also, and I don't think we can emphasize this enough, at least three of your throws pushed the dart through the board and into the wall. So what's up?" Aiden rolled his bottle of beer through his hands, making it scrape against the table.

It grated on Levi's nerves.

Just because he had a few strong throws didn't mean something was bothering him. He certainly wasn't upset. Levi Walters didn't get upset. He focused on the job at hand until it was done. Then he focused on the next job. He didn't get upset. He didn't get bothered. He didn't wonder why good things happened to other people.

Which made it all the more weird that he couldn't seem to stop thinking about the guys and their new relationships.

But he definitely wasn't bothered.

"What do you guys think about the bike trail they're talking about? The one that will follow the old railroad tracks?"

Collin and Aiden exchanged a look. Neither said anything.

"I don't think it's a good idea. That land is undeveloped, but it's adjacent to the ranch, and to the Harris property, too. Could lead to mischievousness, especially during the summer months."

"He broke out a twenty-five-cent word," Aiden said.

"Still avoiding the actual conversation, too," Collin replied. As if Levi weren't sitting right there with them. As if he weren't trying to hold a legitimate conversation instead of whatever it was the two of them were trying to get him to admit to.

"Nothing's bugging me." He settled his shoulders against the back of the booth. "Just here to throw darts." The guys stared at him. "And that bike trail could lead to all kinds of other prob—"

The door to the bar opened, and Levi stopped talking. He couldn't breathe, and that didn't make any sense at all. It was just a woman. Pretty brown hair pinned up on her head. Pale, creamy skin. He couldn't see her eyes from this distance, but her lips were red and turned up at the corners. She twirled a set of car keys on her finger, and gathered the train of her dress—a wedding dress, and that was weird—in her other hand, saving it from the closing of the door.

"You were saying?" Collin prodded him, but Levi couldn't remember what the three of them had been talking about. He'd been a little annoyed with them. Something about the bike trail that still hadn't been decided on by the county commissioners.

His mouth went a little dry, and he forced himself to take a long breath. Tried to make his heart stop galloping in his chest. She was… the most beautiful figment his imagination had ever created.

"Something's definitely wrong with him," Aiden said. And Levi realized his friend was right.

There was something very, very wrong with a man who hallucinated a beautiful woman in a wedding dress. Something really wrong.

Maybe it was a brain tumor, only instead of giving him migraines, the tumor was causing him to imagine beautiful women. Or maybe Adam's epilepsy was catching. Airborne or something. Didn't he say that things went fuzzy and stopped looking normal when a seizure was starting?

A beautiful woman, in a wedding dress, in his favorite bar was definitely not normal.

Levi blinked. The woman was still there, standing just inside the door of the bar, looking a little lost. She wasn't fuzzy around the edges or anything.

So she wasn't a hallucination, then. He could

cross brain tumor off the list of things that were wrong with him. That left the epilepsy. Except that couldn't be it, because a person didn't catch epilepsy because he hung out with someone who had the disease. That left...jealousy.

Was he jealous of the relationships his friends were in?

Levi Walters didn't get jealous. He had everything he needed at the ranch. More than he needed when he thought about the plans he had for the business that had been in his family for three generations. He didn't need a girlfriend. Definitely didn't need a woman in his life who walked into a bar in a wedding dress. That was a little too desperate, even for a guy who hadn't had sex in...more months than he cared to recall.

She focused in on Merle, the bartender, and crossed the room, the heels of her shoes click-clacking across the hardwood floor.

"I'm lost," she said, and Levi found himself leaving the booth and crossing the bar.

He wasn't looking for anything. He knew who he was, knew where he was going. He had good friends, and he was happy for those friends.

But there was something about the woman who'd just walked into the bar that was different.

Maybe, just this once, he should let himself consider something different.

CHAPTER TWO

CAMDEN CROSSED THE hardwood floor to the bar, wishing she'd at least grabbed the ballet flats she'd worn to the wedding venue that afternoon. The ballet flats wouldn't echo so much in the cavernous space. At least there weren't hundreds of people crowding the dance floor, staring at the strange woman in the wedding dress. She really should have thought this whole thing through. Should have taken five minutes at her mother's house to shed this ridiculous gown.

She couldn't stop now, though. She was probably the only person in the world to get lost in such a small town. And she wasn't even really lost. She knew she needed to get on the highway—it was those stupid one-way streets that were causing the problem.

The older man at the bar wore a faded Kansas City Royals T-shirt and was wiping down a mahogany bar that already looked pristinely clean.

"I'm a little lost," she said, trying to keep her

voice low. The only full table was in the back of the bar. What appeared to be three locals were sitting there, and they probably couldn't overhear her. Still, she didn't want to advertise her predicament to the whole town. "I'm trying to get on the highway, but every time I hit the intersection, the one-ways make me go the wrong direction."

"You want a beer?" The older man's voice was gruff, but he didn't seem annoyed.

"No, just the directions, please." He looked at her for a long moment. "Okay, and the beer."

He grabbed a bottle from below the bar and slid it across the shiny surface. The mountains on the label were icy blue. She eyed the amber bottle for a long time, hearing her mother's voice in her head. Telling her wine was a lady's drink, but that a lady never had more than half a glass. As if she were living in the 1800s and not the twenty-first century. Real women drank. And she was tired of living by rules that were not her own.

What the heck? She was in a bar, in a strange town, wearing her wedding dress. "Do you have a bottle opener?"

"Twist-off cap," the bartender said. He put the cleaning rag away.

Camden twisted the cold cap and grinned

when it popped off in her hand. She put the bottle to her lips and grimaced as the beer hit her tastebuds. Maybe her mother had been right about this one thing; wine was very definitely preferable to the contents of this bottle, pretty amber color or not. She pushed the bottle away. "About those directions?"

"Sure. The mayor ordered new signs after the tornado. Only the crew working that area were supposed to put them just past that intersection. You go one more street past the light, then hang your right and follow the signs from there."

That seemed simple enough. "Great. Thank you."

"No problem." He seemed to consider his answer. "Course, you could also just take this street out to the bridge and catch the highway there."

Even better, she wouldn't have to make her way around the one-ways again. "Thank you, again. How much for the beer?"

"Three dollars. You taking it with you?"

Camden eyed the bottle. "No. No, I've had enough. You wouldn't have a white wine?"

The older man narrowed his eyes and snatched the still-full bottle from the counter.

"This is a bar, lady, not a nightclub. We serve beer, whiskey and tequila."

"Don't you let this old geezer bother you, honey." A Hispanic woman came up to the bar, holding a round serving tray. "I'm Juanita, and this is Merle. He's harmless, but he has definite ideas about the differences in bars, nightclubs and bar-and-grill-type places. We have a nice boxed blush—"

"You said I only had to keep those frou-frou drinks on hand during the summer."

"Summer ended about a week ago—"

"A month and a half ago, woman, it'll be Thanksgiving tomorrow," Merle put in, but Juanita kept talking.

"We're still working through the supply. Don't worry, you'll be disappointing your customers with the limited menu in another few days." She turned back to Camden. "So you want that glass, honey?"

"Sure." As much as she wanted to get out of this dress, she still hadn't figured out what she was going to say to Calvin and Bonita when she showed up on their doorstep.

Hi, how've you been? seemed a little too breezy, especially as she hadn't seen them in more than a decade. She wasn't up to spilling the whole sordid tale about her mother's expectations, the life she'd hated and the colossal mistake she'd made when she accepted Grant's proposal. Not yet.

Juanita delivered the glass of wine, and Camden took a sip. It glided down her throat, tasting sweet and soothing. So much better than the beer. She hooked her heel around the rung of one of the bar stools and settled herself at the bar.

Calling her grandparents was probably the best next step, but what if they were already asleep? Or didn't want to see her? She'd sent Christmas and birthday cards, had invited them to her graduations, but other than that, her grandparents were strangers to her over these past few long years. All she knew about them was that they were far away from Kansas City. And that there was no love lost between her father's parents and his former wife.

This was childish, wasn't it? Running away from her problems instead of facing up to them wouldn't solve anything. But what was done was done, and she was too exhausted to drive all the way back to Kansas City tonight. Maybe she should get a hotel room and wait until the morning to see her grandparents.

"You seem a little lost," a man suddenly said beside her.

Camden took another sip of her wine, weighing her options. "No, I have the directions. Thanks, though."

If she went to a hotel, chances were she would talk herself out of visiting Calvin and Bonita at all.

If she drove back to Kansas City, chances were her mother would convince her Grant would change his ways once they were married.

She didn't want to be married to Grant. Not because it would cement her stepfather's place at the firm, and not because Grant wanted a former beauty queen on his arm at political events. She didn't want to be married to Grant. At all.

For the first time since she found Grant and Heather in the closet, Camden felt as if she could breathe. She didn't want to be married to Grant. That was settled.

"A woman doesn't walk into a bar wearing a designer wedding gown, alone, without being a little lost," the man said, and there was a teasing note in his deep voice.

"I don't want to be married," Camden said, testing how the words sounded when spoken aloud. No twinge of anxiety. No guilt. She didn't want to be married. "I didn't pick out this monstrosity of a dress, and I didn't pick the groom, but I am picking where I'm going from here. And I'm not going down the aisle."

"That's good, since we don't seem to have an aisle." The words seemed to rumble from his chest, vibrating between them and making the little hairs on her arm stand up. Weird. Camden rubbed her hand along her arm, and the engagement ring she'd forgotten to take off winked at her in the dim light.

"Wow," he said, taking her hand in his and letting the light catch the different facets of the three-carat ring from Tiffany & Co. Camden kept her focus on the half-full glass before her. Her skin tingled where his hand held hers, and tension set off butterflies in her stomach. Camden snatched her hand away. How could she have forgotten the ring? And how could she have a physical reaction like this to a guy she'd known for only a minute? Her stomach never got jumpy like this with Grant. At best, she was lukewarm around him, but suddenly, the bar seemed hot and humid, as if hundreds of people were crowded into it on a steamy summer day. Not a handful of people on a chilly fall night.

"Nice rock," he said, leaning against the bar, facing the big dance floor she had crossed only a few minutes ago. Camden kept her focus on the wineglass. She wasn't interested in marrying the man she'd been engaged to for the last few months, and she wasn't interested in flirting with the man who'd sidled up next to her in this bar.

"I didn't pick it out." Now, where had that come from? She'd been blown away by the ring when Grant presented it to her back in the summer. Sure, it was heavy on her hand, and it snagged on everything. But it—

No, Camden shut down that train of thought. Yes, Grant had bought the ring for her. But Grant had also been screwing her maid of honor in a closet about fifteen minutes before they were supposed to pledge their love—or at least fidelity—to one another. So…she had no reason to feel sentimental about this ring or guilty that she was happy she could now take it off and never wear it again.

Camden wasn't quite sure what she wanted, but she knew diving into a flirtation with a stranger wouldn't help her figure it out. She needed to focus.

"It's a nice-looking dress, though."

"Not my style."

"I find that hard to believe. You wear it too well."

Because she'd been trained to wear it well. Her mother had started her on the pageant circuit when she was nine, and after her father died, the pageants had become almost weekly occurrences. Still, having a stranger comment on her appearance was nice. Maybe a little stalkery, but nice. "Yeah, well, it's not like it takes a special set of skills to wear designer clothing."

"I don't know about that."

Okay, that upped the stalker level a little too high. She was not going to let some cowboy in a small town take her to his trailer just because she'd walked out on her old life.

"I'm going to finish this glass of wine and be on my way. You can scurry back over to your buddies now and tell them what a hateful witch I am."

"You don't seem all that hateful. Maybe a little sad. But not hateful." His voice was kind, kinder than she probably deserved after walking away from everything and everyone the way she had done. But she still wasn't letting a stranger talk her into bed. No matter how sexy his voice sounded in the darkened bar. "You're wearing a ring you didn't pick out, and a dress that isn't your style. Seems to me like this has not been your day."

"Try lifetime," she said and twirled the stem of the wineglass between her fingers. And she was not going to keep talking to a perfect stranger about her life. She was not feeling like herself, but she wasn't completely desperate.

"How much do I owe you?" she asked Merle, who was looking from Camden to the man at the bar and back again.

"Ten dollars," the older man said.

"I'll take care of it."

"I pay my own bills," Camden said and turned to look at the man standing beside her.

He was tall, built like a football player. His skin was a rich brown, and there were golden flecks in his brown eyes.

And she knew him.

He was taller than she remembered. His shoulders wider. His voice deeper. But the laughter in the gaze was the same, as was the crooked tilt to his mouth. Camden clapped her hand over her mouth. Oh, God, she wanted to sink through the floor of the bar.

Of all the bars, in all the world, why did she have to walk into Levi Walters's?

"Camden?"

Levi blinked once, twice, then a third time. This brain tumor–epilepsy thing was getting out of hand. He'd gone from imagining a beautiful woman in a wedding dress to imagining Camden Harris—a girl he hadn't seen since he was fourteen. Not girl. Woman. From the tilt of her pretty head to the smooth shoulders, full bust—

Levi slammed his hand against the bar, and Camden jumped. So did Merle. And he was pretty sure he'd gotten the attention of everyone else in the bar, too, from annoying Collin and Aiden to Juanita, who stuck her head around the corner of the door leading to the kitchen.

"Sorry." He swallowed. "I'm not crazy, right? You're Camden Harris."

"Hello, Levi."

Her voice was the same. A little twang, which was odd, because she lived in a fancy part of Kansas City and competed in beauty pageants. At least, she'd been on the posters of several pageants around the university campus where he played football.

Slight southern drawls weren't welcomed in those circles. For beauty pageants it was full-on, south-of-the-Mason-Dixon drawl or what he considered broadcaster cool, with no hint of an accent. From anywhere. Or maybe he was reading too much into a short conversation.

He needed to get a grip on himself or he was really going to lose it. Levi didn't like to prove people right on the crazy side of things. He was steady. Not impulsive. He considered options, developed a plan of action. He didn't rush into decisions.

He didn't even usually rush into flirting with women, especially women he didn't know. So, naturally, now that he had, it had to be someone he used to know.

"What are you doing here?" she asked, and the question threw him. What was he doing here? What was she doing here? And in a wedding dress?

"I live here." Levi sat on the stool beside her. "What are you doing here?"

A half smile crossed her wide mouth but didn't reach her eyes. Camden shook her head. "Paying my bill." She stood, and her high-heeled shoes clacked against the hardwood. She pulled a ten from the little bag strapped around her wrist and left it on the bar. "I'll see you around, I guess."

"I live here," Levi said and felt like an idiot for repeating himself. And in such a lame way. Of course they'd see one another—Slippery Rock was a small town. His ranch and her grandparents' farm were next to each other. It would be a miracle if he didn't bump into her now and again.

He reached out, and a sharp little burst of attraction hit him hard when his hand brushed her arm. Which was just weird. Sure, he'd felt a little heat when he took her hand to look at the glimmering rock on her finger, but that was when he'd been in the mood to seduce the sexy stranger at the bar.

Camden Harris wasn't a sexy stranger. She was the girl next door. The girl with the big brown eyes who tagged along after him during her summer visits with her grandparents.

The girl who hadn't been back to Slippery Rock in at least a decade and, as far as he knew, whom her grandparents hadn't seen in at least as long.

Calvin and Bonita had pictures of Camden, though, and he'd seen them on several occasions when he stopped in to check on them. One more reason he should have recognized her as soon as she walked into the bar. But he hadn't. The girl—no, woman—in those pictures was confident. Happy.

The Camden standing next to him at the bar…wasn't. Something had changed. Whatever that something was, it wasn't his business.

He should just back off. Camden Harris was a childhood acquaintance, not a personal friend.

"Yes?" she asked, and Levi realized his hand still gripped her arm, holding her in place. He let go quickly, and her arm fell to her side.

"Nothing, nothing," he said, and she turned to go. "Wait! You didn't say what you were doing back in town."

She turned to face him, and those big brown eyes went soft, her mouth turned down and Levi wondered what might have happened in Camden's privileged life that would make her look so sad.

So lost.

So…familiar.

And that wasn't right. Of course she was familiar. Her hair was the same walnut brown he remembered, and her eyes were still big and round and had those honey-colored flecks that mesmerized him. She was taller, but that was normal. What twelve-year-old didn't grow a few more inches in their teens and early twenties? He'd put on about fifty pounds of muscle and added nearly three inches to his height since graduating high school.

Only it wasn't the color of her hair or her eyes that drew him in—it was something else. Something to which Levi didn't want to get too close. Something that might be a little bit dangerous for a man who liked to consider and think his way through life, because his impulse was to pull Camden Harris into his arms to make that look go away.

Levi Walters had too much going on in his life to let a woman with a sad look on her face distract him, though. He had very specific plans, and those plans had specific goals, and getting distracted with Camden Harris was definitely not part of the plan.

"I'm just here for a few days. Visiting my grandparents," she said, but he didn't think she was telling him the whole truth.

"In a wedding dress."

She shrugged, and the half smile that crossed her face made a little of the lost disappear. "I already told you the dress isn't my style."

"And the ring wasn't your choice."

"Something like that."

The evasive answers were interesting. More interesting than the conversation he'd been avoiding with Collin and Aiden. More interesting than the fact that he had a video conference with his investment counselor in the morning about making an offer on a portion of the Harris land he'd been renting for the past two years.

"Is coming here your choice?"

She looked around, and he wondered what she saw in the weathered floor, the neon signs and the dim lighting. He saw familiarity. Safety. Home. The sign behind the bar had been partially unlit for as long as he could remember. The juke in the corner had played the same songs since he was in high school, with the exception of Merle adding Savannah's single a few months before. The vinyl on the booth seats was cracked, and the chairs were scuffed.

It was perfect to him. Not a shiny disco ball in sight.

"Yeah. Coming to Slippery Rock was my choice," she said, and when she looked at him again, he thought he saw more confidence in her expression. In the set of her shoulders. That zing of attraction buzzed a bit brighter. "I'll see you around, Levi."

"See ya around, Camden," he said as she crossed the room. Her footsteps seemed to echo in the bar long after the door closed behind her.

Camden Harris was back in town. This might be the most interesting thing to happen to Slippery Rock in...okay, that wasn't fair. A lot had happened over the past year. Savannah had scandalized the town, as had the revelation that Sheriff James Calhoun had been having an ongoing affair with the favorite local rebel, Mara Tyler. The tornado had nearly destroyed the town. And Aiden Buchanan had finally come back.

But Camden...

That was interesting on a whole other level.

"I guess we figured out what's bugging Levi," Collin said, coming up behind him at the bar. He pulled his wallet from his rear pocket.

"Yeah, we thought there was trouble at the ranch. Turns out, Levi Walters just needs to get laid," Aiden added. Levi started to give a sharp reply, but that would only encourage the two of them. And they weren't wrong.

Not that he was going to sleep with Camden Harris. That zing of attraction was just a zing. A reminder that it had been too long since he'd taken time away from Slippery Rock to be with a beautiful woman.

Like Camden. Levi shoved the thought away. "What do we owe you, Merle?"

"Thirty'll cover it," the older man said.

"I got it—loser buys, remember? And who was that, anyway?" Collin leaned against the bar, holding out a handful of bills to Merle.

"She looked familiar. Kind of," Aiden added.

"Camden Harris." Levi turned his attention to the door again and then pulled a few bills from his wallet, but Collin pushed the money away. Right. Because Collin and Aiden lost at darts. Levi needed to get his mind back inside the bar. "You remember. Calvin and Bonita's granddaughter. She used to spend her summers here." Neither Collin nor Aiden said anything, and that brought Levi's attention fully back inside the bar, not out there in the night with Camden. "She used to tag along with us to the lake on really hot days. Camden Harris."

Aiden snapped his fingers. "That's how I know her. She did the beauty pageant thing with Julia while they were in college. The two of them traded off winning and losing there for a while. Until Camden was crowned at the state level and went on to the national competition."

"Julia competed in pageants?" Julia was a beautiful woman, but she didn't have the slick polish Levi associated with beauty pageant contestants. She was too genuine for that. For that matter, so was Camden. At least, the Camden he remembered. The woman he'd spoken to a few minutes before was a stranger, in a wedding gown, wearing a ring she said she didn't want. Weird.

"Something her mom got her into. After her parents died, it was a way to keep that connection going. Plus, she wanted to save the money they left her, and academic scholarships only went so far. The pageant circuit paid the difference." Aiden leaned an elbow on the bar. "I wonder if Julia knows she actually came to town?" he muttered.

"Julia's been talking to Camden?" Even more interesting. Camden had made it seem like this visit was a spur-of-the-moment thing, but if she'd been talking to Julia, it probably wasn't. So what was up?

"They text, Facebook now and then. She was supposed to be getting married this weekend. Today, actually. Obviously that didn't happen."

Obviously. Levi watched the door for a few more minutes. Camden was engaged. Or had been engaged. Was still engaged? And now she was in Slippery Rock, wearing the dress and the ring, but apparently alone. Interesting on that whole other level.

"You fellas gonna leave sometime tonight? I'd like to close," Merle said. He was leaning against the counter on the back side of the bar, arms crossed over his flannel-clad chest. He tapped the toe of one well-worn boot against the rubber matting on the floor.

"Sorry," Collin said, pocketing the change Merle had left on the counter.

The three of them walked out of the bar, got into their cars, and each went in a different direction from there. Once Levi was out of town, he considered what might have brought Camden to town.

It could be she was just running away.

It could be that the deal he was about to close with her grandfather had brought her.

It could be anything, really.

The narrow road leading to the ranch and the Harris property split, and Levi paused, watching the lane that would lead to Harris land, for a long time. No taillights shone down the lane, not that he'd expected any, and despite the late November date, the foliage blocked out any light that might have shone from the porch or yard lights at the Harrises'.

Probably she was tucked up in one of the guest rooms Bonita kept in pristine condition despite the fact that no visitors had been at the farm since Levi was a teen.

Probably she was just here for a quick visit, like she'd said.

Probably he shouldn't wonder what might have brought Camden back to Slippery Rock.

In a wedding dress.

He really needed to stop thinking about what she looked like in that dress.

Levi put the truck back in Drive and turned to go down the road that would lead to his parents' home and then around to his own. All the lights were off at the main house, which meant Bennett and Mama Hazel had gone to bed and Savannah was spending the night at the orchard.

He shouldn't let Camden's reasons for coming to Slippery Rock get under his skin, but her evasive answers in the bar were doing just that. The memory of her soft hand in his still made his palm hot. But her evasiveness, that was the issue here. He had a deal going with Calvin, and he didn't want that deal messed up. More than that, he liked the older couple. They were like grandparents to him, and maybe it was crazy, but Camden showing up now, when they'd decided to sell—it only made sense if she wanted something from them.

Like money.

Levi gripped the steering wheel as he crossed over the cattle guard separating his drive from the county road.

He would find out what Camden was up to. Then he'd get back to his plans for Walters Ranch. And he'd take a weekend off, maybe go to Little Rock or Tulsa for a few days. He knew women in both cities who would be glad to hear from him, who wouldn't expect more than a weekend's worth of fun.

He turned off the truck and went inside, toeing off his boots in the mudroom and slinging his beat-up jacket on the wall hook.

Camden Harris was back in town, and he would find out what she was up to.

CHAPTER THREE

CAMDEN BLEW TWO sharp blasts into the whistle. The border collie who had been working his way through the course of inclines and tunnels stopped and his head swiveled to look at her. She held him there, not moving, for a slow ten count, then blew into the whistle again, giving him the go-ahead to complete the course.

She'd been back in Slippery Rock for only two days, and already she felt like the Camden she remembered from childhood. Not the worried, sheltered, bored woman she'd been in Kansas City. She wanted to stay here, and she was beginning to see a way she could. Maybe for a long time.

"You haven't forgotten," her grandfather Calvin said. He stood beside her, looking so much older than she remembered. And shorter, somehow. She didn't think the shorter was just because she'd grown taller since her last visit to Slippery Rock. God, she'd been a jerk to have stayed away.

Yes, she had only been twelve when her father died and her mother took her away from Slippery Rock, but she'd been an adult for many years now. She could have come down here on her own.

"I practiced," she said. "Mom had me in pageants, playing piano. I wanted to work a cattle dog as my talent, but she insisted piano was more ladylike."

"She wasn't wrong about that." His voice was gruff, and he put the stopwatch he'd been using in his pocket. "He's dropped three seconds, and it's not because of me."

"It's just a fluke."

"You said you'd been practicing."

"I did, for a while. Mom didn't care that I hated piano, and I wanted to do something else. So I found a dog trainer whose wife taught piano. I was obnoxiously horrible to every piano teacher in the Kansas City metropolitan area until she worked her way to the teacher with the dog-trainer husband, and I made that teacher a deal. I'd get Mom to spring for two hours of lessons if I could use half the time to work with the dogs."

Granddad chuckled. "And the teacher went for it?"

"She'd heard how obnoxious I could be."

"Sneaky. And a little bit brilliant."

Camden wasn't so sure about the brilliant part. Desperate was more to the point. And somehow dumb seemed to fit, too. Because a truly brilliant person would have stood up to her mother about the pageants in the first place.

A truly brilliant person wouldn't have gone to sleep the last two nights thinking about a two-minute conversation with Levi Walters. Or woken up the past two mornings still thinking about the man and half dreaming more conversations with him. Camden shook her head, hoping to dislodge the Levi train of thought. She refocused on her grandfather.

"Let's take him through one more time," Granddad said, and Camden blew three whistles. Jake, the collie, lined up at the starting line. When Camden blew the whistle, he started through the course.

Jake was one of only a handful of dogs left at Harris Farms, and the pup of a dog Camden remembered from her childhood. When she was younger, there had been at least thirty collies, Australian cattle dogs and other working dogs on the farm. Her grandfather had trained them to work on ranches all over the United States, Canada and Mexico. Working cattle, sheep, llamas. She'd come here hoping to work with Calvin for a while until she found her footing again, but the dogs he had now were mostly old favorites. They liked the course work, but they were more pets than working dogs.

Still, it was nice to be out here in the bright sunshine, watching the big collie go through the paces. She wondered what Levi was doing this morning. She knew he was running the dairy his family had owned for several generations. Would he still be milking cattle at almost noon on a Friday?

Not that it mattered if he was. Levi was a childhood acquaintance; she was a recently unengaged woman who was not—repeat, *not*—looking for a one-night stand. No matter how cute the boy she'd known so many years ago had grown up to be.

He kept the hair she remembered as dense and curly nearly shaved now. His eyes—eyes that has mesmerized her as a young girl—were rich and brown with a few hints of hazel or amber in the depths. His skin a shade lighter than his eyes. His smile a bit crooked, but that only made him more memorable to her.

The breadth of his shoulders made her heart skip a beat, and she could still feel his hand on hers.

Calvin snapped off the timer as the collie crossed the finish line, and that snapped Camden back to the course.

She would not let her childhood crush on Levi Walters take hold. Not again. He was her grandparents' neighbor, that was all. A guy she used to know.

"I think he could be ready for sheep or goats soon," Granddad was saying.

"Do you still have sheep and goats?" she hadn't noticed any early morning feeding runs, the pasture near the farmhouse was empty, and she hadn't hear any distant lowing or bleating from a small herd.

Granddad shook his head. "Hasn't been much need for a herd lately." A wistful expression crossed his face. "Probably won't be again, but it's nice to consider the option. I'm too old for full-time training."

"I'm not." She snapped her mouth closed. Camden wasn't a professional stock dog trainer. A couple of lucky runs, and a year or so of training lessons for competition dogs might have given her a little experience, but she didn't know the first thing about running a working stock dog school. And if Calvin still wanted to run a school, wouldn't he be running it?

The idea though, kept nagging at her. What

if Granddad wanted to rejuvenate the school? For her time with the trainer in Kansas City, she knew competition dogs were sought after and could sell for high amounts of money. Training fees on top of that…

If she could get just one dog ready for competition, she could help her grandparents rejuvenate Harris Farms. Could have a real reason to stay here rather than return to Kansas City.

"You want to train stock dogs?"

"There's a stock dog competition in Tulsa in a week. I couldn't train a dog in time, but if you want to build the school back up, it might be a good place to start."

Calvin turned an assessing eye on her. "That isn't an answer."

Did she want to train stock dogs? Camden blew out a breath.

Training dogs was something she'd done as a kid, something she'd done with her father and Granddad. It was miles away from training pageant contestants, a business she'd gone into with her mother after her last competition. Elizabeth always said to go into business with someone who was a success. Calvin Harris was a world class stock-dog trainer. His collies and Australian shepherds and cattle dogs were working cattle ranches and smaller llama and sheep farms all over North and South America. Cattle, llama, sheep. Camden gave Jake a rub behind his ear and tossed a treat into the air. The dog snapped it between his jaws, swallowing it whole.

"I might want to train dogs," she said, and although the words sounded weak, saying them aloud made her stand a little straighter. As if saying them had woken up something deep inside Camden. The way walking away from Grant had woken something else. "I'd at least like the chance to try."

Calvin nodded. "We haven't had sheep or goats around here for more than three years. Other than the cows Levi boards on the north side of the property, Jake and his buddies are the only livestock around."

The two then started toward the farmhouse where Camden had spent two of the best summers of her life. Before her mother married Darren Carlson, a rich lawyer from Kansas City. After that, visits to her father's family farm stopped abruptly. Her grandparents came to Darren's Mission Hills mansion a few times for Christmas dinners or the odd birthday, but she'd never been allowed to come back here after her father was killed in a drunk-driving accident.

When she called her mother Thanksgiving

morning to tell her she would not be coming back to Kansas City for a while and that she wasn't marrying that two-timing weasel, Grant, Elizabeth Carlson had hung up the phone. She hadn't called back. Hadn't texted. She probably expected Camden to snap out of it and show up for their traditional Black Friday shopping marathon.

Elizabeth would be shocked to see Camden in knee-high rain boots, nondesigner jeans and a hoodie instead of the high heels, designer jeans and cashmere sweaters she'd worn in Kansas City. Camden chuckled.

She'd never been more comfortable than the past two days, and that included wearing the baggy sweat suit she'd borrowed from Bonita on Thanksgiving afternoon to go into town to get a few items of clothing from her old friend, Julia's, store. Julia bought into Shanna's boutique earlier in the fall, and had plans to run a destination wedding business here eventually. She'd taken the polish and poise she'd learned from pageants and turned them into something real.

Camden wanted, desperately wanted, to turn her life into something real.

The rain boots, a deep navy, the only pair Julia had in stock, rustled through fallen leaves.

She had three more pairs coming, bought on-line just the night before—one with butterflies, another with little umbrellas, and a third with unicorns—and bought them all, along with several pairs of jeans, flannel shirts, tees, and a few tunics. It felt good to buy clothes that struck her as cute, that she liked, rather than clothes designed to impress others.

Although she wouldn't mind impressing a certain former football player. And that was a road she didn't need to start traveling down. The little hairs on her arms stood up and her tummy did a flip-flop. No, not going there. She'd just walked out on an engagement only a couple of days ago. Jumping into something with Levi Walters just because he made every last inch of her stand up and take notice was dumb. Worse than dumb—it would likely blow up the very life she wanted to build in Slippery Rock.

She needed to figure out who she was, without her mother's input and without an ill-thought-out relationship distracting her.

"Granddad?"

Calvin tilted his head and watched her but didn't say anything. It was his familiar way. He had been more talkative when she was a kid—at least that was how she remembered it.

Now, he almost seemed like a functional mute, only speaking when he'd measured each and every word.

"I'd like to train Six on my own, if that's okay with you." This was step one in the plan she'd been working on for roughly five minutes. A plan that seemed solid, despite its short life. She hadn't been here forty-eight hours, but even she could see the dog school was barely hanging on.

"Okay. He's not big enough to be a working dog, not even for smaller livestock."

"I'd like to train her for showing, not real-world herding," she added. Six was the youngest dog in what was left of Calvin's stable. The small dog was still a puppy, really. Calvin had found it on the side of the road last summer, and brought it to the farm. He was a smart little thing, and in the five minutes it took to get his food and drink into the run, she'd seen his eagerness to learn. She didn't care that she'd only met the dog, had only been back in Slippery Rock, for a little over a day.

The "for showing" bit got a raised eyebrow from her grandfather. "I trained stock dogs for working conditions. Not show rings," he said.

She'd only planned to be here a day or so, and then had vague thoughts about going back to Kansas City to figure out what she would do with the rest of her life. Running the pageant business with her mother held no appeal, but there had to be something else she could do back in the city.

But the rickety dog runs used to be solid. The handful of dogs remaining used to have dozens of friends, and the pastures around the farmhouse used to hold sheep and goats and a few ducks, too.

Then, there was the silly, slobbering Six. The little puppy was a runt and had likely been dumped on the side of the road by a breeder who couldn't sell him. But Six was all border collie—eager to learn, eager to please and eager to do. Camden fell in love with the little ball of fur that licked her face every time she picked him up. And she picked him up too often, she knew. Granddad treated his dogs well, but he treated them like workers. They received praise for a good job, treats, plenty of food and water. When the day was over, though, the dogs went into their runs for the night.

When the other dogs piled on one another, Six was left outside the group. Camden felt a camaraderie with the little dog. She'd felt left out of so many things in her life—from

decisions about pageant dresses to her actual
college degree program. Before running away
from the wedding, the only decision she'd
made in her life was to stop pageanting after
losing the national crown. And even then, she'd
fallen right in line with her mother's plan to
open a pageant coaching studio in the city.

Now she was here, and she was remembering how much fun she'd had with her grandfather's dogs and the dogs at the trainer's in
Kansas City. This was something she could
do, something that held value. Something that
would keep her near her grandparents. After
only a couple of days with them, Camden was
already dreading leaving them again.

Six clambered up to her when they stopped
at the barn. When the older dogs went inside,
Six stayed, looking up at Camden with excitement vibrating through his little body. She
took the green tennis ball from her pocket and
tossed it. Six took off at a run to chase it down.
The three other dogs with them this morning watched Granddad for an opening, but he
closed the kennel door, and they lost interest.

"Six is too little for real stock work," Granddad said. "He'd make a better pet than a working cow or sheep dog."

Six caught up with the ball and turned

around, the neon green of the covering showing between his teeth. He dropped it at her
feet and waited. Camden bent, tossed the ball
again and watched the puppy chase after it.
Granddad had stopped to watch, too. One of
the dogs in the run whined. He shot the dog a
look. It stopped.

"I was thinking, if it went well, I could train
a few others for showing. You know, stock-dog
showing is popular at fairs and things. People
who don't have ranches or farms can be just as
passionate about the training. About the sport
of it." Camden winced. Comparing her grandfather's work to a sport was probably not the
best wording. Other than baseball, she didn't
think he was interested in any sport.

"The sport of it, huh?" he said after a long
moment.

"If it goes well, we could maybe build the
dog school back up. It would create another
way to make money for the farm. More people would bring their dogs to you. You might
even have more outlets for runts like Six." And
she would have something to do. Something
that was hers.

Something she could be proud of doing—a
kind of fulfillment she never found while competing in pageants and then training contestants.

The beauty queen thing was never something Camden wanted—that was always her mother's dream. And the irony of her walking away from a world that required training only to go into a different sort of training wasn't lost on her. The difference was that the dogs she'd train would have a skill that required more than good genes.

Six returned, and she held the ball until he quieted. "One more time, then into the run. Okay?" The little dog's tail wagged, and he seemed to smile at her. "Last one, ready?"

The dog vibrated a bit harder. Camden threw the ball, and Six took off like a shot.

Camden knew she wasn't being fair about the pageants. There were legitimately good reasons to take part. The scholarships opened educational avenues for a lot of women. Pageants taught poise, even if they focused a little too much on appearance, in her opinion. They also celebrated talents like music and creative writing and put a focus on charity work.

But she didn't particularly care that she wasn't being fair; competing hadn't been her choice.

It had been her responsibility.

When her mother was floundering after her

father died, Camden competing in pageants seemed to lessen Elizabeth's depression.

Camden knew a lot of beauty queens who were smart, who were passionate about their work. Maybe if her mother had let her choose her talent or her volunteer work, she could have been passionate about pageanting. But Elizabeth Camden Harris Carlson had only cared about winning. As a Kentucky Miss and then a North America Miss herself, she knew what it took to win, and she hadn't allowed Camden to veer from the chosen path. Camden had worn the same color dresses as her mother, had sung the same song her mother sang during competitions and used the same platform her mother had used during her days as a pageant girl.

Hell, even if she'd chosen something of interest to her, Camden wouldn't have liked parading around on those stages, smiling until her cheeks hurt. That was what made it so easy to walk away, not only from the pageant world, but from the rest of her life. She only regretted that it had taken until now to walk out.

"Showing at fairs, huh?"

"It could be fun. Challenging," she corrected. Not once in her twenty-six years had she won a conversation with her mother or stepfather by describing something as "fun."

How ridiculous was it that she hadn't realized until she was twenty-six that she'd made only a handful of decisions about her own life?

"Nothing wrong with doing something just for the fun of it, kiddo," Granddad said. "You think I'd've trained dogs all my life if I was only in it for the money?"

She'd never thought about her grandfather as liking anything. "I, um…"

"I trained dogs because it was fun. It was challenging, too, but so was accounting. I hated accounting. Hated sitting at a desk all day just to come back the next and do the same thing again."

"You were an accountant?"

Granddad grinned, and it was the first smile she could remember passing over his face since she'd come back. "Did the books for most of the businesses in Slippery Rock at one time or another. Until I decided there had to be more to life than sitting at a desk fifty weeks out of every year. I didn't start the dog school until your daddy was in school. And I didn't start it because it was challenging, I started it because Bennett Walters needed a new stock dog to help keep the dairy cows in line."

Camden blinked. This was more information than she'd ever known about her grandfather. "You started the school on a whim?"

He shrugged. "I liked dogs. I didn't like the way the dogs were being treated when the trainer Bennett hired brought a few to his place. Figured it was something I could do that would get me outside a little more, especially during the summer months. So I trained that dog for Bennett, then a few more area ranchers asked for dogs, and within a couple of years I was spending nearly all my time training the dogs. Shut down the accounting business and haven't worried about it once."

"Then why aren't you training any longer?"

"A man has to retire at some point, Camden. I thought it was time." She started to protest, but Granddad held up a hand. "Why don't you tell me more about stock competitions."

"They use sheep, goats, chickens. A few calves. One trainer works a few dogs to get the animals from one pen to another, and they're judged on speed, agility and time."

"Sounds like what I did when I was training."

"It's a lot like a training session, actually." Camden couldn't get the thought of her grandfather retiring out of her mind. He wasn't that old, maybe in his midsixties. Sure, it was the age when a lot of people retired, but he'd loved working the dogs. How could he just stop? "That competition show in Tulsa I mentioned? Six couldn't compete in that one, but you could get an idea how the show circuit differs from the working circuit. If you wanted to go."

"Your grandma's not going to want to go to Tulsa this close to the holidays," Granddad said. He opened the run for Six. The dog went in and began sniffing. Probably for water. Camden grabbed an empty bowl from a shelf and filled it from the sink on the wall. Granddad did the same for the other dogs. "All these runs used to be full," he said after a while.

"I remember." She'd come out here every morning that last summer, watching Granddad and her dad and the collies from the hayloft above. Listening to the men talk about training methods. Elizabeth never set foot in the barn. She'd rarely left the porch, insisting that the dirt would ruin her shoes. God, her mother had hated this place. It was no wonder she had never wanted to come back.

Camden looked around. How could anyone hate the smell of fresh hay and summer sunshine? Even the gray November sky today couldn't take away the smells that lived in her memory. She remembered traipsing over these fields with Levi when the sun was high and the temperatures much hotter than on this chilly morning. He'd had this sky and these smells all of his life. Did he know how lucky he was?

"Your dad wanted to train a few dogs for the show circuit."

"I remember." He'd been so excited about the prospect. Her father, Bobby Harris, liked his job in the marketing department of the television station in Kansas City, but he'd loved coming back to Slippery Rock for vacation every year. Had been talking about getting a dog for the city, not a cattle dog, but a retriever or something.

"You don't have to train dogs because it was something your dad liked to do. Not even because it's something I like."

"I know. I just liked working with them. I'd like to work with them again." She didn't want to live her life in a quiet office, watching girls try on dresses and perfect their makeup.

"Then you should do it."

She inhaled, deeply. "Yeah?"

Calvin nodded.

Camden grinned at her grandfather, and he swung his arm around her shoulders the way she'd seen him embrace her father so many times in the past. "I'm glad you came home, kiddo."

"So am I," she said.

In the kitchen, her grandmother Bonita was just taking toasted cheese sandwiches off the stove. "You two are back early." She wore a neon-orange hoodie with black yoga pants and sneakers with bold orange, green and yellow striping on them. Her bobbed hair, dyed a crisp black, was perfectly arranged, and she'd put on lipstick.

Camden hung her jacket on the peg in the mudroom, slipped the muddy boots off her feet and smoothed her hands over her long brown hair.

"Couldn't stay away any longer." Calvin put his arms around his wife's waist, pulling her back against his chest and nipping her earlobe with his teeth. Bonita slapped at his hand and blushed as a grin spread over her face. "Camden wants us to hit Tulsa for a dog show in a week."

"Tulsa in the middle of the holiday shopping season?" Bonita shook her head. "I'm going into town this afternoon. Groceries. And then I need to stop in at the boutique. They're holding a pair of earrings for me. Want to come along?" Bonita looked pointedly at Camden. "I don't know what you could need after the five packages that were delivered this morning, but you might find something."

"I was going to—"

Bonita held up a hand. "Play with the dogs, I know."

"*Train* Six," Camden corrected. Bonita and Calvin exchanged a look.

"We're going to reopen Harris Farms," he said after a long moment.

Bonita's smile grew wider. "He's been pretending to be retired and complaining about having nothing to do for nearly a year now. Yet on only your second day back in town, you got him to agree to reopen? That is reason enough for a little celebratory shopping. You can help me pick out a few things for Tulsa, because while he's only going for the stock, I'm thinking I can get him to agree on at least one fancy restaurant."

Granddad frowned at his grilled cheese. "This is a business trip, Bonnie."

"Everyone has to eat, Cal. Who says we only have to eat at fast food restaurants?"

Camden watched the two of them bicker and thought it was the cutest thing she'd ever seen. She had been too young to realize whether or not her parents bickered, but her mother and stepfather didn't. Her stepfather made the decisions about schools and household budgets, and her mother made the decisions about vacations. There was something odd about parents who presented logical, spreadsheeted presentations about everything from the type of shoes needed for tennis to a summer spent sailing in the Caribbean.

"I'd like to work with Six a little this afternoon," Camden said when they'd agreed on one fancy dinner and the purchase of at least two new collies.

"You aren't reopening today, and you can't train a puppy for a competition set for only a few days away," her grandmother said. "Come on, woman does not live by dog obstacle courses alone."

Bonita made a good point. And there had been that really cute tunic at the store yesterday. "I guess training could start tomorrow."

NINETY-NINE PERCENT of the time, football held zero allure for Levi Walters. What fans saw as a couple of hours of playing on television he knew was actually six hours in the weight room, another three watching film and a minimum of two more hours of on-the-field practice. He'd been out of the game for nearly three years and could honestly say he didn't miss the grind of the football life.

He did, sometimes, miss the glitz. Red carpets could be fun. The roar of the crowd after a particularly good tackle made him feel alive in a way nothing else did. The women were beautiful.

Although none had made him forget to breathe like Camden had the other night at the Slope.

And he wasn't going to spend another day thinking about Camden Harris. She was a childhood friend, that was all. He had no business wondering about her appearance in Slippery Rock. Or thinking about what she'd look like out of that designer gown.

Wedding dress, dude, wedding dress. He was not going to get hung up on a woman who ran out on her own wedding. Back to pondering football. The things about it he'd liked. The exhaustion after a particularly grueling workout.

An image of Camden, face pinkish with exertion, body naked, popped into his mind. Levi gritted his teeth and refocused on football.

Signing autographs for kids had been fun. Visiting them in the hospital.

An image of Camden in a nurse's costume popped into his mind, and Levi angrily sank the shovel he was holding into a pile of manure and hay. He barely knew Camden Harris. He'd talked to her for all of five minutes. What the hell was she doing in his head?

Football never failed to distract him, so Levi ran back through the things he'd liked about the game. The exhaustion that made his mind blank—he wouldn't mind a bit of that right now. The one-on-one interactions with kids, the roar of the crowd on game day. The bullshitting in the locker room.

Fifty-three sweaty men, some with questionable hygiene to begin with, were definitely better than the two hundred cows he cleaned up after twice a day.

Levi sank the shovel into another pile of manure and hay in the milking parlor. Mucking out the stalls after the herd of dairy cows had done their morning session was one of the times he missed the relative cleanliness of football.

A clump of manure landed on his boot.

In some very specific instances, football was better than being a dairy farmer. Definitely better.

He flicked the clump into the pile in the back of the ranch truck. Brilliant November sunlight peeked over the trees, turning the sky a brilliant blue. Under the smell of manure, there was the scent of dew on the grass, and the leaves were finally beginning to turn. All along the lakeshore, the trees would be laden with deep red and orange leaves with a bit of gold thrown in for good measure. He'd missed the turning of the leaves for four long professional seasons, and for the four before that, when he'd played at the college level.

The few things he missed about football life didn't compare to the beauty of a country sunrise or getting to watch the slow change of the leaves or knowing that the products that came from his dairy were wholesome and healthy for the people who consumed them.

Football was fun, but the best part was that the money he'd made playing the game ensured the stability of Walters Ranch.

Levi put the last shovel full of hay and manure into the truck bed. He'd drive the load to the composting area. It would be ready for the local home and garden store by spring. He should check with Collin to see if they needed more compost at the orchard, too.

Then he needed to check on the cattle over on the Harris property. He'd been renting several acres from the older couple since making the dairy an organic operation; the cows couldn't mix with the organic cattle, but that didn't mean they had no value. Of course, they didn't have much monetary value, but that was beside the point.

And while he was at the Harrises', he'd probably run into Camden, could maybe learn why she was back in town after being gone for so long. Maybe seeing her again—hopefully wearing something other than that dress— would get her out of his head.

Another image of Camden, naked, popped into his head. Levi rapped his fist against his head, hoping to dislodge thoughts of Camden— in the wedding gown and out of it—from his mind.

He turned on the hoses to begin the rest of the cleanup.

"I still say you should install a sprinkler system in here so you can do away with the shoveling altogether."

Levi turned to see his sister, Savannah, in the doorway.

"Yeah, because what everyone wants to breathe are minute manure particles."

She wrinkled her nose. "Maybe a vacuum *and* sprinkler system then."

"If you aren't going to be helpful, you can just leave." He took the sting out of the words with a smile. Not that he'd intended any sting to begin with. Savannah could be sensitive about things, though. He hadn't known how sensitive until she returned to Slippery Rock last summer. She was settling in now. Practically living at the orchard with Collin, and in another few weeks would be married to him.

Levi couldn't have picked a more perfect man for his sister. It was good to see her so happy lately.

She was dressed for the orchard today, in old jeans and a fleece hoodie, with gloves poking out of the big front pocket. The ripped big front pocket. He tilted his head to the side. The sweatshirt had to be about three sizes too big for her. She looked like a kid with the hoodie hanging past her hips and her skinny legs clad in ripped jeans.

"Is that my sweatshirt?"

"I don't know. I found it in the mudroom. Collin said to dress warmly. We're pruning today."

Another change in his life. Savannah pruning apple trees. Savannah working, in general. She'd waited tables in town for a while then run off to sing in a talent competition. But before returning to Slippery Rock, Levi had never seen her do agricultural work. It was interesting to see that now. Especially because she seemed to enjoy it. Whether it was football or dairy farming, no feeling was better than the knowledge he'd done a solid day's work. It was good that Savannah had that now, too.

"Do you want it back?"

"Nah, you can wear it. As long as you don't mind that it's been covered in cow dung too many times to count."

Savannah gave the hoodie a side eye, wrinkling her nose.

"It's been washed just as much," he added. "You know Mama Hazel wouldn't let anything hang in her mudroom unless it had been thoroughly cleaned first."

"True." She put her hands in the back pockets of her jeans and rocked back on her heels. She wore rain boots today, the rubber kind that reached almost to her knees, with a plaid design on them. "Anyway, I wasn't just here to talk about the sprinkler system. I was wondering what you're planning for the old cows. The ones on the Harris property?"

"Not really planning anything. We'll feed them, make sure they're comfortable. Let them live out their lives in peace over there. Why?"

"I was thinking a few of them might be a nice addition to the camp when it's up and running in the spring. They're so gentle. It might be nice to have… I don't know, not a petting zoo, but actual farm animals that the kids can interact with."

"I thought this camp was a musical one?"

She'd had the idea to form a program like the one she'd volunteered with in Nashville. A music program for kids in the foster care system—kids like she had been before Bennett and Mama Hazel adopted her at the age of seven. Police officers had found her, abandoned and dirty, on the steps of their precinct in Springfield, and Levi vividly remembered her quiet demeanor and how skinny she'd been when they first brought her to Walters Ranch. How she'd jumped at loud noises for a while. That early beginning had left scars on Savannah he hadn't realized until she came back to Slippery Rock last summer. Seeing her blossom like this, planning a camp for kids like her, it was something he wished he'd thought of.

Still, to add dairy cattle? That seemed a little...off.

"It is. I was talking to one of the therapists who has agreed to spend a few days each month at the farm. She told me about horse therapy and mentioned that having other animals around could give the kids more responsibility. You know, feed the cows, clean up after them." She wrinkled her nose again at the cleaning part, and Levi bit back a smile.

"And you're going to teach them this cattle feeding, cattle cleaning stuff?"

"Ah, maybe?" She looked around the milking parlor. "I did learn how to milk them, after all." Levi raised an eyebrow at his sister. She laughed. "Okay, so it took me a while to get the hang of it, but I did. If I can do it, the kids in the program can figure it out. Especially if one former star defensive back from the NFL is around to encourage them."

And the other shoe dropped. She wanted him to be part of the camp. Levi shrugged. "Sure, I'll pick out a couple of the really docile cows." And he'd volunteer as much time as Savannah wanted. After all, wasn't that what family was for?

Savannah rewarded him with a big smile and reached up on her tiptoes to press a quick kiss to his cheek. "We can talk it through more whenever you have some free time. Hey, you're coming to the downtown lighting tonight, right?"

"Do we know yet why Thom has called, emailed and texted everyone in town to be there?"

"Do we ever know why the mayor does something?" Savannah asked and shrugged.

"He invited the TV stations from Springfield to come, too, because most of them covered the Branson lighting on Thanksgiving. My guess is he's trying to drum up more winter tourism. You know, tour the small-town lights, drink hot cider, spend your money in our town. That kind of thing."

"But we don't have anything for people to see. Only lunatics hit the lake at this time of year—the water's too cold."

Savannah shrugged. "Thom always has his reasons. Listen, I need to get to the orchard. We'll save you a spot tonight, though," she said, looking at her watch. She hurried out of the parlor, and he heard one of the ranch four-wheelers start up and then fade into the distance.

Her plan wouldn't hurt anything, Levi told himself as he got into the truck and turned it toward the compost area. The camp wasn't set to open until the spring, and cows were adaptable. Adding another thing to his calendar wouldn't be a bad thing, either. With Aiden, James, Collin and Adam deep in relationship heaven, he was kind of the odd man out.

Levi liked people. He liked conversation and camaraderie. Those were two of the things he'd loved about football. There was never a lack of backslapping or talking on a football field. There had been plenty of both here, too, before his buddies started dropping like flies under Cupid's bow. He didn't want to be a third wheel to any of them, so he needed to find something else to do with his time. Savannah's camp was a good starting place. The new product lines for the dairy would take up more time, too.

At the compost area, Levi began shoveling the manure onto the smoking squares. By spring they would have a good amount of compost for the local home and garden store, and probably enough for the orchard and a few other local businesses, too. He shoveled another pile into one of the compost squares.

It wasn't that he envied his friends falling in love. He wouldn't mind falling like that himself, if he could find the right woman.

The problem was most of the women in Slippery Rock were taken—a hazard of small-town living. If he didn't make the time to either meet someone from a nearby town who fit the bill of farmer's wife or head to Little Rock or Tulsa to find someone to at least take the edge off his physical needs, though, this restless feeling he'd been trying to shake since the summer would keep bothering him. The daydreams about Camden were only the fruits of his too-long celibate streak.

Until he could fit one of those two plans of attack into his schedule, he would just keep himself busy in other ways. The less time he had free, the less time he'd have to brood over...things. Like his lack of a love life.

Like the pretty girl he remembered from childhood wandering back into town looking like a drop-dead-gorgeous woman, complete with a wedding dress.

Finished with the compost piles, Levi tossed the shovel into the truck bed and got behind the wheel. He'd go check on the old cows. His father, Bennett, would have already fed them today, but Levi could check the salt licks. Maybe make some notes for Savannah's new project.

He pointed the truck to the rutted path that led to the fence between Walters property and the Harris farm.

Nothing was wrong. Everything was fine. He'd made the right choice to come back to Slippery Rock, to gracefully back out of football. This was just part of the adjustment period. So it had taken more than two years to get to the questioning phase—that didn't make his decision wrong.

He wanted to be here. Here, he had a purpose. Plans for the future.

Camden Harris was just a distraction. One he would start ignoring right now.

CHAPTER FOUR

LEVI STOOD ON the crowded dock in the Slippery Rock Marina. Two remote broadcast trucks from Springfield news stations were parked on the road, their cameras trained on the Slippery Rock mayor, Thom Hall, as he made a speech at the makeshift podium.

Thom was going on about the resilience of Slippery Rock, how neighbors had pulled together this year and how that togetherness would make this the best holiday season in memory.

Levi shoved his hands into the pockets of his denim jacket, willing away the nip in the air. It didn't work, but at least his fingers didn't feel as if they would fall off now.

People he'd known all his life surrounded him. Buddies he'd grown up with, women he'd watched fall for those buddies. His parents were somewhere on the crowded dock, likely closer to the shore because his mother was afraid of water. It wouldn't matter to her that this part of the lake was no more than eight feet deep, that she could actually swim or that she had spent time on a big ocean liner while in the Peace Corps.

"That's why I invited you all here tonight, to celebrate the rejuvenation of Slippery Rock, and to kick off this wonderful season of giving," Thom was saying.

Levi held back an eye roll.

Thom wasn't exaggerating, but he could use a better speech writer. After a tornado had torn apart the downtown area, leaving several people wounded and causing hundreds of thousands of dollars in damage, the town had come together. Neighbors had put new roofs up, and locals had banded together to build the new grandstand area and rebuild the farmer's market. Still, Thom was talking like some kind of character from *It's a Wonderful Life*.

This was Slippery Rock, Missouri, not Bedford Falls, New York. This wasn't a black-and-white movie. And he was freezing his butt off out here on the dock, where Thom had insisted everyone stand for the lighting ceremony of the inaugural Slippery Rock Holiday Festival.

He'd hired a carnival to come to town every weekend between Thanksgiving and New Year's. There were street vendors, and live music would be in the grandstand that had been erected after the tornado.

The festival would definitely bring in crowds of tourists, and that was good, but if the man didn't stop pontificating about the town, they were all going to freeze to these wooden dock boards.

"Is it just me, or does the temperature keep dropping despite the amount of hot air coming out of Thom's mouth?" Collin whispered.

Savannah shushed them. Levi gave her the eye roll he'd been holding back.

"It's sweet how he's going on," she insisted.

"All he has to do is throw a switch. We've been out here for thirty minutes while he talks about us like we're living in some kind of cross between George Bailey's Bedford Falls and Captain von Trapp's prewar Austria."

Savannah shot him a confused look. Levi shrugged.

"I was going for two heroic dudes."

"And you didn't think John Wayne or Denzel Washington?" Collin asked.

"I was going for heroic and Christmassy."

"*The Sound of Music* isn't a Christmas movie," Savannah offered.

"Then why is it only shown on TV between Thanksgiving and Christmas?"

"Arnold Schwarzenegger was in a Christmas movie, remember? He beat up Sinbad over a children's toy," Collin offered.

Arnold Schwarzenegger probably would have been a better choice. But both Jimmy Stewart and Christopher Plummer had been on late-night TV in their iconic roles this week when he couldn't sleep for the visions of Camden Harris dancing in his head. There had been no sign of Arnold on TV.

"So was Bruce Willis," Savannah teased. She wound her arm around Collin's as she spoke, snuggling closer to him. Levi would never have imagined his baby sister would fall for his best friend, but the two of them were perfect for each other.

Levi rubbed a hand over the back of his neck. Why their perfection annoyed him he couldn't figure out. But the more they snuggled and whispered, the more he wanted to toss them both into the lake. He'd leave them and join James, Slippery Rock's recently elected sheriff, but James was canoodling with Mara at the other end of the dock. Same with Adam and Jenny, although they weren't canoodling so much as looking as if, once they got their little boys back home and asleep, they'd *start* the canoodling.

Canoodling. What the hell was wrong with him? Levi Walters didn't use words like *canoodling*. He didn't watch sappy movies. He took care of his cattle. Played a little football every now and then with the guys. He threw darts and drank beer—all manly things.

So why was he so annoyed that Collin and Savannah were holding hands? That James had wrapped his arms and coat around Mara, holding her close to him? That Adam just kissed Jenny on her forehead when Thom said that line about the "best Christmas ever"? That Aiden and Julia were currently in a lip-lock, ignoring the speech and the crowd entirely?

He definitely needed to get started on either Plan A, find a local girl who'd fall for him, or Plan B, settle for a weekend of fun with a city girl. Maybe tonight.

The cattle weren't in birthing season yet, and even if they were, his dad could handle a few deliveries. The cattle knew their routine, and the dairy was mostly mechanized now, anyway. Maybe he'd get in his truck once Thom stopped chattering on about Christmas and drive south until he hit the Gulf. Spend a few days with his toes in the sand.

Get away from Love Central and have a fling

of his own. Carry around one of those souvenir cups filled with something highly alcoholic.

Someone jostled him.

"Excuse me, just trying to get a good shot of the lighting." The woman, tall and slender, with her hair up in a ponytail that came out the back of her ball cap, pushed past Levi to stand closer to the edge of the dock. She had a camera up to her face, looking through the viewfinder as she moved around in the crowd, and she looked nothing like the woman who'd walked into the Slope the other night in a wedding dress. But this was definitely Camden. His heartbeat revved a little faster in his chest. Levi frowned. "Better," she said, to no one in particular.

"So, let's count it down, people," Thom Hall said, raising his voice despite the microphone before him. Levi winced as the mic fed back through the speakers. "From five," Thom called out.

Everyone on the dock joined in. "Five."

Finally. They'd be off this dock and into the Slippery Slope in a few minutes, and maybe then he could feel his fingers again. Putting a few extra feet between his body and Camden's wasn't a bad idea, either. Levi's entire body had clenched the moment she pushed past him, and he couldn't get the muscles to release.

That settled it. He had to get out of Slippery Rock and into a fling of some sort. Pronto.

"Four," Thom continued, leading the town through the chant.

Once the feeling returned to his fingers, Levi would make a list of things that needed to be done before he took that vacation.

"Three," the town called out.

Savannah kissed Collin. Camden stepped a little closer to Levi, still apparently unaware that he was anywhere near her. Screw the list—he was just going to get in his truck and go.

"Two" rang out over the dock as the countdown continued. Collin and Savannah were still stuck in their lip-lock.

"One!"

Thom raised his arms like the flagger at a NASCAR race, and when he lowered them, a man on shore activated the lights. Streams of fairy lights crisscrossed the streets of downtown; more lights outlined the buildings and the grandstand. New flags had been hung on the street poles, and the school band struck up "Winter Wonderland" from inside the grandstand.

"Oh, it's perfect," Camden said, keeping her

focus on the viewfinder on her camera rather than the people around her. "They're going to love this," she said, moving the camera from side to side.

Making a video, not taking stills, Levi realized. No wonder she was so focused on the camera's viewfinder instead of where she was going. She stepped back, and so she wouldn't land on him and lose her balance again, Levi moved back, too. He put his hands on her shoulders, letting her know he was there.

"Sorry," she said, "I just want to get all the lights." She tilted the camera, he supposed, to get the outlines of the buildings as well as the Main Street lights.

"No problem."

The crowd began to move back to shore. Levi started to inch away from Camden, but when she took another little step back, he realized he couldn't move. He was the only thing between her and the lake. The dock was sturdy, but this area was where the boats tied up, with no railings to stop anyone from diving—or falling—off the side.

He waved at Collin and Savannah as they started moving away. "I'll catch up."

"Playing hero?" Savannah teased.

Levi gave her another eye roll. "Protecting

someone from catching cold by falling into the lake in November."

Collin and Savannah continued back down the dock, along with the other town residents. He saw James and Mara start climbing the steps leading to the street. Adam and Jenny, along with their little boys, were nearly back to shore. He didn't catch Aiden and Julia, but they'd probably already left the dock. Everyone watched the twinkling lights as they walked, and Levi had to admit the downtown area had taken on a bit of a fairy-tale quality.

Something he probably wouldn't have noticed if AMC wasn't in full-on holiday mode with the old movies this week. Old movies beat reruns of those daytime talk shows any day of the week.

Camden took another step back, her heels at the edge of the dock now. Levi reached for her arm.

"Watch your step," he said, but she startled as he brushed her arm.

Camden pulled away from him, quickly, and the move threw her off balance. As if in slow motion, Levi reached for her as she tried to take another step back to regain her balance. But there was no place for her foot to make purchase. She flailed, and Levi surged forward, trying to catch her before her other foot left the dock.

And then they were both falling.

Frigid water splashed over Levi's head, and he gasped, taking in a mouthful of lake water as he did. Levi kicked for the surface, sputtering and coughing when his head found the air.

Camden surfaced just after him, coming up just a couple of yards from Levi, spluttering.

"You okay?"

"What the heck was that?" she asked angrily. The ball cap had come off under water, and long, dark, saturated hair hung over her face. She pushed a mass of it away, but the darkness hid her face from him.

She kicked toward the dock, and Levi followed. She was mad at him? "I was trying to keep us both dry," he said, hauling himself up on the dock while she used the ladder.

"Nice job," she said, and there was a note of sarcasm underlying the anger.

Well, she wasn't the only one ending a chilly November night with a dunking in the lake. "What the hell were you doing watching your camera screen instead of watching your step?"

"I was taking a video of the lighting ceremony, thank you very much." She made it to the top of the ladder, and Levi held out his hand to help her onto the dock. "Granddad and Grandmom stayed home, and I wanted them to see what the lights looked like from the docks."

She ignored his hand and stepped onto the wood, water streaming off her clothes to puddle on the dock around them.

"I'll never find my hat," she mumbled as she gathered the hem of her shirt in her hands and squeezed out some of the water. The camera dangled from a string around her wrist.

Lights were strewn intermittently around the dock, and in the dim light, he could see her bottom lip tremble. Not in fear or hurt, but from the cold. Camden gathered her hair in her hands and wrung out the excess water. He should do something. Offer her his coat. Of course, it was soaking wet, along with everything else he wore.

"I have a blanket in my truck," he said. He shrugged the soaked denim jacket off his shoulders and twisted it in his hands as water streamed onto the wooden slats at their feet, then hung it on a dock post and stripped his shirt over his head.

"What the— What are you doing, Levi?" A hint of panic edged into her voice.

"I'm wringing out my shirt. Don't worry, the feminine virtue of a woman who wanders around strange towns in a wedding dress is safe with me."

"I wasn't wandering around town, I was getting directions. And I told you, the gown wasn't exactly my choice."

"And yet you were driving across Missouri wearing it."

"I needed to clear my head." She frowned.

"Looks like you finally found some non-wedding attire to wear."

"I picked up a few things at Julia's store on Thanksgiving. And thankfully ordered a few more things online, because these clothes are probably done for." A tremor shook her body as she spoke.

Levi wadded the shirt in his hands until no more water dripped out, then held it by the hem, snapping it between his hands. He put it back on and shivered. He grabbed his soaked jacket from the post. "Come on, let's get you somewhere warm and dry," he said. Levi didn't wait; he caught Camden's elbow in his hand and led her toward downtown. For the first time, his skin didn't tingle at her touch. Good—maybe the other night had just been a fluke and he wasn't as hard up for sex as he'd imagined.

He slipped the damp shirt back over his head

and shivered. He needed to get out of these clothes, pronto. Camden shivered beside him. So did she.

"A little cold water hasn't hampered my ability to walk, thank you," she said, pulling her arm from his grasp. But she continued walking beside him. After a moment, she blew out a breath. "Do you make a habit of knocking unsuspecting women into the lake so you can offer them a warm blanket?"

"It's probably not much warmer than we are at the moment, but it's dry. And I didn't knock you into the lake, you stepped right off the dock." They crossed from the dock to the main road, and Levi pointed. "My truck's right over there."

"Because you grabbed at me." He hadn't expected her to fall to her knees in gratitude, but this was a little much on the annoyance side of things. All he'd done was tell her to watch out and then try to keep her from falling. She was the one who overreacted to the situation.

She kicked her legs and stomped her feet as they walked, as if either would do much to get more of the water off her. Her tennis shoes made squishing sounds as they walked. So did his. Levi held back a grin. She looked ridiculous. He probably did, too.

"I grabbed at you because you were flailing around like a bass in the bottom of a boat." He unlocked the truck and grabbed the blanket out of the back seat.

"I was just fine until you—"

"You're welcome," he interrupted, handing the soft throw to her.

She narrowed her gaze at him and didn't take the blanket. "That wasn't a thank-you."

"It should have been."

Streetlights threw a cozy glow on the downtown area, brightened even more by the Christmas lights around the buildings and in store windows. Only a few people were still outside; most had gone into the Slippery Slope or the grandstand, where a local band was playing holiday music. Camden pushed her hair out of her eyes, and Levi's hands tightened into fists.

"And maybe you should have been more chivalrous." She twisted her long hair around her hand, wringing more water from the mass and then leaving it to hang in a twisted mess down her back.

Since she wasn't taking the blanket, he tossed it onto the back seat of the truck and shut the door. "I tried to help you out of the water," he pointed out, crossing his arms over his chest, waiting.

"I meant by not knocking me into the lake in the first place," she said through clenched but chattering teeth. "Is this some backward way of welcoming new people to town?"

"Only in the summer. In winter, we generally wait for people to get bored and leave on their own."

She shot him a look and then froze.

"And you're not exactly a new resident. You're just visiting, remember?"

She swallowed. "True. Although I'm thinking about staying a little longer." She blew out a breath and paused for a moment before saying, "Okay, maybe we should start over. Hi, Levi. And I'm sorry."

"Hello, Camden. And it's not a problem."

She worked a lock of hair free from the twist hanging down her back and twisted it around her finger. "I, ah…"

"What are you doing here?"

"Uh, taking a video of the lighting ceremony for my grandparents—"

"I meant in general. You said you might be staying a little longer." And that was interesting to him in a way that it really shouldn't be. He wasn't going to have a fling with the granddaughter of people he considered to be good friends. Neighbors. People he hoped would sell about half their acreage to him in another few weeks. He didn't need to mess that up with a night of hot sex with their granddaughter, no matter how gorgeous she looked in that wedding dress or how adorable she looked with lake water dripping off her. She trembled again, and Levi grabbed the blanket out of the back seat of his truck to settle it over her shoulders.

"Thank you. Again. Granddad is letting me train a pup he found on the side of the road last summer. We're thinking about reopening the dog school."

This made no sense at all. Camden Harris, the girl who had spent summers with her grandparents at the farm next to Walters Ranch, was running away from her wedding two days ago, and now she wanted to work at a defunct dog training school? After not setting foot in town for nearly fifteen years? She'd gone from summers running after her grandfather's stock dogs, and hanging out with Levi and his friends at the lake, to Kansas City once her mother remarried. And she'd never looked back. Levi would have known if she had. After all, he was the one taking care of Calvin and Bonita Harris for the past few years. Watching the stock-dog school go downhill because, no matter how good a trainer Calvin was, he was also now sixty-seven years old. After the tornado, it had been Levi who helped Calvin sell off the few dogs who could bring in some decent cash.

Camden had avoided all of that. But now she was here?

"Reopening the school?

She nodded. "Training working dogs for shows as well as real-world work. Doubling the income stream of the farm." Camden slipped the camera strap off her wrist and put the device into her back pocket. "Well, I guess I'll see you around," she said after a long moment. "I live here now."

She backed away, and he realized her grandfather's truck was parked just a few spaces beyond his. The older truck had a white stripe down the side and a few rust pockets over the rear wheel wells. The bench seat was covered with an old Mexican blanket.

How many times had Levi encouraged Calvin to sell the old bucket of rust?

The door creaked as Camden opened it. She slid inside and drove away, offering a limp wave as she passed him on the street. She was still wrapped in his blanket.

Levi frowned, more annoyed by her revelation that the fact that his emergency blanket was now tucked around Camden.

Calvin was too old to try to start over, and what did Camden know about training dogs? The last he'd heard, she was a beauty queen in Kansas City. There had to be more to Camden's plans than a sudden interest in her grandparents' lives or dog training. Something like the value of the one hundred acres of prime ranch land they held.

Now that he knew why she was back in town, he just had to figure out a way to stop her so that Calvin and Bonita could retire to Arizona like they'd been talking about for the last few years.

SIX TOOK TO the training course like he'd been running it since the summer months. The little dog stopped short when Camden blew her whistle and waited for her to signal him again. When she did, he took off like a shot, circling training barrels and crossing over the fallen log her grandfather had used as an obstacle when she was a young girl.

This training session was good for her, too. It kept her mind off her fall into Slippery Rock Lake with Levi Walters last night. A small piece of her heart wanted to insist he'd caused her to fall in, but the truth was he'd tried to keep her on the dock. She could still feel his hands on her upper arms, and the empty space under her foot as she stepped off the dock.

God, how embarrassing. And she wasn't going to keep reliving it. Accidents happened, and at least no one else had seen it. Nor had there been anyone to witness the wet, mucky mess she'd been after climbing out of that frigid water because her grandparents had retired to their bedroom before she got back to the farmhouse. There was also the fact that she'd escaped without even a hint of a head cold. Probably she should call Levi, just to make sure he was okay, too. At the very least, she should return the blanket she'd laundered with her wet clothes last night.

A new round of butterfly wings flapped in her belly at the thought of calling Levi. And that was the most ridiculous thing of all, because she barely knew the man. All she should be feeling toward him was embarrassment that he'd caught her at her worst. She had to get past this nervous, excited, attracted feeling. At all costs. Running into him in the bar and again—literally—on the marina dock didn't make him anything more than an innocent bystander in the chaos that was her current life.

She definitely, absolutely was not going to call Levi Walters. Except to return the blanket.

Finished with the course, Six returned to Camden's side, sat and waited. She gave him a strong rub behind his ears and offered a dog treat as she praised his work. When she started back toward the house, the dog fell in beside her.

Camden breathed deep, enjoying the smells of the crisp fall morning. She knew it was too far away, but she thought she could smell the apples from Tyler Orchard, and in the distance, she could swear she heard cattle lowing. Leaves crunched under her feet as she walked along the path back to the farmhouse. In the timber, something rustled, and Six's body went on point. His head swiveled in the direction of the noise, his legs were stiff and his body seemed to shiver in excitement. The rustle sounded again, and the dog whined softly.

"No," Camden said. "No chasing."

The dog didn't turn to look at her, but his ears seemed to droop a little.

Once more whatever it was rustled in the timber, and then a big, gray rabbit shot from the brambles. It paused for a moment when it saw Camden and the dog, twitched its nose and then it was hopping like mad into the trees on the other side of the path.

"No," Camden repeated, but the rabbit crossed ahead of them again, and Six was off. The little dog pounced, but the rabbit was faster. It made it back into the brambles and trees, but Six was undeterred. The little dog followed, thrashing through the thicket, despite Camden's repeated shouts of "No" and "Heel!" She blew the whistle, but he kept chasing.

She waited a moment, hoping Six would return when he couldn't find the rabbit, but the sounds of the dog and rabbit making their way through the underbrush and timber continued. There was nothing for it, Camden decided after a long moment—she would have to go in after them. She studied the brush and weeds and grasses.

She should have paid more attention in science; she had no idea if those brownish-green leaves were new tree growth or poison ivy or oak. And if there was a snake in there… Camden pushed the thought away.

She could handle a little garden snake. Didn't they hibernate, anyway? It was late November—surely the snakes would be in hibernation by now. And for that matter, if those leaves were poison ivy, it was late enough in the year that the poison probably wouldn't transfer to her hands. Just in case, it wouldn't hurt to put on the gloves she'd shoved in the pockets of her hoodie this morning on the way out for Six's training run.

As she drew closer, the thrashing sounds from the dog and the rabbit got louder—well, she hoped it was the dog and the rabbit coming back and not something larger and more dangerous that had been flushed out of its den. Were there bears in this part of the state? Camden stepped off the path just as a blur of gray and white fur flashed past, followed by a larger blur of brown, black and white fur, and then Six and the rabbit were bounding down the trail back toward the training area.

Crap.

Well, at least she wouldn't have to brave the weeds and brambles and possible poison ivy. Camden took off after the dog and rabbit, her booted feet crunching through the fallen leaves and twigs along the path. When the trail opened up to the training area, Six was nosing through an area of underbrush, and the rabbit was nowhere in sight.

"Come," she said, and the dog looked in her direction for a moment before going back to smelling the ground at one edge of the training space. "Six," she said, but the dog ignored her. Camden blew on the whistle, and the dog finally stopped nosing through the brush.

He watched her for another second, and she stared him down, keeping her expression serious. Finally, Six trotted obediently to her side.

"Bad dog," she said, and the dog thumped its tail, a goofy grin on its face. "No chasing. We herd. We gather. We don't chase." Levi's handsome, scruffy face popped into her mind at her mention of that act. The dog thumped his tail again, twice, tongue hanging out of his mouth. "Yeah, okay, chasing is sometimes fun."

Not that she'd ever chased anything. Joining the pageant circuit had been thrust onto her. Every guy she'd dated had been in her limited social circle. Levi's face flashed into her mind again. She hadn't chased Levi as a kid. And she wasn't going to chase him now, no matter how hard that crooked smile of his made her knees wobble, or how excitedly the butterflies in her stomach flapped their wings when she caught sight of him.

Especially not because, after falling into the lake with him the night before, she'd seen his bare chest, resembling her favorite milk chocolate from a little store on the Kansas City Plaza, glistening and wet from the lake.

Definitely not because she'd gone to bed still feeling his hands on her arms, his heat surrounding her when he put that blanket around her shoulders.

Camden didn't need that kind of heat in her life. She wasn't in Slippery Rock to have a rebound affair with Levi Walters. She was here to take control of her life, to build something of which she could be proud.

"But we don't chase," she said, and repeated the words silently in her mind. *Definitely don't chase.* "Come on," she said, motioning the dog to start walking with her. They arrived back at the barn with no more rabbit-chasing incidents. Camden filled the pup's food and water bowls.

In the barn, she flipped on the old TV sitting on a dusty table in a corner. The only channel that came in was a Springfield news network, the anchors joking about the unseasonably warm fall. It didn't feel all that warm to her, but then she was working in the outdoors and not under hot studio lights. With the chattering as background noise, Camden filled the dog food bin and, because it didn't appear to have been done for a while, swept the concrete floors. Granddad and Grandmom had gone into town that morning, leaving her to begin working with Six. For a first training session, it hadn't been half bad. Six learned quickly, and Camden remembered everything from those sessions in Kansas City.

She should have taken charge of her life a long time ago. Not that Camden expected everything to go as smoothly as the last few days, but she knew what she was doing. She had plenty of money, money she'd earned on the circuit and then from the pageant coaching business she'd started with her mother.

Mom. She hadn't spoken to her mother, not in a meaningful way, since walking out on the wedding. She pulled her cell phone from her pocket, thumb hovering over the home button that would unlock the device, when the chatter on the television stopped her in her tracks.

"Okay, this is footage we first aired on the morning show, from the holiday lighting ceremony in downtown Slippery Rock. Although the actual lighting went off without a hitch—" said the male anchor.

"Look how adorable everything looks outlined in red, green and white fairy lights," the female anchor interrupted. "The town has done such a tremendous job rebuilding after that awful tornado that went through last spring."

"This will be the first year they'll host a winter carnival, and most of the weekends leading up to Christmas will include live music at the new grandstand area. You can check our community calendar for more details," the male anchor went on. "But, DeeDee, not everything was quite as adorable as the lights. Watch as one of the residents is filming the lights and obviously not paying attention—"

The female anchor chuckled. "This gets funnier and funnier every time. Look, Greg! She's stepping all over that poor farmer. Wait a second. Here it comes," DeeDee said, glee in her voice. Camden's heart sank as she focused her attention on the small TV. She and Levi toppled off the dock.

"We have splashdown," Greg said. "Let's watch that one more time."

The tape began rewinding on the screen, and Camden saw her body rise miraculously from the water and tangle in reverse with Levi's. She wanted to look away, wanted to turn off the TV, but instead found she couldn't tear her eyes from the sight of herself tripping over Levi and falling into Slippery Rock Lake again. And again, as the anchor team made jokes and kept rewinding the tape that must have been picked up from one of their cameras at the lighting ceremony.

"Here's the really funny part, though, DeeDee.

The woman tripping over the farmer is none other than former Missouri Miss Camden Harris. One of our eagle-eyed interns—herself a former beauty queen—realized who we'd caught on camera this morning. We have to wonder what Ms. Harris is doing in Slippery Rock—"

"And wearing that awful ball cap and ugly flannel shirt," DeeDee interrupted again. Camden leaned the broom against one of the stalls and wiped her hands over the jeans and hoodie she'd worn to work with Six this morning, feeling self-conscious, despite the fact that no one was here to see her. She ran her hands through her hair.

"We haven't been able to confirm why she is in Slippery Rock, but we do have a call in to Harris's reps…just to make sure she's okay after taking that tumble."

Camden checked her phone. No missed calls. They obviously hadn't tried very hard to track her down to check on her well-being. Which was just as well. Camden didn't feel like explaining what had happened last night. She rubbed her hands over her arms. Or why she could still feel Levi's hands on her.

Her phone buzzed in her hand, and Camden jolted back to the present. The anchors were still droning on, although they'd gone from her falling into the lake to an elephant giving birth at the National Zoo in Washington, DC.

Grant's name and face scrolled across her phone screen. *Don't answer it, Cam*, she told herself. Nothing good could come from talking to Grant now. Not when she'd just been on TV falling into a lake.

Of course, he probably didn't know about her frigid night swim; the Kansas City stations wouldn't have picked up something as silly as this, surely. He probably wanted to talk about her calling off the wedding. Camden didn't want to talk about that, either, and she didn't care if it was childish.

Grant knew why she'd walked out, and she didn't want to go through another it-was-an-accident conversation with him. As if he'd merely fallen on top of Heather and his penis had accidentally found her vagina.

Camden sighed in relief when the phone flipped over to voice mail. She'd call him back later.

Much, much later.

A moment later, the phone buzzed again, and Grant's face scrolled across her screen. The man was nothing if not persistent in whatever case, cause or catastrophe was at the top of his massive to-do list.

Crap, crappity, crap.

Camden sighed. Now or later. Her ex was not going away.

She slid her finger across the screen to accept the call. "Hello, Grant."

"Camden, sweetheart, are you okay?" His smooth voice—and his use of the endearment that always made her feel like she was five—made her cringe despite the fact that he was hundreds of miles away. "I saw that news story this morning. Were you hurt?"

Camden squeezed the bridge of her nose. Damn it. Must have been a slow news cycle in Kansas City if they'd picked up the footage from the Springfield station. It wasn't as if Camden were some Hollywood star in red carpet attire taking a tumble. "I'm fine, Grant, thank you. It was nothing."

"Of course it was something. You have to pay more attention to your surroundings, sweetheart."

"I took a less than two-foot fall into about eight feet of calm water. It isn't as if I took a header off the Santa Monica Pier during a storm. I appreciate—"

"How many times have I warned you about daydreaming when you should be focused on the task at hand?" Camden rolled her eyes as Grant continued talking. He'd never once reprimanded her about daydreaming, because she wasn't a daydreamer. That habit had been trained out of her before her first pageant.

Until Levi Walters came back into her life.

Not that he was technically in her life.

"It isn't like you to do this kind of thing," he was saying. "My Camden is a planner, even though she gets in her head sometimes. Why don't you just come home? You've only gotten into your own head about—"

"I'm not *your* Camden," she interrupted.

Silence filled the phone. "What?" he said after a long moment.

"I'm not your Camden. Yes, I like to plan things, but no, I'm not in my head about not marrying you. You've been sleeping with Heather, who I thought was my best friend. You're the one in the wrong here."

"And I want to make that up to you."

"You can't make it up to me. Even if you could, that isn't what I want. I want to move on with my life."

"In Slippery Rock?"

"I want a fresh start."

Grant sighed. "Camden, be reasonable. We can reschedule for the spring, or if you don't want to wait that long, we'll elope and throw a big party afterward."

"I don't want to reschedule, and I'm not eloping with you. And I'm not going to become Mrs. Grant Wentworth. Ever."

"We like all of the same things, we have all the same friends. We're the perfect couple."

"You slept with Heather Abbott."

"I've spoken to Heather. We'll stop seeing each other."

"Gee, thanks," Camden said, but Grant either ignored or didn't catch the sarcasm in her voice, because he kept talking.

"Heather and I have known each other for years. We flirted a bit in college, and things just got out of hand when she struck up her friendship with you."

As if that made it any better. He made it sound as if Heather sought out a friendship with Camden just to get to Grant. Thinking about it, Camden wouldn't put it past the other woman. Heather could be fun, but there was a hard side to her, a side that was never satisfied with what she had. A side that felt no qualms about taking what she wanted, even if that hurt another person.

And Camden had ignored those traits because Heather's mother and her mother had been childhood friends. Camden shook her head. It was as if, before finding Grant in the closet with Heather, she'd had no backbone at all.

"You shouldn't call things off with Heather, Grant. The two of you deserve each other. Just leave me out of it," she said and clicked off the call. Then she blocked his number and deleted his contact information from her phone.

The old Camden let other people think for her. Her mother thought she should be in pageants. Grant thought they should get married. No one cared what Camden thought.

But she wasn't going to be that meek girl any longer. She was through being Elizabeth Camden Harris Carlson's daughter.

It was time she was Camden Harris. Whoever Camden Harris chose to be.

LEVI THROTTLED DOWN the four-wheeler he'd been riding at the gate separating Walters land from Harris land. He'd installed the gate when Calvin agreed to let him rent a few acres for the older cattle in his herd. Before installing it, they'd had to go around the long way; now it was a quick seven-minute ride from his doorstep to Calvin's.

And he had no reason to go to Calvin's on a Saturday.

So why the heck was he sitting here staring at the gate? He was positive Camden would be dried off from their little dip in the lake last night, and if she wasn't, he was not the man to dry her off.

Although the memory of a few water droplets slowly making their way down her neck and disappearing beneath the vee of her flannel shirt made his heart beat a little harder than it should.

This whole thing was ridiculous.

Camden Harris was not his type. He didn't go for beauty queens or freckled noses or women who pushed him into freezing lake water. So why couldn't he go about his day without either wondering what she was doing five times a minute or going out of his way to see for himself what she was doing?

Levi put the four-wheeler in Neutral, unlocked the gate and then drove through it, locking it behind him. All the while he repeated *this is stupid* in his head. But his hands ignored his brain and kept the vehicle pointed toward the farmhouse. Levi followed a narrow trail between the two farms until it broke free of the trees. Light smoke drifted from the house chimney, and because Calvin only had a handful of dogs left, the runs were quiet this morning.

Camden exited the big red barn, a hoodie hanging just past her hips. She'd pulled her hair through the back of another baseball cap and wore skinny jeans with a pair of rainbow-emblazoned rain boots on her feet. She looked adorable.

And thinking that was what had him driving over here for no reason, Levi lectured himself. Camden closed the door behind her and looked from Levi to the house as if she wasn't sure whether to wait for him outside or run for cover.

Funny, he'd had the same feeling, only instead of running for the cover of the farmhouse, he'd considered pulling a U-ey and going back the way he came. Levi brought the four-wheeler to a stop near Camden and turned off the engine.

"Hello," she said after a long moment. Levi realized he'd been staring at her rain boots. Which was double weird. He'd seen a million rain boots in his time. There was nothing remotely attractive about the bulky things, but on Camden they looked almost runway worthy.

Probably her beauty queen training.

"Did you need something?" she asked, and Levi realized he still hadn't answered her.

Damn, he was losing it. "Just dropping by to see how you're doing after last night's swim," he said.

Camden pursed her lips, and her eyes narrowed, and neither of those actions should make her look more adorable than she'd looked when she first left the barn, and yet, they did. The amber flecks in her brown eyes seemed brighter this morning and when she cocked her head to the left, her hair cascaded over her shoulder in a long wavy tail. She crossed her arms over her chest, and despite the bulk of the hoodie, he thought her breasts rose and fell a bit faster than was totally called for. Probably just wishful thinking, though.

"I'm doing just fine, thank you."

"Me, too, thanks for asking," he said when it became clear she had nothing else to say.

"Of course you are. It would take more than a hundred thirty pounds of me to do damage to all, what, two hundred forty pounds of you?"

"Two twenty-five, actually. I've slimmed down a bit since my football days." And he looked damn good, if he said so himself.

"Well, good for you." She looked toward the

house again, but no one had come to the door. "What are your doing here?"

"Isn't that my line?" Levi asked, and a small smile spread over Camden's face.

"It kind of is, I guess." She restlessly shifted her weight from one foot to the other, and occasionally looked over her shoulder toward the house and the lane that led to the main road.

Levi looked around. Calvin's truck wasn't in the drive, and the sports car under the big maple tree had to be Camden's. "Waiting for something?" He pocketed the four-wheeler key and stood near Camden in the shade from the barn. Levi wondered what she saw in the weathered building, the rundown dog kennels, the trees lining the yard.

He saw stability, a place that needed a strong back and some hard work. A place that would fund the well-earned retirement of two people he'd come to think of as family. Space that would let him do a major expansion of the dairy in another few years, especially if things went well with the trial run of ice creams and yogurts next year.

"Grandmom and Granddad went into town for groceries."

"And left you in the barn?"

She straightened. "I was working with Six,

if you must know. He's the dog I told you I was training."

"You're a beauty queen. What do you know about training dogs?" When he'd known Camden, she'd been as likely to chase a dog through the underbrush as to wear a formal gown, but that was a lot of years ago. Years she'd spent on hair, makeup and clothes. And she'd done a good job with those assets, he admitted.

"Plenty, actually. My piano teacher's husband trained dogs for competitions. He showed me a few things. And I picked up a lot from Granddad and my dad…before," she added.

"So you walked out on your wedding to train cattle dogs? Really?"

Camden clenched her jaw. "Yes. And why do you care anyway, Levi?" she asked. "You run a dairy farm—it's not like my farm is in competition with yours."

"I think you mean your grandfather's."

She blinked. "What?"

"This is your grandparents' farm, not yours." He watched her for a long moment. Camden shifted her weight from one foot to the other. He didn't care that she wanted to train a dog, but he did care if whatever plans she was making interfered with Calvin's. The older man had loved training dogs, but he deserved a quiet retirement. God knew he'd worked hard enough for it.

"What does that have to do with anything?"

"I just find it interesting that you ignored Slippery Rock for more than a decade and now you're back here, training a dog like it's your life's mission and calling a farm that doesn't belong to you yours. Calvin has his own plans, you know. Plans to retire, plans to take Bonita on a cruise, plans to see Tucumcari and Dodge City and any other Old West gunfighting town he can get Bonita to visit."

"I didn't ignore Slippery Rock. I was twelve when my father died. It wasn't like I could jump in a car and drive down any time I wanted."

"Did you even try?" He leaned a shoulder against the weathered wood of the barn, pushing for answers to questions he knew he had no business asking. Except, Camden interested him.

Not just because he cared about her grandparents.

Because of that sad, solitary look on her face a few nights ago in the bar.

"Again, *why* do you care?" she asked, but it was more of a shout. "Why do you care why I'm in town or what I've been doing since I was a kid? We barely know each other. And Grand-dad is excited about reopening. You should have seen his face when I mentioned training Six." Camden frowned as she said the words, though, and Levi pressed on. Not because he wanted her off the property for his own future plans, but because Calvin and Bonita deserved a restful retirement. Reopening the dog school? It didn't make sense.

"If he were capable of running a fully oper-ating training school, don't you think he would be? He wasn't waiting for you to come back to save the day. Think about it, Camden, he loves dogs and he loved training. Do you really think most of the runs would be empty if he wanted them filled? That clients would be calling or stopping by every day?"

"I know things have slowed down, but I thought…" Camden looked around as if not-ing the old kennels and the handful of dogs for the first time. "Why do you keep demanding to know why I'm here?"

Levi didn't have a good answer for that. Part of him wanted to know because he didn't want whatever Camden was planning to hurt Cal-vin or Bonita. But Camden had never been the kind of person to intentionally hurt another, anyway. People made all kinds of changes

in their lives, but something as fundamental
as caring was hard to fake or to learn after a
certain point. The reason he wanted to know,
well, that was harder to nail down. He wanted
to know why she'd seemingly picked up and
walked out on her life, simply because she interested him. And nothing about that truth was
simple.

People in Slippery Rock were an open
book, one he'd been reading for most of his
life. Camden Harris wasn't an open book, and
behind that bit of fire shooting from her big,
brown eyes right now was something bigger.
An emotion he couldn't quite put his finger on.
And that probably made him all kinds of an
ass, because he kept prodding with only curi-
osity in his mind, not concern or caring. And
that look in her eyes…it nearly screamed for
caring. Concern.

And Levi was not in the market for either.
He had a dairy to expand, a sister starting a
new business, parents who depended on him,
friends who…okay, so his buddies were self-
sufficient. For that matter, so were Mama
Hazel and Bennett. So were Calvin and Bonita
Harris. So was his sister. That didn't mean he
needed to add whatever problems made Camden's eyes go all mushy and soft into his life.

He reached out, brushing his fingers across her chin. Her skin was pale, but a hint of pink brightened her cheeks at his touch. Her gaze met his, and under the fire, under that other feeling that he couldn't name, something else blazed to life. Something that made his belly tighten and caused him to lean in until he could feel her breath on his cheek. Camden swallowed.

"This...isn't a good idea," she said, her words sounding strangled.

But it was too late. She was there, a breath away from him, those wounded eyes drawing him in closer. And then his mouth was on hers, tasting the sweetness that was Camden Harris, a woman who was so far from the type of woman Levi typically spent time with that it made no sense.

Whatever brought Camden to Slippery Rock would complicate his life, and Levi liked to keep things simple. When he played football, training was his focus. At the dairy, his cattle were the focus. With Camden...

Her small hands rested against his chest, and her mouth opened to him. Levi deepened the kiss, wanting more of Camden and not understanding why. Camden's arms locked around his neck, holding him in place for a long, lingering moment. He pulled her body closer to his, feeling her heat through their clothes, breathing in more of the soft, feminine scent that was her.

With Camden things weren't going to be focused or easy. She would complicate the hell out of his life, and so he should stop this kiss. Stop thinking about her all the time. Stop remembering how much fun she used to be, or wondering if she still had a bit of that reckless, excitable girl in her. Levi pushed the ball cap off her head so he could bury his hands in her hair.

Who cared about complications? Kissing her was enough to focus on.

She pulled away from him. "Really, really not a good idea," she said, and this time her words were breathless, her chest rising and falling unevenly. Levi shoved his hands into his pockets, breathing heavily himself. That had moved so much faster than he expected.

"Yeah," he said, stepping back, putting an inch of space between them. He didn't want the space, though—he wanted to bury his hands in her hair again, to feel her body curve around his.

"I, ah, should finish cleaning the barn."

"I should get back to the dairy." So why

didn't he walk away? Levi couldn't make his legs work, didn't want to let Camden get back to her dog training or barn cleaning or whatever else she was doing here, not yet.

"Whatever brought you back—" he started, but Camden cut off his words.

"Let's just drop it." She put her hands in the pockets of her hoodie and walked away. At the corner of the barn, Camden turned back. "I'll see you around, Levi."

"See ya, Camden," he said as he started the engine of the four-wheeler.

There was no reason for his chest to feel light at the thought of seeing Camden again. But then, nothing else about Camden made sense, so why should this be any different? Levi shook his head.

He really should have taken that trip to the Gulf or, hell, just to Springfield for the rest of the holiday weekend. He hadn't, though, and now a trip anywhere that Camden Harris wasn't didn't appeal. That was the most ridiculous part of this. He'd had exactly three conversations with the woman, none of which lasted more than a minute or two. He'd seen her wandering around in a wedding gown, which, sure, made him wonder all kinds of things about her curves under all that gauzy white fabric.

He'd seen her drenched and annoyed in jeans and flannel and lusted after those silly striped rain boots she was wearing. Not once had she seemed interested in him as anything more than a former acquaintance.

But she'd kissed him like there was more than childhood friendship between them.

Levi took the narrow trail back to the gate separating their properties. Camden Harris wasn't his friend.

But, then, he had plenty of friends already. Maybe Camden Harris could be something else entirely.

CHAPTER FIVE

"IF WE COULD just focus, people," Thom Hall said, his voice heavy with annoyance. He stood behind a podium in a large meeting room at town hall. Levi noted that most of the business owners were in the audience. Merle from the Slippery Slope, Bud from the bait shop. Julia Colson from the dress shop and her new destination wedding business, Vows at Slippery Rock. Collin, Aiden and Adam sat across the aisle from Levi, Bennett and Mama Hazel. Mike from the grocery store.

Mostly, though, Levi was focused on the tall brown-haired former beauty queen sitting in the second row with her grandparents. The woman who hadn't so much as glanced in his direction since she walked in.

The woman who didn't own a business in Slippery Rock, who didn't even technically live here, but who had been welcomed as if she'd been here her entire life.

Why that annoyed him, Levi couldn't quite

explain, but it had been a week since that kiss outside the barn and he had yet to make it through a full day without thinking—or dreaming—about Camden.

It was ridiculous, really. He hadn't acted like this around a woman since…ever. Levi dated plenty of girls through his college and high school days, and there was always a woman around when he played in the pros, but none of them had captured his attention like Camden Harris. She leaned over to whisper something to Bonita that made her grandmother chuckle. Camden tucked a lock of hair behind her ear, revealing a bit of her delicate neck. Levi swallowed hard and pushed thoughts of kissing Camden out of his head.

"The company would like to start construction right after New Year's, but we need those landowners affected to grant access rights to the old railroad track areas by the end of next week so that we're definitely on their schedule." Thom shuffled the papers at the podium. "I don't have to tell you what a tourist boon this could be to Slippery Rock. Our section of the old trail would connect the section that runs up to Springfield and then on to St. Louis with the section connecting Joplin and Tulsa. This would be one of the longest rail trails in the US, putting Slippery Rock on the map for not only hikers and runners, but also for bike races. It's possible we could host a triathlon at some point, which would be another tourism draw. With the downtown rebuilt, and the bass nationals definitely on the schedule for this spring, this hiking and biking trail is another reason for visitors to come to Slippery Rock instead of stopping their vacations in Branson or Eureka Springs."

Thom's explanation of the benefits didn't make Levi feel any better about the tourism plan than the last time the man had brought it up, at a town meeting in October. At the time, the bass nationals had just officially signed a contract to host a major fishing tournament here next spring. But the other businesses seemed to like the trail idea. Of course, most of them wouldn't have annoying tourists tossing empty water bottles and candy wrappers in their fields.

The rail trail would cut across a large section of Walters Ranch, and with the winding nature of the old tracks in that area, he'd have about five miles of trail to clean up every day. He'd have to hire someone to patrol it or take time out of his day to deal with the rubbish.

The mayor handed a thick stack of manila

envelopes to Calvin Harris, who took one and passed the rest on.

"The town council has taken the liberty of creating the easement contracts. You can read through them, sign and return the packets at next week's council meeting," he said.

The stack of envelopes made it to Levi, who took one and passed the rest to Collin across the aisle. "Taken the liberty," Levi grumbled under his breath. "Because this section of the trail could just as easily follow the highway and not inconvenience any of us and you know it." Of course, then the Slippery Rock section wouldn't be a rail trail at all. It would be a highway trail. Not what the state wanted, and probably not what hikers or bikers wanted, either.

It would definitely make things easier for ranchers like him, though.

No one overheard Levi's grumbling, which was just as well. He didn't want to start some kind of town feud—he just didn't want random people wandering across his land all summer.

"Are there any questions?" Thom asked, waiting barely a second before continuing. "No? Then we'll see everyone at the town meeting next week. Don't forget, our first grandstand holiday concert is Saturday night.

We've got several area bands lined up, and Savannah Walters has landed an amazing act for our New Year's Eve concert—the band Backroad Anthem will be with us."

Everyone clapped. Levi shot a look at his sister, sitting between Collin and Aiden, who was beaming. She'd met the members of Backroad Anthem when she entered a talent contest a couple of years before and had started on the same label as the band before leaving Nashville for good.

With the meeting over, everyone stood and began talking about the plans. Thom made his way to Levi and clapped him on the shoulder. "I'm sure the town can count on your support for this project, son."

"I still think we'd have more control over the trail if it followed the highway. It wouldn't be as disruptive to those of us with working ranches, and it would be easier for the sheriff's deputies and emergency squads to respond to accidents that way, too."

"But we'd lose the scenic nature of the trail, and the rail trail feel," Thom pointed out.

"I think it's a great idea," said the last voice Levi expected to join the conversation. Camden continued, "The Katy Trail near Kansas City follows old railroad tracks, and it's a great addition to those areas. Thousands of people hike and bike it, nearly year-round."

"Exactly my point. We don't have time to clean up after thousands of tourists."

"So you'll post signs to pack out everything that's packed in and provide trash cans at the trailheads."

Her answer was too reasonable for Levi. As if he hadn't considered that people would pick up after themselves. The only problem with that was he'd been a professional football player, and before that had played at a big-time college. He'd seen cleanup crews walking the stands for hours after a ball game, picking up everything from empty beer bottles to partially eaten hot dogs. People didn't clean up after themselves.

"I think Levi has a point," Calvin put in, joining them. He held Bonita's hand in his, the familiar gesture one of Levi's favorite things about the couple. "The last thing an active dog school needs is tourists disrupting training sessions."

"Nonsense, you don't even use that area of our property. The runs are far enough away that the dogs won't notice a thing," Bonita added.

"Doesn't affect the orchard, and added tourism would be nice in the summer. It could mean more customers at the farmer's market," Collin put in.

"More people browsing the storefront Jenny is planning on opening after we finish renovating the empty building next to Buchanan's," Adam put in, and Aiden nodded in agreement.

"More tourists means more traffic to all our stores. More people thinking about getting married at the lake," Julia added.

Levi frowned. More people sampling the organic products from his dairy. Only he didn't want to think about the positives when the big negative would mean time taken out of his plans so he could police the trail for trash. Although he could probably hire a couple of high school kids to make a trash run every few days during the busy season.

For that matter, wouldn't there be some kind of grounds crew making sure the trail was free of weeds and in good shape for hikers, runners and bikers? That would include trash pickup.

"It will mean an extra patrol or two for the department, but we already patrol the area around the tracks to make sure teenagers aren't having wild parties out in the boonies. A trail might keep some of them from getting into trouble out there, actually," James added, the "sheriff" addition to his badge somehow making his words sound more official.

Well, his friends were just no help at all. Hell, maybe he was being persnickety, as Mama Hazel liked to say. Making a big deal out of something that would really only be a minor inconvenience.

"Local service groups would probably join in the cleanup every few weeks," Camden added. "I did a bikeathon on the Katy Trail a couple of years ago, and it was pristine. People loved it."

Of course she had. The former Missouri Miss had probably donned a bikini or an evening gown for her bike ride through the wilderness on her quest for world peace.

And that wasn't fair at all.

Thom was asking Camden questions about the bikeathon event. Getting even more ideas, no doubt. Levi tuned them out, forming his own argument against the trail, which he'd never really wanted but had never truly objected to, either. Not until tonight, and he didn't care to consider why that was. His objections to the trail were one thing.

The bigger problem was that Camden was too adorable. Standing there all earnest and enticing in jeans, a flannel shirt and a puffer vest. Clothes that were as ordinary in Slippery Rock as apples from Tyler Orchard. The rain boots weren't ordinary. This pair had neon flowers emblazoned on them and should look more suited to a toddler than an adult. Damn it, those boots should not make his heart beat faster in his chest. For that matter, all those enticing curves he'd been dreaming about since seeing her at the Slope that first time were completely covered in flannel and denim—not the most seductive of fabrics. Although the denim was definitely curved in all the right places. And that vest was fitted to her slender torso, showing off the rest of her to perfection.

And, damn it, he was not getting all hot and bothered by Camden Harris in a vest, jeans and a ridiculous pair of rain boots. The second ridiculous pair of rain boots he'd seen her wear. He was annoyed at a proposed bike trail that was going to cause him a lot of extra work. He was not excited that Camden was still in town more than a week after her arrival. He was definitely not thrilled at the prospect that she was staying, or that Calvin was talking about reopening the dog school he'd been ready to sell only a few weeks ago. Camden and her dog-training plans could throw a definite wrench in his plans to expand the dairy. That was another thing to be annoyed about.

Annoyed at the trail.

Annoyed Camden could muck up his business plans.

Not attracted to the woman who was running away from her problems.

"They can love that other trail all they want. This is Slippery Rock, and when the town council agreed to them damming the river to create the lake all those years ago, they wanted the area to remain as undeveloped as possible. One marina, no condo developments. They wanted to keep Slippery Rock the same small town it's always been."

Several pairs of eyes swiveled to him, all confused about his newfound objections to a trail that was a potential tourism boon to their little town. Levi straightened his shoulders, ready to defend the position he wasn't even sure he wanted to champion. What the hell was wrong with him lately?

Daydreaming about Camden and that stupid kiss. Thinking about Camden wearing nothing but those silly rain boots. Making multiple trips to check on the old dairy cows, a herd that was getting lazy and fat and had shown no interest in trying to escape their new home. He was losing it, and for what? A woman who had sad eyes and probably a long, self-indulgent story? He needed to get his eye back on the ball: his dairy, his plans, building a strong business that would create jobs for the people in his community.

"No one is talking about turning Slippery Rock into the kind of vacation rental–strewn place that Branson is," Thom objected. "We're talking seasonal tourism, something that will benefit all of us."

Before Levi could offer up another argument against the trail that he wasn't positive he didn't want, the door to the hall opened and closed, and Camden's eyes grew as wide as quarters. She blinked, as if she couldn't believe what she saw. Levi turned to see a tall clean-shaven man wearing khakis and a blue-checked button-down shirt and an open leather jacket. He had blond hair, cut short. Levi had never seen him before.

"Grant?" Camden said, pushing out of their group.

"Camden, sweetheart." The man reached for her hands, but Camden pulled back from him. The ex? The one who didn't know the kind of ring his woman wanted to wear? Levi studied the stranger. Slicked-back hair. Perfectly pressed trousers. Manicured hands. He leaned in to Camden, as if he might kiss her, but she wrinkled her brow, pulling away from him.

Definitely the ex.

The man looked…like exactly the kind of man a beauty queen would marry. But seeing Camden next to him was wrong. Levi couldn't picture her, not even the wedding gown–wearing version of her, with whoever this guy was. The rain-booted, flannel-wearing version fit even less.

"What are you doing here?" she hissed at him. Then she looked back toward their group, grabbed Grant's arm and dragged him toward the door, out of earshot.

Levi watched her for a long moment, animatedly waving her hands as she spoke. It was the most lively he'd seen Camden since she arrived back in town. Well, aside from the moment she flailed around with him on the dock, but that wasn't the same.

"…and if you really have these concerns, raising them during the meeting would have been better than talking behind the council's back," Thom said, drawing Levi's attention back to the people he'd grown up with and the town mayor. A man who was only guilty of trying to improve Slippery Rock. A goal Levi shared, although his plans included more jobs and less tourism. He was being an ass about the trail, and it had more to do with Camden's enthusiasm for the project than the project itself.

Which was just plain dumb. What was arguing with Camden about something he was going to do anyway going to accomplish?

Levi waved his hand. "I'm in the minority, and I've never been one to stand in the way of progress."

Satisfied with the answer, Thom nodded to the group. Calvin and Bonita were watching Camden and the ex carefully.

"Going to the Slope?" Collin asked. "Savannah and Mara are already there, holding the table."

"You mean they're sweet-talking Merle into breaking out the blender for margaritas," Julia said with a laugh. "They're convinced they can make him see the benefits of mixed drinks. I'm not so sure. But I'm in."

"I go where she goes," Aiden said, grinning when Julia elbowed him.

"I'll call Jenny's dad, see if he's up for watching the boys so Jenny can come by for a bit," Adam said, already dialing his cell phone. His service dog padded along behind Adam as he strode from the room. Levi hadn't noticed the dog, which he supposed was normal. Sheba was part of the gang now, part of Adam, although his friend had not had a seizure in nearly two months.

Levi nodded. "Sure, I've got nowhere to be," he said, but he couldn't take his gaze off Camden.

Calvin and Bonita bypassed them on their way out of the building, waving at their granddaughter as they passed. Camden crossed her arms over her chest, shutting out whatever the ex was saying, just as she'd shut Levi out that day at the barn. Before he had kissed her.

Collin slapped Levi on the shoulder. "See you in a few," he said.

"Yeah." Levi offered a half wave, his focus across the room. He shook himself and looked around.

Thom and a few council members were across the room, stacking envelopes as they talked, probably about construction dates. James, Aiden and Julia had left. Calvin and Bonita were nowhere to be seen. Levi's parents watched him from the doorway.

He crossed to them, but part of him was still focused on Camden and the man she argued with in the corner. "We're meeting up at the Slope, if you want to stop in for a drink."

"I'm missing *NCIS*, and you know how I love my Gibbs," Mama Hazel said. "But we'll leave the light on for you and Savannah."

"She'll probably be staying at Collin's. And I've been moved into the new house for weeks now."

"Still, we'll leave it on." Mama Hazel patted his face, her walnut-colored skin nearly identical to his, her brown eyes with a hint more amber at the iris.

His father eyed the woman across the room. "You sure you know what you're doing there, son?" he asked, his deep baritone seeming to boom across the room. No one else seemed to notice, though, which was odd.

"I'm just going to the Slope."

"Yeah," Bennett said. He put his big hand at the small of Mama's back, leading her from the meeting room. "See you in the morning," he said.

There was no one left to talk with. Nothing holding him back from heading to the Slope to shoot darts with his buddies. Levi looked across the room.

Camden pointed a finger at her ex, still annoyed about something. His being here? His taking more than a week to get here? Levi had no idea. Not his problem.

He pushed the door open and glanced back one more time before leaving the room. It was none of his business, and he shouldn't care.

So why did he?

"SWEETHEART, I KNOW. I embarrassed you at the rehearsal dinner with that speech," Grant said placatingly.

Camden held back an eye roll. While his rehearsal dinner speech had had very little to do with *her*, it was small potatoes compared to her finding him with Heather in the closet down the hall from the bridal suite minutes before their wedding.

Grant was still talking, but Camden had no desire to listen or to even be in his presence.

"I don't give a fig about your speech at the rehearsal dinner. I care about the fact that you've been sleeping with my supposed best friend. For how long, Grant? A month before the wedding? Two?" Grant looked uncomfortable. "Three? Six?" His spray-tanned complexion reddened. "Since before you proposed?"

"Camden, it didn't mean anything. Heather and I dated for a while in college, when you were at Mizzou and we were both at KU—"

"You said it was just a flirtation before."

"Flirtation usually leads *somewhere*. In our case, it led to sex."

"So this has been going on for more than five years?"

"Having sex with Heather doesn't mean I don't want to marry you."

Actually, she was pretty sure it did. Especially the way he'd gone about that last encounter. In a closet or not, he'd been inside their wedding venue, where servers and planners and guests and their parents and the bridal party were rambling about.

Camden sighed. "Why didn't you just propose to her instead of me?"

Grant blinked. "Because your father is on a partnership track with my father's firm, and hers is a cardiovascular surgeon."

Something clutched in Camden's chest. Not hurt, not entirely. Not betrayal, although the bile at the back of her throat tasted like it. Not sadness. She'd realized several weeks before finding him in the closet that she didn't love Grant. But at the time she'd looked to her mother and stepfather for inspiration. They had made a marriage of common interests work, and it had never seemed like such a big deal. It had, in fact, seemed so much more safe than to wait for the kind of love she'd seen between her biological parents.

The kind of love that sent her mother whirling into a months-long depression and then severing every tie that reminded her of the man who'd had the audacity to be killed in a drunk-driving accident.

She poked at the emotion she didn't want to name. There should be a word that encompassed sadness and betrayal and relief and anger all at the same time. Not miserable, though—she was too relieved to have gotten away from the mistake she might have made to be miserable. If there was such a word, it would be something like *sangerbelief*, maybe.

"Don't be mad," he said, and the placating tone was back in his voice.

"I'm not mad. I'm not even all that sad. I'm relieved that I walked out before I made the biggest mistake of my life."

Camden looked past Grant to the nearly empty meeting hall. Her grandparents were probably waiting outside. God, she was going to have to tell them everything at this point. What would they think of her? Camden closed her eyes for a moment. When she opened them, she saw the mayor standing near the front door, looking everywhere except in their direction.

She needed to get Grant out of here. Out of the hall and out of Slippery Rock entirely. He didn't belong here, and she didn't want him here. A lick of the anger she'd been trying not to feel heated in her belly.

Looking at Grant now, Camden felt entirely naive to have once thought that the two of them had, at least, a deep enough friendship to build something solid. But friends didn't have secret sex meet-ups in closets behind the backs of other friends.

Or maybe they did and it was one more part of life in the twenty-first century that she'd missed out on while she'd been the playing the role of pageant queen.

"We can still get married, sweetheart." Grant reached for her hand, and she felt nothing at his touch. Not familiarity, not a spark of heat. Not the kind of sizzle that seemed to encompass her body every time Levi Walters was within a thousand-yard radius. "We can make this work. I don't have to sleep with Heather," he said, and for the first time, his voice lost the placating edge. "And you don't belong here. What are you going to do? Wear faded jeans and those silly rain boots for the rest of your life? Drive for hours on end to get to a good restaurant? Order designer shoes online because the nearest store is three hundred miles away? You can't be happy here, Camden. This place isn't you."

He'd summed up the woman she'd been pretending to be in two sentences: a woman concerned with nothing more than a great pair of shoes and the right place to have lunch. God, how had she allowed herself to become so shallow? Camden rocked back on her heels, the comfortable boots squeaking against the tile floor. This pair had just been delivered and featured neon-tinted magnolia blossoms. What kind of woman needed seven different pairs of rain boots? Most got by with one. Some with none.

"I may have a slight shoe problem, but that doesn't mean I belong in Kansas City, waiting for you to get done visiting whatever closet you've hidden Heather in. You don't want to be with me, Grant. If you did, you wouldn't have gone after a quickie within a couple of hours of when we were supposed to be saying our *I do*s." He opened his mouth to object, but Camden kept talking. "And I do belong here. I've always loved it here."

"You've never once talked about Slippery Rock, not in all the years we've known one another."

"You never once talked to me about Heather,

but that obviously didn't put out the torch you've been carrying for her."

Grant narrowed his eyes.

"I'm not the person you thought I was. Or maybe I'm just realizing that the person I was isn't who I want to be any longer. I don't want to do the Junior League circuit for the rest of my life, and I don't want to coach pageant girls, and I don't want to marry you. I'm sorry, but I don't."

"But I drove five hours to come and get you."

Camden ignored him. "These boots I'm wearing?" She pointed to the magnolia-splattered rubber. "These boots let me walk through underbrush and a little stream that's only a few inches deep. They keep my feet dry and warm and I wear them when I'm training my dog—"

His blue eyes widened. "You're training dogs?"

"With my grandfather, yes. And maybe the boots are a little silly, and probably I don't need all seven pairs that I ordered, but they're fun. They represent the person that I'm trying hard to become."

"You want to be a woman who wears faded jeans and flannel and ridiculous rubber boots?"

"All the best jeans are faded these days. Some are even ripped before you buy them. It's wonderful." A smile spread across Camden's face. "I do want to be here. And I want to work with my grandfather. I want to make up for all the time I missed with both my grandparents. I want to do something that has meaning."

"I'm not sure training dogs is meaningful."

Camden shrugged. That, right there, was the crux of the problem between her and Grant. They didn't actually think the same way about anything. They attended the same functions, were members at the same clubs, but he saw meaning in profit-and-loss statements. She saw meaning in training dogs. In nature. In the small town she wasn't really a part of. Not yet.

Thom caught her attention and looked pointedly at his watch.

"We should go. Thom's waiting to lock up."

When they were outside and Thom had continued down the street toward the Slippery Slope, Camden turned to Grant. His blonde hair nearly glowed under the streetlight. His polished shoes made a clacking sound against the concrete sidewalk, and his camel coat might be perfect in Kansas City or Chicago or New York, but it was out of place in Slippery Rock.

"I'm sorry you wasted the trip, Grant. Move

on with your life. Move on with Heather or whoever else you might have hiding in a closet somewhere."

"You don't know the kind of mistake you're making."

"And you don't know the kind of mistake we'd be making if I went back with you."

He put his hands in his pockets and watched her for a long moment.

"Goodbye, Grant." She turned toward her car, parked next to her grandfather's old truck. Inside, in the glow from the dash, her grandparents watched her closely. Camden gave them a small wave and walked away from the man she'd been prepared to marry just a week ago. She knocked on the window, and Calvin rolled it down.

"Are you guys thirsty? I could go for a drink."

"Are you okay, Cam?" Grandmom asked after a long moment. She looked past Camden to where Grant had been. Camden didn't look back; she didn't want him to interpret a backward glance the wrong way.

"I'm fine," she said, and realized that she was. That *sangerbelief* feeling was gone, replaced by full-on relief. Like she'd been released from something—or someone—that had been weighing her down. "We could go to the Slope. If I remember correctly, Merle serves the coldest beer and the worst onion rings in town."

"He's added buffalo wings and burgers, and they leave a lot to be desired, too," Grandmom said.

"How about dinner and drinks, then?" she suggested.

Her grandparents exchanged a look, and then Granddad nodded. "I could eat."

The three of them walked down the quiet street. Cars were parked on both sides, but only a few people were out.

"He's the reason you showed up wearing a wedding dress?" Grandmom asked.

"He's the reason." Camden sighed. "He was sleeping with someone I thought was my best friend. I found them, just before the actual wedding."

"Oh, baby," Grandmom said, squeezing her hand. Camden returned the squeeze.

"It's okay. I'll tell you the whole ridiculous story some time."

"You sure you don't just want to go home?" Granddad asked.

"Positive. I'm really okay. I'm not sad or mad or…anything but relieved, actually."

They passed the now quiet grandstand. The next Christmas concert wasn't slated until Saturday, and Camden had spent so much time talking to Grant that the hot-cider and roasted-chestnut vendors had packed up for the night. More cars were parked outside the Slope.

Thom Hall exited his car and offered a wave. Her grandfather waved back, and when they got to the door at the same time, Thom held the door open for them and then continued to the table where his wife waited.

The bar was much as she remembered from her first night back in town: the same polished hardwood floor, the same country music on the juke, the same middle-aged waitress delivering drinks. But there were more people. A lot more. Only a few tables were available.

Levi and his friends, most of whom she recognized from her childhood, were in a corner playing darts with women she didn't recognize. Her tummy did a little flip-flop when her eyes locked with Levi's. Silly. Didn't mean anything—just her girlhood crush rearing its ugly head.

She hadn't walked away from an engagement only to start an even more reckless relationship with a man she barely knew.

"Sit anywhere," Juanita called to them from across the room. "I'll be there in a second."

The three of them found a table near the bar and sat. Camden grabbed a menu from the stand, but Grandmom took it from her. "You want buffalo wings, garlic parm. They're the best."

"Of the worst?"

Grandmom chuckled. "We only really say 'the worst' because all his food is deep fried and consists mainly of salt and fat and empty calories. Well, other than the maraschino cherries and mandarin oranges Juanita keeps on hand for some of the drinks. Despite the empty-calorie thing, though, it's some of the best food in town."

Juanita made it to their table. "I think everybody in town must've come here after that meeting," she said.

"Looks like," Granddad said. "We'll have the garlic parm wings, all around, some onion rings and a few of them mandarin orange slices from the bar."

"The orange slices are for drinks, Cal," Juanita said, putting one hand on her rounded hip.

"Then tell Merle I'm inventing something new. Whatever's on tap, infused with orange slices."

Juanita grimaced. "I'll just bring the bowl."

"I'll have a white wine spritzer," Grandmom

said, and Camden realized for the first time that they shared the same taste in drinks. It was perhaps an odd thing to make her feel as if she'd come home; regardless, warmth spread through her at the realization.

"Same for me," she said.

Once Juanita left, Camden sat back in her chair, taking in the room. The neon behind the bar was partially burned out and made only half-hearted occasional blinks. The patrons talked animatedly. Conversations surged about the odds that the Chiefs would make it to the Super Bowl, about plans for the concert Saturday and whether Santa should come to Slippery Rock via pontoon boat at the marina before going to the little gingerbread house the city had built on the grandstand grounds, or whether a sleigh was the better option.

Santa on a boat seemed like a fun idea to Camden, especially since the chances Slippery Rock would see any snow before Christmas were practically zero.

The dart game in the corner drew her attention; the competition seemed intense. She watched Levi and his friends for a long moment. Collin Tyler had the same enthusiastic grin she remembered from her childhood. Aiden and Adam Buchanan, twins who were practically impossible to tell apart, laughed loudly at something James Calhoun, the newly elected sheriff, said. One of the twins—Adam, she thought—had a dog sitting patiently at his feet. Odd. Animals weren't normally allowed in restaurants or bars. Levi's sister—Camden couldn't remember her name—and Collin's sister, Mara, cheered when Aiden's dart missed the bull's-eye by several spaces.

Levi had changed the most, Camden thought, as she really took in those physical differences. He'd always been tall, but the years training as a professional football player had taken all the gangly off him, replacing it with muscles that made her want to touch. He had a tattoo on his upper arm that she didn't remember. Of course she didn't remember it. She'd seen him a handful of times before tonight, and each time he'd worn a jacket. Well, except for that moment after their tumble under the lake, but she'd been so entranced by the dark skin covering his muscled, bare chest it was no wonder she hadn't noticed a shoulder tattoo. His smile was the same, but somehow it seemed more dangerous coming from the twenty-eight-year-old Levi than it had from the fourteen-year-old. His mouth full. Unbidden, the memory of their kiss outside the barn popped into her head.

Nope, not thinking about kissing Levi. Not thinking about Levi at all.

Her grandparents were deep in conversation across the table, so Camden watched the people around them. But none of them were as interesting as the man standing up to throw darts at the wall target.

His head was nearly shaved, and he had a bit of five o'clock shadow. Suddenly, Camden realized she wasn't just watching Levi. Levi was watching her watching him. She felt trapped in his gaze for a long moment and then forced her attention away from the dart game to the TV behind the bar. A couple of college football teams were pummeling one another.

Camden didn't know a thing about football, but trying to figure out what was happening on-screen was so much better than getting sucked farther into Levi Watching. She glanced toward the corner of the room. He faced the wall, focused on the dartboard. With a graceful flick, he sent the red-tipped dart in his hand to the center of the board.

A smile spread over Camden's face. The man had a way with sports, that was certain. Not that she should pay attention to that.

"So, Six is coming along well," she said, hoping to jolt thoughts of Levi from her mind with plans for the dog school. Her grandparents continued to talk quietly across the table so Camden raised her voice a little. "Are you both still coming to the show in Tulsa with me?"

Their attention swiveled across the able to her. "We made our hotel reservations this morning," Grandmom said then frowned, and seemed to consider whatever she was about to say carefully. "Honey, what was all that about at the hall earlier? Are you sure you're okay?"

"Of course I'm sure," Camden said, without really thinking about it. She *was* okay. Better today than she'd been yesterday or the day before, or, heck, for longer than she cared to admit. "Grant and I…accepting his proposal was a mistake, and waiting until the day of our wedding to walk away was a mistake." Her grandmother's eyes widened. Camden shook her head. "I mean a mistake because I should have done it so much earlier. I just…haven't been myself for a long time."

Granddad reached across the table and brushed her hand with his. "But, kiddo, are you sure you want to train dogs? Because if you don't—"

"Camden, I believe you're making a mistake," Grant said, interrupting them—and stopping the conversations at several nearby tables, too. It seemed to Camden as if every eye in the bar—Levi's included—was suddenly focused on her table. She wanted to sink through the floor.

It had been bad enough to be the focus of attention for the few minutes it took for the hall to empty earlier. At least most of the town didn't know she'd arrived fresh from her almost wedding, still wearing the dress. At least, she hoped they didn't.

"Grant, what are you doing here?" She'd told him to leave. Told him to move on with his life. Made it clear she was moving on with hers. But the man standing before her in polished wing tips, pressed khakis and a camel coat was definitely Grant Wadsworth, and he was definitely not a figment of her imagination.

Automatically, her gaze went to the darts area in the opposite corner, but all Camden could see was Grant's torso in the camel coat.

"I'm here because we had an arrangement—"

"I think you mean engagement," she corrected and then bit her tongue. It didn't matter what Grant called it—it was over. And it didn't matter.

He waved his hand. "You can't just walk away from me."

"I can and I did," she said, keeping her voice low. Granddad started to stand, but Camden motioned him to stay put. She stood and pointed to the door. "We should talk outside."

He didn't move. "You should drop whatever this small-town act is that you've got going and come home with me."

"You don't love me, Grant."

"What does love have to do with it?" He seemed genuinely confused about that, but Camden was his ex, not his teacher. Explaining the ins and outs of relationships—especially when she wasn't all that versed on the subject herself—didn't seem like good use of her time. Or his. And she needed to get him out of here.

"Fine, forget the love angle. You don't want to marry me. I'm not even sure how I factor into the decision at all. My father is on a partner track at your father's firm. A strong contract with a strict noncompete clause is what your father and the firm need. I'm not some princess who can be used to unite warring factions in medieval Europe."

Grant shook his head. "I told you I'd stop seeing Heather."

"Heather isn't the problem."

"Then why did you bring her into this at all?"

"Heather isn't the problem. Heather is what you use to ignore the problem. We liked each other, Grant." She lowered her voice, hoping that between Keith Urban singing from the juke box and the few muted conversations still going on across the room, their argument would remain mostly private. "We were friends whose mothers set them up on a date, and neither of us could come up with a good reason to let either of our mothers down. That isn't a reason to get married, though."

"I still don't see the problem."

Camden squeezed her eyebrows together in annoyance. "The problem is that you don't want to be with me any more than I want to be with you."

"Then who do you want to be with?" Grant asked, as if she had another man on standby. Which made perfect sense, as he'd had Heather on standby in at least one closet while engaged to Camden. Camden wondered what other places he'd used to hide her. The kitchen pantry? The pool house? The trunk of his car?

Someone moved behind Grant, his shadow nearly engulfing the other man. *Crap. Levi.* The last person she wanted to hear about her broken engagement or her idiotic past choices. Grant's question echoed in her mind, along with the image of Levi's face. And that was just stupid.

Twenty-six-year-old Camden did not want to be with Levi Walters. Twelve-year-old Camden had, but that was a long time ago.

"Well?" Grant asked.

Of course, Grant didn't know that. And Levi was only a couple of feet away. And the two of them had nearly burned down Granddad's barn with that kiss a few days before.

Not a good idea, Cam, she told herself. But Grant was watching her expectantly, along with everyone else in the bar.

"Him," she said, moving to Levi's side. Camden took his hand in hers as Grant watched them with a shocked expression on his face. "I want to be with him. Grant Wadsworth, this is Levi Walters."

"The football player?" Grant asked.

"Ah, Camden—" Levi began, but Camden didn't let him finish.

"Yes, the football player. You saw that video from the lighting ceremony. We, ah, reconnected when I came back to town, didn't we..." Camden couldn't think of a proper endearment for Levi. *Darling* was too shiny, *sweetheart* made her think of all the times Grant had called her that, and *honey* was what her grandmother called her. Maybe the two of them didn't need pet names for each other. Did anyone in a fake, would-only-last-a-few-minutes relationship need pet names? "Didn't we, Levi?" she said, gazing up at him. When he didn't say anything, she squeezed his hand as hard as she could.

"I'd say it was more of a dunking than a reconnection. But, sure," he said after a long moment.

Grant eyed the two of them, taking in Levi's short-sleeved T-shirt, jeans and work boots, and Camden's flannel, jeans and rain boots. Probably thinking that the two of them had been shopping at Goodwill or something. Camden didn't care as long as his assumptions drove him straight out of Slippery Rock.

"I have a six-figure salary and you have a serious shoe addiction, Camden—you said it yourself," Grant said after a long moment. He held out his hand. "Come on, let's go back to Kansas City. We can announce our reconciliation in time for Christmas."

"I'm not reconciling with you. I'm with Levi now," Camden said and pasted what she hoped was a sappy, head-over-heels expression on her face. Levi raised his eyebrows and smirked at her, but at least he didn't contradict her.

"No, you're just mad at me about Heather and lashing out," Grant said, and the placating tone was back.

Camden clenched her jaw. "I don't sleep with one man just to get back at another, Grant. Levi and I—" she smiled up at the man who was currently gaping at her "—we're in love." And Camden raised up on her tiptoes and pressed her mouth against Levi's.

The room around them seemed to vibrate with energy, and a rumbling of surprise pulsed through the bar from table to table. She wanted to open her eyes but was afraid of what she might see in Levi's gaze, so she kept her lids squeezed closed and concentrated on selling the kiss to Grant.

Levi's lips tasted like beer, and his mouth was hard against hers for a moment. Then it softened. His tongue pressed against the seam of her mouth, and Camden opened for him. His hand gripped hers, holding it between their chests, and her other arm snaked around his neck.

A wave of heat washed over the room, and the rumbles of the other customers seemed to fade, Grant seemed to fade, everything faded except the man before her. He was real and strong and the heat from him seemed to scorch straight through her.

Camden slipped her tongue into his mouth, deepening the kiss, not for the audience, but just for her. Just because this was Levi, and she'd wanted to kiss him since she was a kid. Had dreamed about the one kiss they'd shared for the last few days. And she wanted to experience his mouth just one more time before she became a celibate dog trainer.

The heat between them in this bar on that first night had been an inconvenience, and when he'd kissed her outside the barn, it had startled her.

This kiss could burn out of control, leaving her shivering and alone in a heartbeat. The thought should petrify Camden. Should send her running from Levi's arms, but she couldn't find the strength to disengage from the kiss. She wanted to stay here, like this, for another year or maybe two. Tasting him, feeling his heart—or was it her own?—pound beneath their joined hands, taking in the rich, outdoorsy scent of him. She could stay like this forever.

"We can talk about this more when I call you tomorrow," Grant said, and the words washed over her like a bucket of cold water. He turned on his heel and left the bar, leaving Camden to face her surprised grandparents, a shocked Levi and a too-interested bar filled with people she barely knew.

Levi released her hand. "We're in love?"

Camden shrugged, hoping the move was more nonchalant than it felt, because in that moment she felt anything but casual. She felt as if her body was on fire. She wanted to wrap her arms around Levi's neck again. Arms, hell, she wanted to wrap her body around Levi and forget the last six months with Grant had ever happened.

But they had happened. She'd gotten engaged to a man she didn't love because he was a good catch, his father was her stepfather's boss and her mother thought Grant was the type of man who was perfect for her.

The truth was, Camden didn't know what she wanted, and until she did, it didn't matter that Levi Walters made her feel more than she'd felt in a long time.

"He needed a reason to let me go."

"And you walking out on him wasn't enough?"

"You don't know Grant."

"I know his type."

Something in Levi's voice caught her attention. "What do you know about his type?"

Levi grinned. "I know his type leaves your type cold and lonely."

"And what is my type?"

He considered her for a long moment. "Trouble," he said, and Camden grinned at him.

She'd never been called trouble before, not even in her wild childhood days of following Levi around in the woods between their properties. She realized most of the bar patrons were still staring at them. So were her grandparents. Since Grant had left, Camden held out her hand. "Thanks for the assist."

"I'm not sure it was an assist. I was on my way to the bar for another round."

And she'd hijacked him. He hadn't been coming to her rescue. Not that she needed him to come to her rescue, but the thought that he might have been had been nice. "Oh. I'll, ah, let you get to it," she said.

Levi watched her for a long moment and then turned on his heel to return to the dart game.

Juanita delivered their food and drinks, and when she left, Grandmom said, "You and Levi?"

Camden shook her head. "He's just a friend."

"That didn't look like a friend kiss to me," her grandfather offered.

Camden speared a buffalo wing with her fork and tasted it. The spice burned her tongue the way Levi's hand at the small of her back a few moments before had sizzled through her clothes. She watched him with his friends for a few seconds.

He hadn't gone to the bar for that next round, she realized. And he hadn't just let her kiss him—he'd kissed back.

"This is good chicken," she said, hoping her grandparents wouldn't press the issue. She needed to figure out how she felt about kissing Levi—tonight and at the barn—and what that meant moving forward.

No, Camden Harris had never been trouble for anyone, and the idea that she could be was intriguing.

LEVI WANTED TO pound his head against the paneled walls of the Slippery Slope. He hadn't intended to get in the middle of whatever was going on between Camden and Khaki Pants. Didn't care what was going on between the two of them. All he'd wanted was another beer, but the Slope was so slammed tonight, Juanita was running in fifteen different directions. He should have gone straight to the bar for the pitcher Merle put out for their table, but no, he'd taken the long route, weaving between tables. And gotten sucked right in to Camden's drama for his trouble.

Everyone at their corner booth was watching him as he closed the gap between Camden's table and their own. Everyone would have questions. And he still didn't have the beer. Damn it. Before he could turn on his heel to go grab it, though, Juanita buzzed past him, carrying two pitchers.

"Anything else y'all need?" she asked, and when no one put in a request, she turned to Levi. "So you and the Harris girl, eh? Wouldn't have seen that one comin'."

Levi didn't know what to say. He and Camden weren't a thing. He and Camden barely knew each other, aside from the two scorching-hot kisses they'd exchanged since her return to town. She obviously wanted people to believe they were, though, and it wasn't exactly a hardship kissing her. Still, he should set the record straight.

Instead, he grabbed one of the pitchers and his glass and poured. "Who's up next?" he asked the group.

Juanita clucked her tongue but didn't ask

anything more about the kiss or Camden before heading to her next table.

"When did this happen?" Savannah asked when it was just the nine of them again. When had their four- or five-man dart game morphed into nine people? And why did all nine pairs of eyes have to home in on him so intently?

"Nothing's happening," he said, hoping they'd all back off. Julia, the newest of their little group, was the only one to stop with the staring. Collin chuckled, James exchanged a glance with Mara and Adam folded his arms over his chest.

"If that kiss was a nothing, I'd like to see a kiss you consider something," he said after a long moment. Jenny smacked his upper arm. "Ow! What? You said the same thing ten seconds ago."

"I *said* it's about time some girl makes Levi think about something other than football and dairy cattle."

"And?"

"And that isn't the same thing *at all*," she retorted.

Levi picked up a dart, considered throwing it at the board and ignoring the pointed looks and conversation surrounding them. Instead, he looked over his shoulder to the table in the middle of the room. Camden and the Harrises were chatting as if nothing had happened. That was annoying. If he had to face some kind of inquisition from people who weren't even related to him—well, aside from Savannah—Camden could damn well face the same line of questioning.

It was only fair, to Levi's way of thinking.

But he wasn't about to cross the room for a second time that evening; that would only lead to more speculation. More questions he didn't have answers for.

Just what had that been about? Obviously, she wanted to get the ex out of the picture, but what did that have to do with Levi? He didn't know Khaki Pants, and Khaki Pants didn't know him.

Were they supposed to duel for her hand?

Was the mere sight of Levi supposed to send the other man running?

Or was the sight of Levi supposed to make Khaki Pants throw Camden over his shoulder Neanderthal-style and carry her back to Kansas City?

Levi tossed the dart at the board. It landed on a twenty spot. Aiden grabbed another dart and took aim while everyone else chatted at the tables. Probably about him. Levi tuned them out the way he'd trained his mind to tune out the noise of a football stadium on game day. Aiden's dart landed on a twenty, too.

The thought of Khaki Pants hauling Camden around like a caveman made him frown. He aimed and threw the dart. It missed the target and embedded in the paneling. Aiden pulled it from the wall and whistled low.

"You don't embed a dart all the way to the barrel in a wall without something being wrong," he said, handing the dart to Levi.

"Nothing's wrong." He aimed again, and this time the throw was true. The dart landed in the bull's-eye. He crooked his head. All the way to the barrel. So maybe the thought of Khaki Pants and Camden was a little annoying. That didn't mean anything.

Aiden threw and hit another twenty position. "Whatever is going on, it's upped your dart game to post–knee injury levels. At least, according to what Adam told me about those duels to the death the four of you would play when you were first came back."

"It's just a dart game." Levi threw his final dart and hit the edge of the board. No score.

"Sure, and whatever that thing was over there wasn't a kiss." Aiden aimed, threw and hit just outside the bull's-eye. He won the round. "It was nothing, right?"

From the corner of his eye, Levi saw Camden and the Harrises leave the bar. As if nothing had happened.

Nothing *had* happened. Kissing Camden, wanting to kiss Camden, didn't mean anything.

Levi Walters wasn't looking for the distraction of a relationship. Not now. Maybe not ever. He liked the company of women, but a long-term relationship had never been something he needed. Being back in Slippery Rock didn't mean he needed that now.

He watched James and Mara, Savannah and Collin, Adam and Jenny, and Aiden and Julia for a long moment. Each couple part of the group, but each also an entity unto itself. Savannah was saying something to Collin that made him grin and nod. Mara had laid her head on James's shoulder. Adam twirled a lock of Jenny's curly hair around his finger, and Aiden slid into the booth next to Julia and put his arm around her shoulder.

Levi swallowed hard and turned back to the dartboard. He pulled the darts from the board and put them back in the holders.

He didn't need a relationship. Before Camden had returned to Slippery Rock, hadn't thought about a relationship at all. He'd considered that run to the coast, hitting a few clubs and scratching the sexual itch, but a relationship? Not something on his mind.

Grabbing his jacket from the bench seat, Levi turned to go. Letting a single kiss—correction, *two* kisses—change his frame of mind where relationships were concerned. He had nothing against love, but he'd never gone looking for it. Somehow, he didn't think being Camden Harris's rebound guy would lead to the type of relationship his friends had found.

"Where are you going?" It was Savannah. She scooted off the booth seat she shared with Collin.

"Home."

She looked at him for a long moment and then said, "Wow."

Collin, James and Mara continued their conversation at one table; Aiden, Julia and Adam talked quietly at the other. No one paid attention to him talking to Savannah. Why that relieved him, Levi wasn't sure.

"Wow, what?" he asked, already knowing he wouldn't like her answer but unable to resist asking just the same.

"One kiss and a few questions from your family and you're running off into the sunset?"

Levi hooked his thumb over his shoulder, pointing toward the one small window that kind of overlooked the street and the marina. If a three-by-three square of the kind of block glass that was usually used in showers could be called a window. It did let in light, though. "Sunset was about three hours ago. And I have an early morning."

"You know what I mean. Finish the game—"

"No one else seems interested in playing. And we already played through one tournament."

"Or just have another drink."

"Maybe another time," he said, and because Savannah looked as if she might have one more suggestion, Levi reached out and tugged a couple of the small braids that covered her head. She hated it when it pulled on her hair, had hated it from the day their parents brought her home from the foster care agency. Levi needed her distracted and off this line of questioning, though, and annoying her about something else was the quickest way to reroute her train of thought.

She wrinkled her brow and brushed her hair

behind her shoulders impatiently. "We always have drinks after town meetings."

"You never attended town meetings until you came back last summer."

"I wasn't interested," she said, straightening her shoulders. "Also, they didn't used to have town meetings at the drop of a hat, not before the tornado tore through. And, anyway, you didn't answer my question."

"Sure I did. You asked where I was going. I said I was going home."

"Not that one, the other one."

"You didn't ask another question."

"You know what I mean. Are you running after *her*?"

"Her who?"

Savannah squinted at him. "It wouldn't be the worst thing in the world, you know." He reached for her hair again, but she brushed his hand away. "It won't work. You're not going to distract me by treating me like I'm seven. I didn't know Camden back then and I don't know her now, but I do know chemistry. And I haven't seen you have chemistry with a woman since I've been back. That can't be, ah, healthy. You know, for a strong, healthy, apparently virile man."

"I'm not talking to my baby sister about my sex life."

"That's because you don't have one."

"Hear, hear," said either James, Collin, Aiden or Adam. Levi had been so focused on Savannah, he couldn't be certain which of his friends was turning traitor at this moment. All four of them seemed engrossed in their conversations. Adam reached down absently to scratch Sheba behind her ears.

"I'm fine, Van. I don't need your help to get…a date or…anything."

"That's why you should stay," she said earnestly. "We could come up with a plan for you to woo Camden Harris's socks off."

"I think you mean bra, Van," Collin said, a stupid grin on his face.

"And panties," James chimed in.

"Pull her hair out of that ponytail," Mara added, a devilish glint in her eyes.

"Point of fact—Camden doesn't wear bras," Julia said. All eyes turned to her. "What? You learn things about the girls you pageant with. She jokes that she's a lowercase A cup, so why bother? Some of us wish we had that problem," she added ruefully, looking at her own full chest.

"Some of us like the quadruple-D cup

you—" Aiden began, and Julia slapped lightly at his hand.

"They're a C cup, and I didn't say I didn't like them, but it would be nice every now and then not to deal with underwires. But we're talking about Levi's girl problem, not my issues with my girls. So, you want the scoop on Cam?"

No, he didn't want the scoop on the woman. He didn't want her at all. He wanted…to kiss her again, damn it, and that was wrong. Camden Harris was the granddaughter of two people he respected and thought well of. On top of that, she'd shown up in town wearing her wedding dress, and now her ex was in town and obviously wanted a reunion.

"I'm going home now, and the next person to bring up Camden Harris or my sex life will live to regret it," he said, pointing his index finger at each of his friends. "I'm. Not. Interested." He turned on his heel and started for the door.

"Methinks," Collin said behind him, and Levi paused.

"He definitely protesteth too much," James added.

Levi kept walking toward the door. They could think whatever they wanted about Camden, about him, about the possibility of the two of them. They were wrong. Levi didn't need that kind of crazy in his life. He liked order.

Camden was chaos, he was positive of it.

CHAPTER SIX

CAMDEN WOKE THE next morning with the feel of Levi's mouth on hers, the smell of him close around her. She stretched, enjoying the sensations in the haze of sleep.

And then sat up straight and knocked the palm of her hand against the side of her head, trying to knock the memory loose. She didn't want Levi Walters. She didn't want a rebound relationship. She didn't want a relationship at all.

What she wanted was to do a good job training Six, to begin rebuilding the dog school with her grandfather, to build a life she could be proud of. A life that didn't involve primping before mirrors and showing off her assets— especially those she'd padded and taped to appear larger than they actually were—to a panel of judges. One that didn't include marrying a man simply because her parents—and his— thought it was a good match.

She pushed back the covers and slid out of

bed, catching a glimpse of herself in the mirror. Her brown hair was mussed from sleep, and in a pair of sleeping shorts with unicorns on them and a gray T-shirt, she looked about twelve. Not at all the kind of woman Levi Walters was likely used to waking up to. Not that she cared. Camden turned toward the door to her adjoining bath rather than the door leading to the hallway and the tantalizing smells of toast and bacon coming from the kitchen. Shower first, then food, then training.

Fifteen minutes later she stepped into Grandmom's country kitchen with its green-checked wallpaper, dairy cows decorating everything from the pot holders and table runner to the magnets on the refrigerator. Three plates were stacked beside the stove, along with silverware. Grandmom turned a few slices of bacon in the pan, humming a tune Camden didn't recognize.

"Good morning," she said. "What can I do to help?"

"You could grab glasses for juice and coffee. Everything else is ready, and Granddad should be back in a second."

Camden set about her task, filling juice glasses and setting them around the circular oak table and then grabbing coffee mugs from the rack under the upper cabinets. "What's he up to, Grandmom?"

"Levi stopped in, talking about the rental agreement for the north forty," she said and began sliding slices of bacon onto plates she pulled from the warming oven.

Camden's heartbeat sped up at the mention of Levi, and she shook herself. Levi wasn't here to see her. He was here to talk with Calvin about business. Nothing to get excited about. Still, Camden craned her neck to look for Levi through the kitchen window.

"I heard his four-wheeler take off a few minutes ago."

Camden snapped back to the kitchen. "I was checking to see if Granddad was coming in," she said, and Grandmom raised an eyebrow at her. Camden set the coffee mugs down, along with the carafe, and then took her place at the table as the back door opened then closed.

"Smells good," Granddad said. He moved to the sink to wash his hands before sitting down and heaping scrambled eggs over his bacon. He proceeded to tear apart a piece of toast from another plate and then mixed the concoction up before eating. Camden had never seen another person eat eggs the way Calvin did. She knew all the food ended up mixed up in the stomach, but how Calvin could look at it all like that was beyond her.

Carefully, she put a spoonful of eggs on one side of the square green plate, bacon on another and toast at one corner. Everything together but nothing touching. Perfect.

Calvin grinned at her and shook his head. "Never did get over your fear of foods touching, did you?"

"It isn't a fear. I just prefer to only taste eggs when I'm eating eggs. Same goes for the bacon and the toast."

"You eat sandwiches, though."

Camden forked up a bite of egg and considered the implication. "That's different. A sandwich is a single entrée. It's supposed to be all squished together."

Granddad chuckled. "You going out with Six this morning?"

Camden nodded. "I thought I'd take him to the course first and then maybe hike around. See how he does outside the course setting."

"Good plan. Dogs can get too used to a course—they need the variety. I was thinking about going over to Joplin Monday morning. There's a dog sale we could hit, then make our way on to Tulsa for the show on Wednesday," Calvin said.

Bonita sighed, but there was excitement in her voice and in her eyes. "Tulsa for two and a half days in the Christmas season. It's going to be crazy."

"But you could visit that craft store you like instead of ordering stuff online for the church bazaar," Calvin said, a cajoling note in his voice.

Bonita finished a slice of bacon and then tapped another against her fingers as if counting off something. "True. And since I'll be spending hours watching dogs herd goats and sheep in a ring, you can spend hours helping me pick out the right ribbons and beads and other supplies for the craft booth. I was just checking and I'm going to need paper clips and craft foam paper and ribbon to finish those bookmarks for the sale on the fifteenth." Bonita turned to Camden. "Will Levi be joining us?"

Camden choked on her eggs, picked up her coffee mug and gulped down a mouthful, burning the roof of her mouth in the process. *What? Levi? Tulsa? No. Not just no but no no no no no. No.* "Why," she began, but her voice sounded as if she'd spent last night screaming at a football game instead of kissing Levi like she'd never kissed another man in her life. She cleared her throat and tried again. "Why would Levi join us?" she asked, fanning her face.

"After last night at the Slope, why wouldn't he?" Bonita asked innocently. She cocked her head to the side, set her bacon on the plate and picked up her cup of coffee. "I didn't realize the two of you had been spending time together," she said over the rim of the mug.

"Now, Bonnie, Cam is capable of picking her own dates. Although that khaki-wearing fella didn't seem like her type at all," Granddad added.

This wasn't happening. She'd never had a dating talk when she was a teen; she wasn't going to start now. She was twenty-six years old. Perfectly capable of dating whoever she chose. Should she choose to date anyone, that was. And when she did choose, her date wouldn't be a Levi type. Levi made things too upside down. He wouldn't be a Grant, either; Grant made things too steady, too predictable.

The man Camden would invite into her life would be a Lent or a Gravi—a man who was nice to look at and who made her stomach do that roller-coaster thing, but who didn't make her question every other thing in her life.

"I'm not dating or doing anything else with Levi. He was just…helping me out of a sticky situation," she said. Camden folded her napkin and put it on her empty plate. "No need to invite him to Tulsa."

"I didn't realize you were the kind of friends who helped one another out of sticky situations by exchanging bodily fluids. In my day, a woman knew a little more about a man than his name before she kissed him in quite that way."

Camden's face burned. She'd kissed Levi—not once, but twice—and Bonita was right. She barely knew the man. In the heat of the moment, with Grant showing up at the town meeting and at the bar, she'd thought she needed a drastic move. Kissing Levi, though, was probably too drastic. Too extreme.

Granddad grunted. "'In your day,' my left foot. Did you or did you not jump off the cattleman's float to plant a kiss on me in the middle of the Founder's Day parade?"

"That was different. We went to school together. I happened to live on one side of the lake and you the other, but we weren't strangers."

"You'd never said two words to me before that kiss, and we were in a class of less than one hundred people."

"Still—"

Granddad shook his head, but Camden

jumped into the conversation. "You jumped off a float? To kiss Granddad?" This was the first she'd heard of this. Her grandparents were affectionate with each other, but jumping off a float in the middle of a parade? Grandmom had always seemed more reserved than that.

"Of course I did. Hattie Mallard was making eyes at him at the time, and I had to get in there quick before she put the best-looking senior in the whole school under her spell." Bonita's gaze was much softer than her voice when it landed on Calvin. "Calvin Harris was quite the catch back then," she said and reached across the table to squeeze his hand. "Still is, as far as I'm concerned."

Granddad smiled back at her. "And Bonita Walsh is still the prettiest girl in any homeroom," he said. Grandmom blushed.

"I'm just going to go grab Six," Camden said, excusing herself from the table. Neither of her grandparents seemed to notice her leaving. That was just fine with her.

Camden pulled a light jacket over her shoulders as she headed for the barn. The sun was just beginning to burn off a bit of fog from the early-morning hours, and the sky was a crisp December blue. Fitting, she supposed, since it was December 1. If she'd gone through with the Thanksgiving wedding, they would just be returning from their honeymoon in Antigua. She'd be at the small office suite in Kansas City this morning, prepping one contestant or another for the holiday season pageants. Deciding on red velvet and fur-trimmed dresses in which her contestants would sing "Silent Night" or "Hallelujah." But she'd walked away from that—some would say recklessly—and she was now wearing jeans and rain boots ready to train a dog in herding techniques.

It was a life she'd imagined as a young girl, but one she'd put into a box in her mind, chalking it up to wishful thinking.

She glanced back to the farmhouse that hadn't changed since she was a preteen. Same black shingles on the roof and shutters at the windows. Same green front door that was so seldom used it squeaked when you opened it. Same mudroom where boots and coats were removed, even if said boots weren't muddy or dirty. Same kitchen, same bedrooms. Same grandparents, people she had never envisioned as reckless at all. They'd always seemed so settled, so in their routine. Like she'd been for most of her life. Now, she wondered how it had taken her more than ten years to finally stand up for what she wanted in her life.

Maybe she wasn't—

Camden stopped short just outside the barn. The door to the runs was open, but instead of Six's usually excited barks at her approach, she heard nothing. Camden peered into the kennel area. The run with the older dogs was full; most of them appeared to be snoozing, although one of the collies raised a lazy eyelid as if questioning why she was there.

"Six," she called, even though she could see the dog's run was empty. The door was latched securely, but the collie was nowhere to be seen. Camden contemplated the options. Either Six had spontaneously combusted and then cleaned up the mess from the beyond, or he'd escaped the runs. Escape seemed like the more realistic option. The dog had been watching closely as Camden opened and closed the run for several days now, and just yesterday Camden had caught Six trying to climb the chain link of the door.

The question now was where would the dog go? And what were the odds that Camden would find him before he caused havoc somewhere?

It only took a few minutes to hike to the training area, Camden's first choice for Six's escape destination, but there were no puppy sounds coming from any of the training apparatus, and no chasing sounds, either. In the distance, a few cattle mooed, but other than that, the chilly morning air was still and quiet.

Wait a second. Cattle were making noise. She never heard the cattle Levi had parked on the forty acres to the north of the training area. If she hadn't walked that area with Granddad and the dogs a few days before, she wouldn't have known the cattle were there at all. Knowing Levi rented the land for the cattle when he could just as easily have put the cattle down when they lost their usefulness to the dairy made her heart clutch in her chest.

Levi might not be thrilled that she was back in town, but he wasn't a monster. No man who created a retirement farm for his old cattle could be a monster.

Camden started for the field where the cattle spent most of their time and, hearing a yip from the same area, quickened her pace.

Darn that silly dog, anyway. He had probably chased another rabbit into the field, only to disturb the cows in the process. Camden felt around in her pocket for the whistle, and when she found it, put it to her mouth, ready to signal Six to stop.

Around the last corner, Camden stopped

short. Six hadn't chased a rabbit into the field, or at least, it wasn't a rabbit he was trying to catch now. The little dog worked tirelessly around a small grouping of five cows, pushing them closer to one of the fences separating this part of the Harris farm from Walters Ranch next door. The cattle not being herded ignored the dog to either chew their cud or lick a big white salt lick as if it held the last scrapes of fudgy brownie batter. While most of the cattle in the pasture relaxed in the late-autumn sunshine, the few cows Six tried to herd bawled or lowed as he moved them closer and closer to the corner of the fence.

Camden forgot about blowing her whistle and simply watched the little dog work, wondering how he'd figured out what to do. The two of them hadn't worked on actual herding yet; so far their training had been about learning the signals so that while Six herded, he was also listening for Camden's instructions. Was it instinct that had him pushing the cows to a corner area? Or was Six simply trying to play with cows who didn't want to play with him? It was impossible to tell.

For a few more minutes, Camden watched the dog, trying to decide which was going on. When one of the cows started to move away from the corner, Six countered, directing her back with the others. The six of them—five cows and the dog—moved in a kind of dance across the area of pasture. When the cattle veered left, Six countered by pushing them back to the right. The sound of a four-wheeler in the distance brought her back to the pasture, and the fact that she and Six weren't supposed to be in this area. Hell, if it was Levi on the four-wheeler, he would probably take that even farther and insist Camden wasn't supposed to be in Slippery Rock at all.

She couldn't blame him after the way she'd used him the night before. She hadn't explained why she'd kissed him, hadn't offered to introduce him to Grant. She hadn't told him anything about her life before or after arriving in town.

She had barely spoken to him, hardly knew him at all and yet she'd kissed him. Twice now. Kisses that made her think things that simply weren't possible. Like that maybe the two of them were fated lovers or something. Camden eyed the crisp December sky. Had to be the holiday season talking, although it certainly didn't feel like a cold Christmas Day right now. The sun was bright in the sky, the fog had burned off the ground and before long she wouldn't need the light jacket she'd grabbed this morning. Sounds of the four-wheeler grew louder.

Camden blew the whistle, and Six stopped in his tracks to look toward the gate. Letting the whistle fall from her mouth, Camden climbed over the gate separating the area of pasture on Harris land and the portion rented by Levi. When the dog saw the whistle drop, he went back to herding the cows into the corner.

Another of the dairy cattle wandered into the area, and Six joined her with the rest of the tiny herd. Watching the dog's smooth movements, Camden was proud. She couldn't take any credit for what Six was doing right now, but the dog's actions reinforced to her that training was how she wanted to spend her time.

She blew the whistle again, but this time Six ignored the sound and continued to work until all six cows were huddled into the corner of the pasture. The animals didn't seem scared, and once the dog backed off a little, a few of them went back to chewing grass. Six trotted to Camden's side, looking expectantly at her.

Camden wrinkled her brow. "We're going to add another rule to your training," she said, kneeling before the dog and giving him a good scrubbing behind the ears. "The other day we learned not to chase bunnies. Today, the lesson is that we don't bother the cows. They're here to enjoy their retirement, not put on a show for you," she told the dog, who seemed to smile happily at her.

The four-wheeler engine grew louder, and when the cattle in the corner became restless, Six hurried to their area again, herding them back into the corner.

Camden blew her whistle, but the dog either couldn't hear it over the sound of the four-wheeler engine or he ignored Camden's instructions. Camden wasn't sure which was worse—a dog that wouldn't listen to her or a dog that was hard of hearing.

Levi stopped the recreational vehicle outside the gate and climbed over, an annoyed expression on his face.

A dog that wouldn't listen, definitely, she decided.

"What the hell are you doing on my land with my cattle?"

Camden crossed her arms over her chest and stepped between Levi and the dog. Not that the dog was paying any attention to the man—he was too busy barking at the cattle in the corner of the pasture for that. "Technically, this is my grandfather's land. You're only renting it," she said.

"Renting to own," Levi corrected. "And that doesn't answer my question."

Briefly, Camden considered pushing Levi, because she didn't owe him any explanations. Except he had legally rented the land from her grandfather, who seemed to like having Levi as a tenant. Plus, with the dog school not operating, renting out part of the land meant extra money in her grandparents' bank account.

"Six escaped. I came here looking for him."

"Because you regularly train him using my cattle?"

"No, because he went chasing after a bunny the other day, and I didn't want him getting lost in the woods. It can be dangerous for a dog out here, especially one used to kennels and dog runs."

Levi continued to scowl at her. "The woods end over there," he said, pointing behind her.

"Are you always this grumpy?"

"I'm not grumpy." But the frown deepened, putting lines between his chocolate-brown eyes. He wore an old Slippery Rock High School ball cap, a Carhartt jacket and worn jeans with work boots. He looked delicious from the top of his head to the soles of his boots, despite the frown. Or maybe because of it.

"Well, I wouldn't go straight to calling you Oscar, but there are no words other than *grumpy* and *grouchy* to describe your countenance since I came to town."

"I'm not a dwarf, and I'm not a Muppet. I'm a dairy farmer who doesn't have time to chase after your dogs."

"Dog, singular. And who's asking you to chase after the pup? I said I was getting him, and I am."

"Doesn't look that way to me."

"That's because you're distracting me with your Oscar the Grumpiness," she said, and before she could talk herself out of it, she blew into the whistle. Hard.

"Son of a—" Levi clapped his hands over his ears. Six stopped in his tracks. Camden released two more sharp, staccato blows of the whistle, and the dog trotted over to her.

"As I was saying," Camden said, looking into the dog's big blue eyes as she spoke. "We don't chase bunnies and we don't herd cattle that don't belong to us. Stay," she said sternly when Six came up off his haunches. Camden's cell rang in her pocket, and when she reached for it, the dog started to move again. Camden pointed her finger at the dog and beetled her brow. "No," she said.

The number on the screen read "unknown" but had a Kansas City area code, and Camden swiped her finger across the screen to ignore the call. Grant. She'd obviously not properly blocked his number the other day. Damn it.

"If you'll excuse us, Six needs an actual training run, and your cattle could—"

The ringing of her phone stopped her again. Same number, same "unknown" above it on the screen.

"You should probably answer that. Seems like an intent caller," Levi said when her finger hovered over the screen again.

"Maybe I don't want to talk to him."

"The boyfriend?"

"Ex," she said, emphasizing the single syllable. "Ex-boyfriend."

"I thought you were going to marry him."

"I don't think that's any of your business." Camden once more swiped the call off her screen, sending it straight to voice mail.

"You made it my business when you kissed me last night at the Slope."

"That was a warning kiss. It didn't mean anything," she said, pocketing the phone. "Besides, you kissed me first."

"That was an annoyance kiss. It didn't mean anything, either." He folded his arms over his chest.

"Is that why you keep going out of your way to see me?" she asked, using her sweetest pageant coach voice.

"I was checking my cattle."

"You already checked the cattle this morning. With my grandfather. Also, doesn't Bennett usually check the cattle in this area? He's the only one I've seen delivering the salt licks, anyway." Not that she had been actively watching for Levi when she worked with Six at the training area or during their post-training walks.

"Yes, my father usually checks the cattle first thing in the morning, but I take the later checks."

"Just how much babysitting do retired cattle need? And since when is—" Camden checked her watch "—nine fifteen in the morning 'later'?"

"Since now."

Camden signaled Six to stand. "Mature, Walters, real mature," she said and began walking toward the fence.

"Kind of like your rain boots."

Camden looked down. She'd slid her feet

into the unicorn-and-rainbow boots this morning and smiled when she saw them. The navy was ordinary, but the bright flashes of neon orange and red, the lime greens, and the crisp whites of the design elements made her happy.

"Functional doesn't have to mean ugly," she said. Her phone rang again, and she swiped to ignore it once more.

Grant needed to take a hint. He had to go back to Kansas City. Start a new life with Heather, or, if their sleeping together was just a distraction like he'd said, he needed to find someone who didn't make him feel as if he needed a distraction. Camden didn't want to be either the distraction or the part of life Grant needed distraction from. She wanted… Her gaze landed on Levi.

She wanted to feel the way she felt when Levi kissed her outside the barn, the way she'd felt kissing him in the middle of the Slope last night. Like the two of them were the only people who mattered. She couldn't be with Levi, not really. Not while he barely tolerated her presence. Grant, though, needed to move on, and since he'd already caught one kiss, it made sense for him to see another. And another. For as long as it took him to realize Camden wasn't going back to him.

A plan began forming in her mind. One that would make Grant move on, and one that might make Levi think of her with a little less annoyance. If it didn't accomplish that last part, at least she could enjoy the distraction of Levi for a little while in the meantime.

"How would you like to help me with a little project?" she asked.

LEVI HELD UP his hands in what he hoped looked to Camden like disgust. "No," he said emphatically.

The truth was, he wasn't disgusted by Camden's proposal at all. He was intrigued by it, and that was the most ridiculous thing he'd felt since she blew into town a couple of weeks before. Levi Walter didn't go for schemes— at least he hadn't since that last prank with Mara and the guys in high school. He was an adult, with plans. Scheming with a unicorn boot–wearing former beauty queen was not part of his plan. Adding those new organic food options, expanding the dairy, those were his plans, and if he found a woman along the way who wanted to share in those plans, great. If not, there were always women around who didn't mind spending a little time with him before moving on.

"It's just for a couple of days. Grant only needs to see us together, maybe at dinner or something, and he'll realize that I've moved on. It will give him the closure he needs to do the same and get out of Slippery Rock. Win-win," she said, putting her small hands on his forearm and squeezing. "Come on, Levi, what can it hurt?"

He didn't have an answer for that. Grant didn't seem the kind of man to be truly hurt by a woman dumping him. Inconvenienced and annoyed? Sure. But hurt? The man was too polished and pressed for that kind of emotion. Levi frowned. "Why don't you just tell him you've moved on?"

"I have told him. Twice. Once on the phone after that video of us falling into the lake hit the news, and again last night at the Slope. Just before that kiss." She held up her phone, which was quiet for the first time in a couple of minutes. "Obviously, he hasn't gotten the hint that we're over. He's a visual learner."

"If the kiss last night didn't convince him, what makes you think a coffee date will?"

"Because everyone loves a great story, and Christmas romances make great stories," Camden said, shrugging her shoulders as she spoke. In addition to the ridiculous unicorn rain boots, she wore skinny jeans with a rip midthigh and a layered combination of T-shirt, flannel and a jean jacket. She had to be sweltering. Levi wore a tee and a light Carhartt jacket, and the late-autumn sun was burning him to the ground. Funny, the meteorologist hadn't said anything about an unseasonable heat wave on the news last night. "Grant needs to see it in context. A little talking, maybe some hand-holding. We could go to that concert tonight at the grandstand. He sees us, he sees the town lit up with decorations and he finally makes the breakup permanent in his mind. We don't have to kiss," she said, as if kissing Levi were suddenly anathema to her.

After the one she'd laid on him last night, he knew she enjoyed kissing him. Her apparent denial of that was intriguing.

The cattle her little dog had herded into the corner dispersed. The dog was about to wag his tail right off his little brown and white and black body, or maybe go after the cows again. Levi knew the pup couldn't hurt the cattle; he was a mere annoyance. Better, though, to get the dog back where he belonged.

Like he needed to get Camden back where she belonged.

Of course, dressed like she was in boots and

jeans, she didn't look as if she belonged in Kansas City. She looked like a local, like any one of the two hundred or so girls with whom he'd gone to high school. "You want a ride back to the farm? I'm sure your little Toto here will race the four-wheeler back."

"He's a collie, not a terrier, and I'll walk."

Levi fell in step beside her. He didn't need to escort her back, but he didn't want to leave her just yet, either.

"What are you doing?"

"Walking you home."

"I thought we weren't pretend dating," she said.

"We aren't."

"Then we're dating? Because my understanding of small-town social convention is that the guy walks home the girl he is romantically interested in. And you just swore up and down you weren't interested in helping me fool my ex into thinking we're dating. Is that because you really don't want to date me or because you secretly do and walking me home is the only way to secretly date me?"

Levi blinked, trying to follow her circular thinking. He failed. "Walking you home isn't a testament of my undying love or attraction. It's an act of kindness."

"In case I trip and fall into a bush of poison ivy?"

"In case you get lost. These trails haven't been kept up in recent years."

"A situation I'm planning to remedy once the dog school is back up and running properly."

"So, you're really planning to go through with that? It's not just an idea to help you pass the time until Khaki Pants whisks you off to another lavish wedding you say you don't want?" Levi wanted pull the words back into his mouth, but they were already out there. Camden stopped walking and gaped at him for a moment.

"You think all of this is an act?"

"You're the one who showed up in town wearing your wedding dress."

"Because I ran away from my wedding."

"And in the four hours it took you to get from Kansas City to Slippery Rock, you didn't have a single chance to change your clothes." Camden clenched her jaw and didn't reply. "Because it seems to me if you really didn't want to get married, you'd have stripped off that dress as soon as possible instead of wearing it into a bar and asking for directions. Or showing up on your estranged grandparents' front steps still wearing it."

Camden stomped through the underbrush, hurrying her pace as they neared the barn. "I'm not acting. I'm not marrying Grant Wadsworth, and I'm tired of living my life as a clone of my mother. I walked away from all of that because finding Grant playing Pin the Penis on the Bridesmaid with my former best friend was the final straw. I'd done everything right. I picked the right caterer, the right dress, the right reception band. I started the business he and my mother suggested after I aged out of the pageant circuit, and in college I majored in the same thing my mother did. I'm tired of living my life like some kind of clone." She stopped walking again, turned and poked his chest.

Levi was still hung up on the Pin the Penis comment. Grant had cheated on Camden? That didn't make sense. Camden might be a little flighty—it wasn't exactly normal, from Levi's point of view, for a woman to walk out on her wedding at the literal last minute—and she might have ignored her grandparents for far too long, but she was a gorgeous woman. One he'd never cheat on.

Not that he was dating her. Or would date her. Or should date her. Or… He needed to get back to this conversation and stop thinking about what-ifs that he shouldn't be thinking.

Damn George Bailey and Captain von Trapp for making him equate Christmas with romance and true love. Camden Harris was not his true love, and dating her would be a mistake. A fun mistake, but a mistake nonetheless. Levi Walters didn't make mistakes. He measured and he calculated and he planned. It was who he was, and it had worked thus far in his life.

"This isn't an act," she continued, not giving Levi time to speak. They'd arrived at the barn, and Camden pulled the heavy door open. "I'm not here waiting to get swept off my feet and taken back to Kansas City by some khaki-wearing Prince Charming. I'm here to take my life back and—" She didn't finish her thought. Camden's wide brown eyes widened, and she clapped her hand over her mouth.

Levi started to turn, but she grabbed his shoulders so that he couldn't see whatever was going on behind him.

"I'm going to apologize in advance for what's about to happen. You'll just have to trust that it's absolutely necessary," she said, and then she jumped into Levi's arms.

Camden wrapped her legs around Levi's

waist and put her arms around his shoulders. Without him thinking about it, his arms went around her waist, not that she needed the extra support. Her body felt good against his. Too good. All the blood in his body seemed to instantly reroute below his waistband. Levi clenched his jaw, willing his body to stop reacting to Camden's. Unlike in football, his body ignored what he told it to do. He was hard and getting harder by the minute.

"Just go with it," she said, and there was desperation in her voice and in those big brown eyes. Desperation that Levi should ignore but couldn't. Maybe he could get whatever this was back on solid ground, though.

He put his hands on Camden's waist so he could lift her off him and pasted a grin on his face. "I've never minded women throwing themselves at me, although most don't literally—"

Her mouth closed over his, cutting off his words. Which was good because the kiss also short-circuited his mind. Levi couldn't remember the point he'd been about to make. He forgot that he was annoyed with her cute unicorn boots and her weird fake-dating-to-fool-the-fiancé plan. All he could think about was the feel of Camden's smooth lips, the rise and fall of her chest against his, and the softness of her body against the hardness of his. He wanted to cup her face between his palms, but without a wall to brace her, he was afraid she would fall. That would put too much space between them, and he didn't want space. He wanted more of her.

Her mouth opened under his, letting him in to taste her. Sweet like orange juice.

Her small hands clasped behind his head, knocking the old ball cap to the ground, and Camden moaned low in her throat. The sound sent a rush of adrenaline through his body and, God, his jeans were now so tight around his erection it was nearly painful. Levi didn't mind; the almost pain turned to pleasure. It would be so easy to take things farther. Take Camden into the barn, put her up against that wall or lay her down so he could kiss every last inch of her.

Gravel crunched behind them.

"There she—" Calvin began saying, and then paused. "Is," he finished after a long moment.

Just like that, reality came crashing down. This wasn't what he'd had in mind when he drove back over here this morning. Checking on the cattle had been the plan. Then back to his office, and then seeing how Mama Hazel's ice cream concoctions were going. Kissing Camden was not in the plan, not right now.

"Granddad. Grandmom." Camden blinked, her gaze hazy, as if she'd forgotten for a moment where they were. Well, at least he wasn't alone in that. She slid down his body, and Levi clenched every muscle he could, ordering his body not to react any more to hers. It didn't work. The curves of her body seemed to fit against his as if made for it. The scent of her shampoo still surrounded him. When she reached for his hand, he didn't pull away.

Then she looked past Levi, past her grandparents to the man walking slightly behind them. Wearing another pair of khaki pants, this time with what appeared to be a pressed polo shirt and an open leather jacket. Levi couldn't suppress the eye roll. The guy dressed like he was starring in some 1990s teen movie or something, not like he was visiting a working farm.

Camden sighed and pasted what he knew was a fake smile on her face, and when she spoke, it was forced surprise in her voice. "And Grant, what are you doing here?"

"I, ah, thought we should talk," the other man said. His short blonde hair was combed back from his face, and a concerned look clouded his expression. "Alone," he added when it became clear Camden wasn't in a hurry to leave the barnyard. Or Levi.

Levi bit back a grin. Why it was important that Camden stood beside him he wasn't certain, but it made him happy to see her not trotting off after the ex who'd been cheating on her. Levi might not be the right man for Camden, but neither was this schmuck.

"I don't think we have anything more to talk about. I'm not going back to Kansas City with you. I wouldn't, even if Levi and I weren't together." She squeezed his hand, and when Levi glanced at her, there was a sense of urgency in her gaze, and those big eyes seemed to beg him not to say anything. "But we are together, and that isn't going to change. Levi's even going with us to a dog show in Tulsa this week."

Levi blinked. Tulsa? She'd mentioned a date or two, and he hadn't even agreed to that. Now they were suddenly going to Tulsa? Calvin and Bonita shared a shocked glance. Apparently he wasn't the only confused person in this barnyard.

"Is that right?" Calvin asked after a long pause.

"I, ah, just invited him to tag along." Camden swallowed, and then some idea Levi already knew he wouldn't like flashed in her eyes. "After he saw Six working a few of the older dairy cows, he wanted to see a fully trained dog. You know, for the dairy."

Now he was practically buying a cattle dog in addition to pretend dating her? "I thought—"

Camden cut him off. "I know, dairy cattle don't wander like beef cattle, but you said yourself there were times a cattle dog could come in handy. Maybe for Mama Hazel's chickens or the lambs."

Lambs? What lambs? What the hell was Camden talking about? Walters Ranch had a handful of chickens, but there were no lambs. No goats, no ducks, no faddy llamas or alpacas. It was a dairy farm, and a damn good one that ran like the well-oiled machine he and Bennett had always planned for it to be.

Camden squeezed his hand again, refocusing Levi's attention, and that desperate, pleading expression on her face was his undoing. Before he could tell himself not to agree with her, Levi did.

"I can't wait to see what a few herding dogs can do at the ranch," he said.

Grant stared at the two of them for a long moment, his mouth gaping open. "You're dating a football-playing dairy farmer?" he said. "You're a beauty queen!"

"I don't categorize people by what they do for a living, but, yes, Levi played football and now he runs a successful dairy farm. And, yes, I was once a beauty queen. Now I'm on my way to being a darn good stock-dog trainer. I'm not going to marry you, Grant, or reconcile with you. Go back to Kansas City. Go back to Heather or whoever else you have there." Her voice was firm, and there was a note of steel present. Steel he hadn't heard in Camden's voice since she came back to town. He wondered which Camden was the real Camden—the one who ran away from her problems or the one who faced them. If pretend dating him was, in fact, facing her problems.

Not that he'd agreed to be her pretend date. That was just the kind of crazy scheme Mara would have cooked up when they were kids. But he wasn't a kid. He was an adult. Adults didn't scheme. Adults planned. Well, except Camden, apparently.

Why Camden, in all her forms, appealed to Levi he couldn't put into a clear thought. She'd run away from her wedding, had jumped right into dog training—and at a training center that hadn't been operational in nearly five years—

and now she was bargaining for a handful of dates. None of this made sense to Levi.

Maybe it didn't have to. As long as her plans didn't mess with his, what did it matter that she'd asked him to be her pretend boyfriend to get her very real ex off her case?

The fact was he didn't know Camden, not really, but the memory of her in that wedding dress in the Slope made him think things that just weren't possible, like that he'd like to be the one she walked toward wearing that dress. That maybe her scheming could be a fun way to pass the time during the perennially slow winter months in Slippery Rock.

He just had to figure out who the real Camden Harris was. Was she the woman who wore jeans and goofy rain boots and made him smile? Was she the dog-losing trainer who bugged his cattle—and him? Was she the woman speaking with steel in her voice as if she never doubted herself? And if the no-nonsense woman talking now was the real Camden, why had she run away from Mr. Khaki Pants instead of telling him off when she found him playing Pin the Penis on the Bridesmaid?

"Beauty queens don't train stock dogs, Camden," Khaki Pants was saying, and with quite a bit of condescension in his voice.

"I'm not a beauty queen anymore, Grant. I haven't been for about five years."

"You have a good business, with top clientele—"

"A business I never wanted. Pomp and Circumstance was always my mother's dream. She started it with me, and she was good at it—"

"You were just as talented," he said, but Camden waved her hand in dismissal.

"Training pageant contestants isn't what I want to do. Just like marrying me wasn't what you want. Grant, can't you see what a mistake it would have been, marrying me when you don't want to be with me? We're adults. We can't keep doing the things our parents tell us to do, especially when we don't want those things for ourselves." Camden took a breath. "I knew it before I caught you with Heather, but I didn't know how to stop the wedding train our mothers started. It took finding the two of you in that closet to realize it was time to walk away."

Levi wondered how much of that was true and how much was show for Grant. Had she merely gone along with her mother's plans for her all these years? That didn't seem like something the Camden he remembered would do, or that the Camden who'd literally jumped his bones a few minutes ago would do. But then, he'd seen how close Camden had been to her father all those years ago. How stressed-out the farm seemed to make her mother. At the time, Levi had decided Elizabeth Harris had a monstrous stick up her butt, but maybe it was more than that. Whichever was true, he had to remember his plans in all of this. Expand the dairy operations. Not get caught up in Camden's scheme.

Grant seemed to consider her words. "You'll come to your senses."

Camden shrugged. "Maybe I will. Maybe he will," she said, pointing to Levi.

"This isn't over, Camden, and I'm not leaving."

"By all means, stay. There is a dance tonight at the grandstand, and a host of other events the town has come up with to ring in the Christmas season. I'm sure we'll see you at some of them," she said amiably.

Grant still didn't seem convinced that what was going on between Camden and Levi was real, but to the man's credit, when Calvin said it was time to go a moment later, he went. Like a gentleman, Levi supposed.

Like a wuss was more like it.

Levi had never been shooed away from a woman in his life; he certainly wouldn't allow himself to be shooed at nearly thirty. Grant got into his rental car—a Mercedes, of course—and drove back down the farmhouse lane.

"I suppose you two have some things to talk about," Bonita said after a moment. She and Calvin turned toward the house.

"No, that's—" Levi said, but the two older people merely waved their hands at him and continued on.

"Pin the Penis on the Bridesmaid," he said when the grandparents were too far away to overhear. "Who is this Heather?"

"My former best friend." Camden dropped his hand, and Levi felt a bit lost at the loss of contact. Which was silly. He knew exactly who he was; holding Camden's hand while she very nicely told off the guy who'd cheated on her didn't change that.

"He cheated on you, at your wedding, with your best friend?"

Camden shrugged. "For most of our relationship, I think. Definitely all of our engagement."

"You don't seem upset about that." And that was the strangest part of everything that had happened in the last ten minutes.

She opened the barn door and began sweeping the hard concrete floor. To avoid him or send him on his way, Levi wasn't sure.

"I'm not. I'm not happy that it happened, but I'm glad I found out about it before we'd actually said our vows. That would have made walking away so much harder."

"And two weeks after calling it all off, you want to not only pretend date me, but spend a few days together in Tulsa?"

"No, I want to spend a few days with my grandparents in Tulsa, but if taking you along gets Grant off my back, I'm willing."

Levi chuckled. At least they were clear on one thing: Camden was using him to get rid of her ex. That would make saying no to the whole silly plot that much simpler. "And that kiss?"

She kept sweeping the open area of the barn, avoiding his gaze. She swept methodically until she reached a button near the front of the dog runs. The back walls raised, allowing the dogs to move to the outside area of the runs. And still she avoided his gaze. Interesting.

"Just setting the scene. I already told you, Grant is a visual learner."

"So we pretend to kiss, we pretend to go off to Tulsa, and he finally moves on?"

Camden shook her head, and the movement set off highlights of deep gold in her hair. "No. We go on a fake date here, he probably follows us to Tulsa and then he finally moves on when he realizes *I've* moved on. With you."

Camden opened the interior door to one of the runs, and the dog that had been herding his cattle before came into the barn. Camden scrubbed her hand over its ears, and then threw a green ball that the dog chased around the barn.

"Will you do it?" she asked, and finally met his gaze with hers. Levi felt something hot fire up in his belly.

"What do I get if I go along with this scheme of yours?"

"My undying gratitude?"

"Gratitude doesn't pay the bills, sweetheart," he said.

"It doesn't seem to me that you have trouble paying your bills." Camden cringed. "Don't ever call me 'sweetheart,' not even in pretend. How about you do this for me and I don't rally up support for the bike trail that you obviously don't want?"

"A bike trail versus dating you." Levi considered the options and laughed when Camden slapped his arm. "I need a bigger return on my investment."

"What?" she said after a moment, eyeing him with distrust. The dog brought the ball back to her and Camden threw it again.

Levi considered the options. There was nothing Camden had that he wanted, although if she did expand the stock-dog school, it could impede the growth of his dairy. With Savannah planning to put her camp for foster kids on the south side of the property, he could use the acreage he'd been leasing from Calvin on a permanent basis. It would give the older, non-organic cattle a place to live out their days, and be a place where all the cows could eventually retire. "I've been renting that forty-acre plot from Calvin for a while. I'll help you convince Grant we're an item and that he needs to leave town if you help me convince your grandfather to sell those forty acres—acres he hasn't used in longer than either of us have been alive," he added when Camden tried to speak up.

"I'm not going to prostitute myself for a land deal," she said, crossing her arms over her chest.

"No sexual favors have to be exchanged."

Camden blinked. "I'm not convincing my grandfather to sell his land to you just to get

Grant off my back. I'll deal with him on my own," she said, cocking her hip to the side. The little dog was back, but instead of throwing the ball for it this time, Camden led the animal to the run, put it inside and closed the door. She put the ball in a basket nearby, and turned to him, her eyes narrowed. "Plus, we still have a dog school to run. Once we pick up a few dogs from breeders."

"I'm only talking about a small portion of land that Calvin no longer uses. Your little training area wouldn't be in danger."

"'Little' training area?" Camden narrowed her eyes. "Those trails run all over the woods and pastures."

"But not the forty I've been renting," he said.

Camden drew her bottom lip between her teeth and seemed to consider the options. "I'll suggest that selling might not be a terrible idea, but that's as far as it goes."

"And our apparent infatuation will *suggest* to your ex that it's time he move on." Levi held out his hand, and when Camden took it, he pulled her a little closer. "Assuming, of course, that I agree to the plan."

"But we already set it in motion. I told him about the dance."

"But you didn't actually ask me to go to

Tulsa or to the dance tonight," Levi said, knowing he was being ridiculous. He didn't need Camden to formally ask him to go along with the plan, but it was fun watching those golden flecks in her eyes sparkle to life in annoyance.

Seeing her physical reaction to him was fun, too. She was close enough to him that he could see her pupils dilate, but Levi didn't pull her closer. Something flitted across her gaze. An emotion that made his belly clench. Then she blinked and the expression was gone, replaced by distance.

"Levi, will you go with me to the Christmas dance tonight, and to Tulsa on Tuesday?" she asked.

"Okay, I'll go with you. Do I get a corsage?" She pursed her full lips, and Levi couldn't hold back the grin any longer.

"You're just messing with me," she said.

"You're cute when you're annoyed."

"You're annoying when you speak," she retorted, but she didn't jerk her hand away. "Are we doing this or not?"

"I'll go with you to the dance, and I can carve out a little time for Tulsa."

"Good. And I'll talk to Granddad about your proposal for the acreage. But only in generalities and with no pressure to actually sell."

Camden pulled away from him. Levi followed her out to the barnyard. She closed the big door behind her and then slid the bolt home.

"I'll see you tonight?" she asked.

"Pick you up at seven. We can grab some food at the grill before things get started." Levi wanted to pull the words back into his mouth. Having dinner with Camden wasn't part of the plan, although it might help sell their sudden supposed fascination with each other. Before he could say anything else, Levi turned toward the north pasture.

He didn't want to date Camden. He didn't have time for a trip to Tulsa, and even if he did, he wouldn't make that trip just to watch some cattle dogs round up a few geese and goats. Still, the thought of spending a little more time with Camden was interesting. And the thought of turning his rental agreement with Calvin into a buyer's agreement was even more so. And all for the price of a little acting.

Levi wasn't looking for a relationship, but he couldn't deny that he liked kissing Camden Harris. She made him feel things he hadn't felt in a long time. He liked teasing her. Looked forward to actually talking with her. As little as Levi knew about her now, he knew she deserved better than to be cheated on by a guy like Khaki Pants. *Grant.* What kind of name was that? Preppy and obnoxious, that was the kind of name it was. Just like the man himself.

When he got to the pasture, Levi started the four-wheeler and turned it toward home, still thinking about kissing Camden.

What kind of man messed around with another woman when he had a beautiful woman like Camden already in his bed?

What kind of man pretended to date a woman like Camden, not to get her into bed but to enter into a real estate deal with her grandfather?

Levi frowned at that thought. He wasn't using Camden or their attraction to buy something. It wasn't like that. It was…not entirely unlike that, either.

Damn it, Walters, stop thinking already, Levi ordered himself.

Camden wasn't looking for a relationship, and neither was he. This was just a temporary agreement to get each what they wanted.

Levi just needed to stop thinking so much.

CHAPTER SEVEN

"YOU'RE TWENTY-SIX years old. Living in your grandparents' spare room and dating a man who would probably rather you not have a curfew. So, here," Bonita said, pressing the key into Camden's hand. Camden immediately put the key on the kitchen table and stepped away from it. What she wouldn't give to have waited in the upstairs bedroom until she heard Levi's truck in the drive.

Of course, she hadn't waited, because that made him picking her up for dinner seem too much like a real date, and she wasn't dating Levi. She was using him to get rid of Grant, the same way he was using her to potentially turn a lease agreement with her grandfather into a lease-to-own agreement.

It had been an odd afternoon. After Levi drove off into the woods, Camden had returned to the farmhouse, where her grandparents were conspicuously absent.

Since she had arrived on their doorstep two

weeks before, one or the other of them had hovered around her nearly every minute. It had been nice, but with them both off doing whatever it was they were doing, the house had seemed too big and too quiet, leaving her mind too much time to rethink this crazy scheme.

Pretend dating Levi. What had she been thinking? It was one thing to kiss him last night at the Slope. All eyes in the bar had been on them, but she could have eventually explained that away as too much drinking. They didn't have to know that Camden never drank too much. She didn't like to feel out of control, which was weird, because nothing about her life had felt totally in control since she'd walked away from the wedding, and she had embraced every minute of it.

Pretend dating Levi, though—that thought left a nervous feeling in her stomach, like maybe she was closer to out of control than she thought.

"We hardly ever lock the doors, so the key is mostly symbolic. Live your life," Grandmom was saying.

"I don't need a key. I don't have anywhere to go that you two won't already be." Besides, it would be too weird. She'd lived in her mom and stepdad's Mission Hills mansion for most of her adult life, but that was different than living with her grandparents. At the house in Kansas City, she had practically an entire wing to herself, but here she was sharing four bedrooms with her grandparents, with a rickety staircase and barely two thousand square feet separating the three of them. Which meant she had no plans to come and go. Even with a key, they would hear her coming and going, and this conversation was awkward enough with her grandparents just thinking she might have sex with Levi at some point in the future. She couldn't imagine dealing with either of them over Grandmom's scrambled eggs the morning after she actually slept with the man.

Besides which, Camden wasn't ready to jump back into dating—pretend dating Levi aside. She needed to figure out who she was, standing on her own two feet and without a spreadsheet created by her mother to guide her.

Jumping into bed with Levi would only muddy the waters. Her toes curled involuntarily at the thought of her body so close to his during their most recent kiss. Well, maybe she wouldn't mind seeing a little bit more of that hard body she'd felt so intimately this morning.

She was getting off track. Levi's body might turn her body on, but that was the end of it.

Camden was not going down Hormone Alley with exciting Levi Walters simply because she'd walked away from Marriage Avenue with boring Grant Wadsworth. Shaking her head, Camden waved her hands toward the key on the table. "I really don't need a key. But thank you."

Bonita exchanged a look with Calvin and said, "We love you, but we aren't that interesting. You need life and young people. You need to get out and live your life." Bonita elbowed Calvin, who looked incredibly uncomfortable with the conversation as a whole. He shrugged, and Bonita went on. "Honey, we don't know everything that happened in Kansas City, and we're not asking you to pour your heart out to us. You can stay here as long as you like, date whomever you'd like—not that Grant fellow, though, he's a little too shiny for my taste— but anyone else will do." She motioned to the key. "This way you don't have to worry about us. You can come and go as you please."

Camden blew out a breath. "Like I told you, Grant was cheating on me, which is why I left, but I should have left or called off the wedding long before that. I didn't for a lot of reasons— fear of disappointing all the people who had worked so hard on the wedding chief among them. But I didn't come here looking for another man, I came here to find myself."

"Levi's a good man. You couldn't do better," Granddad said. He held out the key.

Camden wanted something to fill her hands with, something that would make it impossible to take the key and their implicit approval of Levi as dating material. But if she told them this was a setup to get Grant out of Slippery Rock, she would also have to tell them about the whole deal with Levi. She didn't want Granddad to sell the land, but she'd made a deal with Levi, and she wouldn't renege on that deal.

"I didn't come here to hide. I came back here because this is the last place I really felt like me. Like Camden Harris, human being. Not Camden Harris, Elizabeth's daughter, or Camden Harris, pageant queen." Granddad was still holding the key, so Camden took it and slid it into the pocket of her jeans. She'd come here to figure things out, and she'd known if she went practically any other place in the world her mother wouldn't be far behind. Elizabeth hated the farm enough that she wouldn't willingly set foot here. Before Camden could figure anything out, she needed to get her past out of her present. "Will it make you feel better to know I'm going out tonight?"

"Infinitely," Grandmom said. "To that dance with Levi, right?"

"And dinner beforehand. Why don't you come with us? I remember watching the two of you dance until midnight one year during the founders' weekend celebration."

"Psh. You're twenty-six years old. You don't need your grandparents horning in on your date. We can make it to the dance on our own, and we can drive ourselves home and *you* can enjoy that young man."

"I'm sure I'll be home by ten." Eleven at the latest. Pretend dating Levi didn't have to mean staying out until midnight. In fact, the earlier he brought her home, the easier it would be to keep things between them impersonal.

"You don't need a curfew."

"If she wants a curfew, Bonnie, I don't see—" Calvin began, but Bonita stopped him with a glance.

"We won't wait up." Her grandparents exchanged another look, and Camden had the uncomfortable feeling they had plans of their own for the evening. Bonita took Calvin's hand, leading him into the large family room with the big-screen TV—an addition since

Camden had visited here as a child—and an old-fashioned jukebox that played only country and pop hits from the 1960s. It should be strange to hear the Beach Boys followed by Willie Nelson; instead, it was comfortable.

Camden pulled the key from her pocket and turned it over in her hand, feeling a little like a teenager who had been given the keys to her father's sports car. In the other room, the evening news came on, with an anchor talking about holiday festivities in the area. She mentioned the concert at the grandstand, along with some bigger events in larger, more established tourist communities.

Camden had no intention of sleeping with Levi. She had no intention of having a real relationship with the man at all. Before she even considered that, she needed to figure out who and what she was on her own. Was she the novice dog trainer happy with life in a small town? Was she the professional beauty queen who now coached pageant girls and did the Junior League circuit? Whoever she was, how did she go about keeping that identity without letting someone else—either her mother or the man she loved—mold it in their image?

The sound of a big engine pulling down the drive interrupted her thoughts. Had to be Levi;

Grant's Mercedes had been practically silent that morning, and she didn't know anyone else who would be coming to the farm. That overly warm feeling returned to her belly, followed by the flapping of about a dozen butterflies.

Camden willed the feeling away. This wasn't a date. Even if it was, Levi was so far from the type of guy she usually dated—not that she had dated much, even before Grant—that it wasn't funny. Levi was too big, too handsome, too much.

And if she didn't leave right this second, her grandparents would be too present, watching her get into that big truck like she was going off to the prom instead of a holiday dance with a local band performing. Camden shoved the key back into her pocket, grabbed the vintage denim jacket she'd found in a thrift store when she was in college and the small bag that held lip gloss and a few other essentials, and hurried out the door.

She stopped short, gaping at the giant black truck parked in the drive. Levi was a big man, tall and muscular, and filled with confidence. His truck was painted a matte black, she'd missed the color when he pulled the blanket out of the back seat the night of the downtown lighting ceremony, with the Walters Ranch brand on the doors, the truck had dual wheels in the back, a chrome roll bar over the cab and tinted windows. It looked like something Batman might drive if Batman were a cowboy from a small town instead of a crime fighter from Gotham City, and it made her heart rev in her chest.

Silly. She didn't get turned on by trucks any more than she got turned on by overly muscled men with piercing brown eyes, molten chocolate skin and almost-shaved heads. Slowly, Camden made her way to the truck, opened the door and used the step to climb inside the enormous truck.

"You like to make an entrance, I see," she said, fastening her seat belt as if she rode in trucks the size of small planes every day of her life.

"We have that in common," he replied. Levi put the truck in gear, turned around and pointed the truck back down the lane.

"I don't make grand entrances. I blend."

Levi chuckled. "Sure. Waltzing into a bar in a wedding dress is blending. Guess I missed that trend when I moved back to Slippery Rock after football."

He had a point, and that annoyed her more than it should have. They drove in silence for a while, the truck eating up the miles between the neighboring farms as if Levi drove seventy-five rather than the more sedate—and legal—fifty-five. They crossed the city limit, with its welcome sign naming local churches and service organizations. There was a matching sign on the other side of town. They passed the marina, where only a few brave boats and pontoons were still moored, and entered the quiet downtown area. A few people walked around, but the crowd hadn't yet arrived for the concert, and traffic was light. They drove by Mallard's Grocery, where she'd tasted her first Bomb Pop one hot summer afternoon when she was a kid. It was strange to see the empty lot where the old community church had been; the church had been destroyed, along with a few other buildings, in the tornado last spring. The drive took a half hour, yet, when they arrived at the Slippery Rock Grill a few minutes later, Camden wished they had a few more minutes to themselves.

Maybe it was the darkness of the truck cab, but Camden suddenly felt as if she owed Levi some kind of explanation, at least about why she'd asked him to be her pretend boyfriend. When he opened his door, Camden put her hand on his arm to stop him. The light touch sent a zing of awareness through her, and Camden withdrew. "I didn't intend to draw attention to myself that first night in the bar. I just wanted to get home."

"This hasn't been your home in a lot of years, Camden."

Camden sighed. She knew that. Slippery Rock had never truly been her home. At best, it was a vacation spot that her mother hated and her father canonized. Still, it was the place she went to in her mind any time things in her life had seemed off-kilter.

He watched her for a long moment in the dim light trickling in from the sparse streetlights, and Camden wondered what he saw when he looked at her. A lost puppy like Six? An out-of-place debutante? The girl he remembered? Most likely he saw a stranger, because that's what she was. A stranger to Slippery Rock. A stranger to her grandparents. A stranger to Grant—the man she'd been ready to marry.

A stranger to herself. Camden had been here for two weeks, and still she caught glimpses of herself in jeans and tees and rain boots and wondered who the woman was looking back at her from the reflection.

"Nonetheless, I wasn't trying to be a spectacle, and I'm usually the most boring person you would ever meet. No drama." He shot her a look as if he didn't believe her. That was okay—he had no reason to believe that the woman who'd walked into a strange bar wearing a wedding dress was not a drama queen. "I'll probably forget to thank you."

"For what?" he asked, seeming surprised at her words.

She smiled at him, and the expression felt pinched. "For helping me perpetrate a fraud against a man I'd been willing to marry, even though I wasn't in love with him, until I found him…" She trailed off.

"Playing Pin the Penis on the Bridesmaid?" He filled in the blanks, and the way he said it, as if it had happened to someone in a movie and not her, made her smile.

"Yeah. Thank you for that."

"You're assuming he shows up."

"Are you assuming my talking to him at the barn changed his opinion on our compatibility and future plans? Because Grant Wadsworth doesn't give up that easily. He was a member of the Harvard debate club and once argued with a Yalie about who developed the forward pass in football until the man threw up his hands in annoyed defeat. And Grant didn't even know who really had developed the forward pass— he just didn't want to admit he was wrong."

"What kind of self-respecting American man doesn't know Bradbury Robinson threw the first forward pass?" Levi rolled his eyes, and suddenly the dim cab didn't feel like some kind of weird confessional. It was just Camden, talking to her old friend Levi.

"I thought that was Knute Rockne from Notre Dame?"

Levi shook his head. "Rockne and Notre Dame were the first to be successful at it, but Robinson was the first to throw it in a game. His pass resulted in a turnover, but he was the first to throw it." Levi motioned to the restaurant, where a few couples were going inside. "We should eat, if you want this whole fake-dating thing to be taken seriously."

The moment she stepped out of this truck, their pretend relationship would become real, at least to the people of Slippery Rock. It was already real to her grandparents, and Camden wasn't sure how she felt about that. Lying to them made her feel queasy, as if she'd jumped from one fake life to another. Maybe a little white lie like this was what it would take to finally break the ties from her past.

She opened the truck door and climbed down. Inside the restaurant, they were seated at a corner table overlooking a pretty garden filled with flowering quince and daphne. The sun had long since set, but the restaurant had placed a few outdoor lights in the area that shed just enough light that Camden could imagine what the garden would look like during the day.

The waitress stopped by to take their drink orders and tell them about the evening specials of prime rib and lamb chops. Once their orders were placed, the woman disappeared into the dimly lit restaurant.

Camden fiddled with the little packets of sugar and sugar substitutes in the small container near the lit votive candle. She hated first dates—not that this was a true first date—and she hated blind dates, not that Levi was a total stranger. He also wasn't a friend. She wished she knew how to fill the weird void between them.

"What are you doing here, Camden?" he asked, jolting her out of her thoughts.

"Visiting my family. Figuring out my life."

He sat back in his chair. "You haven't been to Slippery Rock in, what, ten years?"

More like fourteen, but she didn't care to think too much about that. She couldn't change the past, and when she was a kid, it hadn't been her choice to stay away.

"I understand about Grant and Pin the Penis, but why come back here? Couldn't you have, I don't know, made off with the honeymoon tickets and come to terms with your life on a beach somewhere?"

She could have. Running off to a Mexican beach had been at the top of her to-do list when she first realized what she was seeing in that closet. Running off to a vacation, though, wasn't the same as running off to start her life. Camden had been afraid that instead of making her confront her decisions, Mexico would have covered those decisions in a haze of tequila, making it too easy to go back to the life she no longer wanted to lead.

She'd known that she needed to fully break out of the mold her mother had been building around her since her father died. Mexico might have made it simple to dump Grant yet continue as her mother's right-hand pageant coach, dressing the right way, doing her hair the right way, wearing the right clothes.

Levi didn't need to know any of that. He couldn't understand the kind of terror that had forced her out of the comfort shell that she'd been living in. Men like Levi, who went from high school football star to college star and into the National Football League, didn't blindly follow what another person wanted for them. They chased their own dreams. Instead of following her dreams, Camden had opted for making her mother happy, and it had taken nearly fifteen years for her to realize it was something she could no longer do. Elizabeth had to make herself happy.

Camden had to learn how to make herself happy, too. She deserved that.

She wanted that.

How to explain that to Levi without admitting how very weak she had been, though?

"I decided it was time to take control of my life. The last place I felt like I had any kind of control was here, so this is where I'm starting." She curled her hands together in her lap as she spoke. "That probably sounds silly to you."

Levi watched her for a long moment. "It sounds brave, actually. But I still don't think we need to pretend date for you to take control of your life back. Look around—no Grant to be seen."

She had to admit that he had a point. There'd been no sign of Grant inside the restaurant or on the streets as they'd driven through town. Still, it wasn't like Grant to go away without a fight, especially when he was convinced he was right. Wadsworth men married beauty queens. Wadsworth men married women in the Junior League. Both were part of Camden's pedigree.

Wadsworth men were all about pedigree.

SHE ISN'T REALLY here with you.

Levi repeated the words to himself for the millionth time since the two of them had arrived at the Slippery Rock Grill. That was two hours and—he checked his watch—seventeen minutes ago. He knew there was more to her taking back her life explanation that she'd offered, but it was the most he'd gotten out of her since first catching her in her wedding dress in the Slope. He knew her secrecy should bother him, but she seemed like the old Camden to him the more he hung around with her. Kissing notwithstanding, of course. He'd wanted to kiss Camden a few times when they were kids, but fourteen-year-old guys didn't kiss twelve-year-old girls.

The old Camden wouldn't be on a mission to hurt her grandparents.

Of course, the Camden he remembered also wouldn't agree to help him influence her grandfather about the acreage on the north side of the property, either.

Still, it was hard to remember she wasn't

here at the dance with him when he was holding her in his arms. Which meant she needed to come back from the girls-only bathroom run with Mara, Jenny, Savannah and Julia. He would never understand the mentality of women who needed entourages to pee.

"They'll be back in a few more minutes. Once Mara and Jenny get the lowdown on what Camden's intentions are toward you," Collin said, interrupting Levi's thoughts.

"Camden has no intentions where I'm concerned." Her intentions were all about Grant, the khaki-wearing ex who still hadn't showed up.

The band switched from "Rockin' Around the Christmas Tree" to a modern Christmas ballad, the singer lamenting being alone over the holidays and wanting her love to return. Like he wanted Camden to return—only she wasn't his love. She was his coconspirator, and he'd better start remembering that simple fact.

"I'd say her intentions are more murky than unintentional," James said, joining the conversation. He wore his sheriff's department uniform, having drawn the short straw for patrol duty that night. He'd dropped in to the dance a few minutes before, ostensibly to make sure there was nothing crazy going on, but he'd spent most of his time flirting and dancing with Mara and not watching the rest of the dancing couples for any signs of bad behavior.

"I'd say she has perfectly clear intentions and those intentions are to turn our resident monk, Levi Walters, into a modern-day Romeo," Aiden added.

Levi looked to Adam, who sat quietly at one of the tables the ten of them had commandeered when they arrived at the grandstand. "You have anything to add?" he asked.

Adam shook his head. "I like her."

"Good for you," Levi said sarcastically.

"She doesn't seem like your type, though," he added.

"I don't have a type," Levi groused. He liked all women. Tall, short, curvy, skinny, long hair, short hair, white, brown or any other color.

The other four burst out laughing.

"You've had a type since we were teenagers desperate to get to first base," Collin said.

Levi folded his arms over his chest. "And just what is my type?"

"Unavailable," his friends said in a chorus.

That was patently ridiculous. He didn't date unavailable women; Levi Walters went out of his way to date only available women. Women who had no expectations where love and romance were concerned and who weren't involved with other men.

"The four of you have lost your minds since you settled down," he said, pointing his bottle of Corona toward the group. Aiden, Collin and James sat with Adam at the table. The dog, Sheba, lay at Adam's feet, taking in the conversation as if she understood it. What was it with all the people in his life bringing dogs into things? First Camden with her unruly Six. Adam with Sheba. Although Adam had a prescription or something for his service dog. He looked around for Camden or the other women, but all he saw were couples in jeans and jingle bells swaying to the music.

"You don't see it because you don't want to, but that doesn't make it untrue. You don't want to be involved with a woman, not in a long-term way, so you pick women who aren't available. They live in other towns, they're groupies from your football days or they've been hurt in the past." Collin's voice was reasonable, and that only annoyed Levi more.

He didn't prey on women like some kind of stalker. Having plans and refusing to let anyone distract him from those plans only made him focused. He'd settle down once he had accomplished the dairy expansion.

"It's called having a life and a business that needs my attention. And, you know, cleaning up our town after that tornado tore through it took up a little time, too."

"It didn't slow *me* down on the romance front," James offered. He finished his bottle of water.

"Me, either," Collin added.

Levi narrowed his eyes. "That's my sister you're not slowing down with," he warned.

"I already proposed. Get over it."

"It slowed me down a little, but I'm catching up fast," Adam chimed in.

Aiden remained silent, watching Levi as if he saw something the other guys didn't. Hopefully he wasn't seeing how hung up on Camden Levi was becoming. Having the guys rag on him about being unavailable was one thing. Their knowing he was having illicit thoughts about a woman who was openly using him was something else entirely.

"What?" Levi asked after a long moment.

"Just wondering what it is about this one that has you smitten," Aiden said.

"I'm not smitten," Levi insisted. He was part of a bargain, and yeah, he was having trouble keeping his hands off the pretty brunette wearing leather knee boots, skinny jeans and a flowing sequined top under her denim jacket, but that didn't mean he was smitten.

"Definitely smitten," Collin said.

Before Levi could dig into those comments, he caught sight of Jenny leading the other women back to the table and lost his train of thought. Camden was laughing at something Julia said. It was the first real laugh he'd witnessed since he got back, and it transformed her face from girl next door to siren, making her skin glow and her eyes light up.

They five of them arrived at the table, and Mara checked her watch. Her face clouded.

"Your fifteen minutes are up," she said, putting her arms around James and kissing him. "And if I'm not home in about twenty, Zeke is going to turn into the bedtime monster and we'll never get Amanda to babysit again."

"I'll stop by the house, make sure he's down. You stay."

Mara yawned. "I'm tired anyway." She waved at the group and then pulled Camden, who had been hanging at the perimeter, into a hug. "We're having lunch when you get back from the Tulsa trip," she said when she released her from the hug. "Come on, Sheriff, get your old woman home for the night." Mara paused when she reached Levi, caught his gaze and winked. "I always knew something might be going on between the two of you," she said.

James put his hands at her waist, propelling her forward. "We're not supposed to say things like that, because he isn't smitten," James said in a faux whisper. Levi gritted his teeth.

God, sometimes having friends sucked. He wasn't smitten with Camden Harris any more than she was smitten with him. This was a scheming relationship, which was one step below the clichéd working relationship.

Now if he could just get his mind off the woman for enough minutes to convince his body it didn't want her, things would be just fine.

CAMDEN COULDN'T KEEP this up.

"It's all an act, you know."

Camden swung around at Mara Tyler Calhoun's words. She vaguely remembered the other woman from her childhood. It would be hard to forget the nearly white-blond hair, the clear blue eyes. She looked like some kind of cross between an angel and a Swedish nanny. She continued talking while the five of them—Camden, Mara, Savannah Walters, Jenny Buchanan and Julia Colson—checked their makeup in the harsh fluorescent lights of the ladies' room at the grandstand.

Outside, the band was riffing through the final chorus of "Do They Know It's Christmas?"

"Levi likes to pretend he's all about football and dairy farming, but he's more than that," Mara said. "Last summer, he and Collin practically led the volunteer crew from project to project as they rebuilt downtown, and he started an amazing charity for underprivileged athletes in his football days."

"Don't forget, he's helping me with the zoo part of the camp I'm developing," Savannah added.

"Saint Levi of the Plans," Jenny said, her voice husky, as if she might be getting over a cold. "Only I don't think you were part of his plans. Not that you shouldn't be," she said quickly.

Camden shook her head. "It's okay. I…"

But she didn't know how to finish the sentence. Camden was nowhere in Levi's master plan, whatever that master plan was. And he was most definitely not in her master plan, not that she had an actual plan in place. She'd mostly been winging her life since landing back in Slippery Rock. "Levi has plans?" she said, hoping to keep the conversation on Levi and off her.

"Are you kidding me?" It was Mara. She leaned lightly on the counter as she reapplied lip gloss. "Levi has had plans for as long as I've known him. First it was the How to Win State plan, then How to Get a Football Scholarship."

"Don't forget the First-Round Draft Day plan," Jenny put in.

"And the Rebuild Slippery Rock plan," Savannah added.

The three of them looked to Julia. "I've been here a month, I don't know the plans," she said, and the other women burst out laughing.

"The Expand the Dairy Because Ice Cream Is the Best Medicine plan," they said in unison.

"He doesn't actually think ice cream is a cure for cancer or something, does he?" Camden asked. She couldn't imagine that was true, but then again, she couldn't imagine Levi expanding the dairy because he had a sweet tooth, either.

Savannah nodded. "Nah, not really. But he does believe the old adage that money can't buy happiness."

"But it can buy cows," Mara added.

"And cows make milk," said Jenny.

"And milk makes ice cream," Julia added.

Then all three of them said, laughing, "And ice cream makes you happy."

The three of them looked expectantly at her, but Camden had no idea what to say.

"So?" Savannah asked.

Camden racked her brain, trying to remember every quote about money and happiness she'd ever heard. None of them mentioned anything about cows or milk or ice cream, though. Was there another part to the saying or was her supposed connection to Levi supposed to fill in this blank?

"So," she said, drawing out the word and hoping against hope that inspiration would strike. The four of them were watching her expectantly, and they'd been so nice since she walked in with Levi, and she didn't want to let them down. Or let him down. She might be trying to get rid of Grant, but Levi had something riding on this, too—the lease agreement. Camden repeated the quote in her mind.

Money can't buy happiness.

Of course, money did make it a lot easier to be happy.

But it could buy cows, and cows made milk, and milk made ice cream and ice cream made you happy.

Now is not the time to mention your lactose intolerance, Cam.

"So money can buy happiness?" she said, hating the hesitation in her voice. If this truly was Levi's saying, and if she and Levi were truly dating, she would know it. Only she wasn't dating Levi, she was dumping Grant. Again.

"Exactly," Mara said. "We'd better get back out there before the boys go off to play darts again."

"At least we always know where to find them," Jenny said as they strode back to the arena.

The crowd seemed to have grown since the five of them went into the ladies' room. The dance floor was crowded with couples wearing jeans, flannel shirts and the odd sweater. One older lady wore a full square-dancing outfit in vibrant red and white, complete with a least a dozen layers of crinolines in the skirt. Little bells hung from the skirt, making jingling noises as she danced with her partner.

This night was perfection, Camden thought as Julia linked arms with her. It was as if she'd had a real conversation with real friends.

If Grant hadn't shown up when he had, she wouldn't even be here tonight, hearing about

Saint Levi. Camden was torn between feeling guilty about lying to these women who had been so very nice to her since the two of them had arrived at the dance and feeling grateful to Levi for going along with her plan so that she had the chance to meet them.

Most of Camden's interactions with women in the past had been from the pageant circuit, where girls would bludgeon one another for the last spray of swimsuit glue. She'd been prepared for backhanded cattiness and even straight-up accusations tonight. What she hadn't been prepared for was the welcome from these four women or the quick acceptance of the men.

Especially since they were all aware of her less-than-graceful Slippery Rock reentry in the wedding dress.

God, they must think she was desperate.

It had been only a few hours since Levi had picked her up for their first fake date, and already it was hard to remember they weren't really dating. That they were barely friends. His chocolate-brown gaze met hers as Mara and James left their little group. She couldn't hear what either of them said to Levi, but whatever it was set the amber flecks dancing. In annoyance? Excitement? She only knew that the fire in his eyes made her stomach go all wobbly again.

Like it had a dozen times since she'd climbed into his truck.

The band started singing the classic "Tennessee Christmas," and then one by one the couples at their tables separated to hit the dance floor, leaving Camden with Levi.

"I, ah, think it's going well," she said after a long moment. Why the realization that their fake date was fooling people she barely knew should make her feel like a phony Camden couldn't explain. But it did. The only person at their table that she could claim to know, aside from Levi, was Julia, and the two of them hadn't been close in years. Not since that last pageant. Like most people who weren't in her mother's circle, Julia had drifted out of Camden's life. It had been nice spending time with her when the shop opened on Thanksgiving.

Maybe she should make a point to call Julia while she was here. Strike their friendship back up, or at least explain why she hadn't made more of an effort to stay in touch.

"Yeah, our performance is top-notch," Levi said, and something in his voice made her turn away from watching the couples on the dance floor sway in time to the music. Had she done something wrong? Before their trip to the ladies' room, he'd been talkative, making it hard for her to remember that this wasn't a real date. He was only honoring their agreement, she knew. Still, the Levi from before the powder room run and the Levi now were two very different people. Before she could ask what was wrong, Levi said, "We should dance."

Camden felt like a teenager at her first dance when Levi pulled her into his arms as the band hit the bridge of the song. Being this close to Levi left her off balance, like she was hearing the echo of the music and not the music itself.

"You want to make this good, don't you?" he asked, settling her closer to his hard body.

Camden barely resisted the involuntary urge to curl her fingers against her palms. Levi didn't need to know how his nearness affected her, not when this was all about the performance. She had yet to see Grant, but he had to be here somewhere. Watching. Waiting for her to slip up so he could debate her back to Kansas City and resume their engagement, just as he'd debated that Yalie into believing the forward pass belonged solely to Knute Rockne.

The band segued into the slightly faster "Last Christmas," but Levi continued to hold her close, swaying slowly.

His hand at the small of her back soothed away the worry that somewhere in the crowd Grant was watching. Levi pulled her a little closer to him, the flannel of his shirt warm and soft and comforting under her hands, and Camden felt herself relax for the first time since she'd heard his truck coming down the driveway several hours earlier. She rested her head against his chest, and the steady *thump, thump* seemed to beat in time to the music. It was dark on the dance floor, couples swaying to the music, talking quietly about whatever couples talked about, and Camden let herself drift.

This might not be a real date, but she could pretend, for as long as this song lasted, that it was. That Levi wasn't her pretend date, that they weren't running a con on Grant, on Levi's friends, on her family. All that mattered was the man holding her close, swaying with her in time to the music.

He wasn't her real boyfriend, but did it matter? For just a little while, Camden was not going to feel guilty for walking out on Grant, for avoiding her mother's calls, for making all of Slippery Rock believe the two of them had fallen in love at first sight.

For just a little while, Camden would pretend that the miracle of Christmas was alive in this small town. And that a man like Levi Walters, patron saint of planners, could fall for an improviser like her.

CHAPTER EIGHT

LEVI DIDN'T LIKE to lie, especially not to people he cared about. Pretending for an evening with his friends was one thing, but actually going on this potential buying trip with the Harrises felt…dirty.

Which made the attraction for Camden he couldn't fight feel even more twisted.

The waitress at the small diner near the arena where the stock-dog show was being held brought the dinner check—hamburgers for Calvin and Bonita, breakfast for dinner for Camden, and a steak for Levi—and before Calvin could pick it up, Levi grabbed it and handed it back with his credit card.

Since he couldn't apologize to them for making them think he was dating their granddaughter, the least he could do was pick up the tab for dinner.

The fact that he couldn't stop thinking about their granddaughter, that part of him wondered what would happen if they were really dating, didn't escape Levi. Nor did his ambivalence on the matter. Just three days ago, he'd been against actually dating her *and* pretend dating her. Now he couldn't stop thinking about her. Hell, for most of the drive over to Tulsa this afternoon, all he'd been thinking about was how her body had melted into his at the dance on Saturday night, and how hard it had been not to follow her inside the farmhouse when he took her home.

And none of that mattered, because Camden wasn't interested in him. She'd chatted breezily about every subject under the sun, seemingly unaware that she shared the front seat of what felt like a very small truck cab—one he'd sat in before with three of his football buddies and never had a problem—with Levi Walters, who couldn't stop stealing glances at her.

"Those dogs know their stuff, don't they?" Calvin asked.

Camden's thigh brushed his under the table, and Levi forgot the question Calvin had just posed. Camden rescued him.

"Definitely impressive, and today was all about the show dogs. Do you see what I meant, Granddad? They take this very seriously. What did you think of the breeder you visited on the way out yesterday?"

Calvin and Bonita began their drive Tuesday—they'd said it would make their trip feel less rushed, but Levi wondered if they had other reasons. Such as giving him and Camden more time alone. It would be like the two of them to give another couple space.

Except you aren't a real couple. You're a pretend couple, don't forget that.

"Nice selection. I have a business card. Once we have the runs renovated, and you've shown Six a few times, the breeder will be our first contact," Calvin told his granddaughter.

Camden looked at Levi, and the excitement on her face was nearly his undoing. He had to touch her, kiss her, something. She'd said she came back to Slippery Rock to find herself—this had to be a big first step in doing that.

The waitress returned with Levi's credit card.

"What's next on the Tulsa holiday tour?" Levi asked as they started for the parking lot.

Bonita yawned. "I'm about done in," she said. "You two should go have a little fun after being cooped up in that arena all day. We'll take Uber back to the hotel," she said and took her phone from her purse.

Camden looked from the older couple to him, and Levi couldn't read the expression on her face. Something about it, though, made his belly clench in anticipation.

"I'm tired, too. The drive, the competition, and there will be more demonstrations tomorrow. Why don't we all go back to the hotel?" she suggested. "If it's all the same to you." Camden looked at Levi expectantly, and his mouth went dry.

She wasn't asking him to take her back to the hotel, he realized.

Camden wanted him to return to the hotel with her. Levi considered faking a yawn but simply nodded. "Yeah, it was a long drive."

All too soon, the four of them reached the hotel. Calvin and Bonita took the elevator to the fourth floor, but Camden and Levi's rooms were two more floors up. When they were alone in the elevator, Camden turned to him.

"I don't normally do this sort of thing," she said. "Sleep with a guy on the second date, I mean."

"Well, since this isn't a date," he said, "maybe it's okay to make that exception. We're here in this hotel to convince Grant to move on with his life. And sex could definitely push that realization farther along."

The elevator door swooshed open, and neither said a word until they were inside the suite.

When they'd arrived earlier, Camden had taken one of the bedrooms and Levi the other, leaving the living area as a communal space. The area was decorated with overstuffed couches, a minibar and a television screen that covered nearly an entire wall. They both stood in the center of it all, closer to each other than it was probably safe to be.

"Except Grant isn't here, and he didn't show up at the holiday dance on Saturday. You probably didn't need to come to Tulsa at all," she said, but she didn't move away from him. "Wait, but there is always the rental agreement for the forty acres."

"That makes this seem a little too much like prostitution. The rental agreement doesn't really matter. I'll find some other place for the older cattle." He stepped closer to her, and her right thumb went under the thin strap over her shoulder, and then she stopped. Levi felt as if he was frozen in place. Less than a foot separated their bodies; her brown eyes were wide in the dim light, her chest rising and falling quickly. His own breathing was rough in his ears, which was odd. He did this kind of thing plenty, but never once had he felt quite like this. As if the world might stop spinning if she didn't push that strap off her shoulder.

Camden took a step back and kicked the rain boots—the rainbow-striped pair—off her feet. "Just how many of pairs of these boots do you own?"

"Four?" she said, but the word sounded more like a question.

"You don't know?"

She blushed, and the pink stain on her alabaster skin made his blood quicken. "I may have ordered another pair. And it may have been delivered while we were driving to Tulsa."

"May have?"

She shrugged. "It could have been two more pairs."

Levi laughed, putting his arms around his middle. Camden really did have a shoe fetish, like Grant had said that night in the Slope. The blush on her cheeks deepened.

"What?"

"Nothing. I was just thinking only a new-to-country-living girl would have not one but six pairs of rain boots." She stiffened, as if insulted at his laughter. Camden dropped her hand from the cami strap, and before she could run from the room, Levi stopped her, putting his thumb beneath the thin strap. "And I was thinking how you're not like any woman I've ever known. *And* I keep telling myself I don't want to know what makes you tick, but I can't seem to stop myself from trying to figure you out."

Camden stepped away from him, moving to the windows.

"Where are you going?"

"Nowhere," she said, her voice soft in the room. She took the curtains in her hands and pulled them across the window. "Just making sure what happens in Tulsa stays in Tulsa."

"Nervous?"

"About having a one-night stand with the object of my preteen affections?" She shrugged nonchalantly. "Why would a partially blue-blooded debutante and former beauty queen like me care about something like that?"

Levi chuckled. "That may be the first time you've referred to yourself as a deb or a social-ite or a beauty queen without a hint of conde-scension in your voice."

"Tonight I don't care so much about who I used to be." Camden took the camisole hem in her hands and pulled it over her head. She wore nothing beneath, and he forgot to breathe for a moment. The pulse at the base of her neck thundered, and a thin vein seemed to darken beneath her smooth, creamy skin. She dropped the garment and her hands went to the fly of her faded jeans. Levi advanced, feeling the predatory linebacker he'd once been. Camden was the quarterback he was tracking.

"What do you care about tonight?"

She shrugged, and a low "Hmm" slipped from her full lips. "Not a single thing," she said finally. "You?"

"I can't think about a single thing except you."

She slid her jeans over her hips and then kicked them across the room, leaving only a pair of pink-and-lime polka-dotted panties to cover her body. She didn't hide her breasts, merely stood in the middle of the hotel suite, letting him look at her.

Levi unbuttoned his flannel shirt. Camden reached out to push it from his shoulders. He went for his belt buckle next, but her soft hands were already there. Levi sucked in a long breath when the backs of her hands came in contact with his lower abdomen. She raised her gaze to his, and for a long moment he only looked. He wanted to memorize this moment, the way he'd memorized every playbook during his football years, the way he'd memorized his father's dairy records. If he memorized her, this night, he could come up with a plan to keep her with him. He couldn't explain when things had shifted. Maybe that first kiss outside Calvin's barn. Maybe the second at the Slope.

Maybe when she'd walked into the bar wearing that ridiculous wedding gown, a gown that wouldn't go with the rain boots she liked to wear, even if some designer added a few yards of camo over the train or on those underskirt things. How could anyone think a tulle dress with a train of roses would be the right wedding dress for a woman like Camden? She needed silk and tulle, but white was…too ordinary for a woman who wore boots decorated with rainbows and umbrellas and unicorns and shamrocks.

God, she'd been in Slippery Rock for less than a month, and already it was hard to remember what life had been like before she'd blown back into town. Levi didn't care that they had no plan for whatever this was between them. He didn't care that he still didn't know what she wanted with Slippery Rock or her grandparents or what was going on between Camden and her ex. He only wanted to feel the softness of her skin, to memorize the curves and valleys of her body like his favorite playbooks, to take in everything that was Camden Harris. At least for tonight.

He raised his hands to her face, cupping her cheeks and tracing the lines of her cheekbones with his thumbs. She licked her lips, and her hands stilled at his waist. Levi lowered his mouth to hers, and it was as if the hotel suite ignited in flames. Her hands fisted at the waist of his pants, and Levi pulled her more securely against his body, trapping her hands at his waist.

And then her arms were around his waist, her hands raking over his back. Levi slid his hands into all that silky brown hair, tilting her head to give him better access to her sweet mouth.

"If we don't move, I'm going to push you against the wall and take you right here."

"Sounds perfect," she said, her words breathy and unsteady.

Perfect, and memorable. Still, Levi didn't want Camden against the wall. He wanted her on that big bed, with soft pillows. Levi lifted Camden in his arms and took her to the bed, where he put her down gently before kneeling between her knees. He wrapped her long hair around his hand and pulled gently to expose her throat to his mouth. She sank back and wrapped her arms around his neck and her legs around his waist, pulling him closer.

He found her breast with his free hand and began teasing the pebbled nipple with his thumb. She arched her back when he flicked his thumb over the puckered skin. Levi nipped at the throbbing pulse in her neck and then released her hair to play his hand over her ribs. While his other hand continued to work her breasts, he kissed his way to them, eventually replacing his finger with his mouth. He sucked her nipple into his mouth, and she hissed. She released his neck to score her nails along his back. Levi had never particularly liked being marked by a woman, but he didn't mind it with Camden.

He'd forgotten how much fun it was to make love to a woman, especially one as responsive as Camden. For every move he made, she had a counter. His mouth at her breast sent her nails scoring down his back. His hands at her ribs sent her hands exploring his pecs. He wondered what would happen if he cupped her center. No time like the present to find out. He slid his hands along her abdomen, liking it when her muscles clenched at his touch. When he reached the thin elastic of her waistband, he slowed, walking his fingers over the cotton until he felt the dampness of her panties against his palm.

Camden sucked in a breath and clutched his shoulders in her hands. Her chest rose and fell in a fast rhythm, and those long, long legs moved restlessly over the fluffy coverlet. He wanted to watch her shatter into millions of tiny pieces. Wanted to hear her shout his name.

She raised her arms, inviting him down, down, down. And Levi felt himself falling even though he hadn't moved a muscle. He couldn't quite explain it, but he knew if he kissed her again, something big would change. There was still time to stop this. Time to turn back the clock before he sent into chaos everything he'd spent so much time and effort planning.

But he didn't want to turn back the clock, and he didn't care what might change. Not in his life or hers. Not with the farm, and not with her dog school. For the moment, he didn't even care how what he was about to do with Camden would change his relationship with her grandparents—the people he thought of as his own family. He wanted to be with Camden, even if he didn't know what would happen next. But he didn't want to think; he just wanted to feel.

Levi took a condom from his pocket and palmed it as he pushed his jeans over his hips. He kicked them off, along with his boxer briefs, and then sheathed himself. As he knelt on the bed, he reached between them, hooked his index finger into her panties and slid them down her legs before settling his hips against hers.

"Levi. Please." Her voice was a whisper in the room as she maneuvered to wrap her long legs around his waist.

He found her center and pressed in. She was warm and wet and ready for him, and this time it was Levi who hissed in a breath. He didn't want this to end, and yet he knew he couldn't make it last. Camden lifted her hips, pulling him farther into her core, and he began to pump.

"God, Camden, you shouldn't have done that," he said, but he wasn't angry. What man could be angry wrapped around five feet seven inches of fiery woman?

"Oh, I think it was the right move," she said and arched her back.

Her breasts pressed against his chest, slipping against his sweaty skin. He nipped at her lower lip, as her hands found his nipples, scratching over them as she met him thrust for thrust.

Levi was close, too close, and he didn't want to leave Camden behind. He reached between them, his thumb finding her clitoris. He flicked over the hard nub and felt her body tighten beneath him. She forgot to move for a moment, her back bowed, her legs tight around his hips. Levi worked the little bud while his hips thrust into her. Camden closed her eyes. Her hands went around his neck to fist in his hair.

"Levi," she said as her body tensed beneath his. For a moment, she was motionless, and then he felt her inner muscles moving against him as the orgasm took her.

Levi rested his weight on his elbows on either side of Camden and let the wave crash over him, too.

"Wow," she said after a moment.

Levi grunted in reply. When he knew he could stand without falling over, he got up, disposed of the condom and then returned to the bed. Camden hadn't moved. She lay there, one arm thrown back over her head, her other over her breasts, eyes closed. She wasn't asleep— he could tell from the still fast rise and fall of her chest. He slid behind her, gathering her to him, her back to his chest. Her legs tangled with his. Arms around her waist, he buried his nose in her neck, breathing her in.

Vanilla but with something spicy under the sweet scent.

She wrapped her hands around his, snuggling into him, and he felt her breathing steady.

He kissed the sensitive spot behind her ear.

"Do that again, and I might require an encore." She wiggled her butt against him.

"Do that again, and you'll get that encore," he returned, feeling his length pulse to life again.

She chuckled. "I'm just going to rest my eyes for a second," she said.

The suite quieted, no traffic noises from outside coming through the thick windows, and no noise from the hotel corridor, only the sounds of their breathing. Camden went limp in his arms, and he knew she slept. Levi didn't mind. He watched the thin shafts of moonlight sneak in around the sides of the closed curtains.

He'd come to Tulsa to prove a point and had ended up in bed with Camden Harris instead. What's more, he couldn't imagine not repeating the experience at least a thousand more times.

Again, he thought about the fact that though

she'd only been back in Slippery Rock for a few weeks, he already had a hard time imagining his town without her in it. Couldn't fathom what the Harris farm would be like if Camden weren't training Six, didn't want to think about how no one else would argue with him about that stupid bike trail.

He'd never, not once in his twenty-eight years, thought about life with a woman at his side for a long period of time. He'd always considered relationships of any sort a distraction from the things in his life that were important: continuing the legacy of Walters Ranch and living up to the expectations of a small town brought to fame because of his work on a football field.

But with Camden, he was tempted. Working together. Playing together.

Collin, James, Adam and Aiden. All four of his best friends had fallen under the spells of their women, and none of those relationships seemed like work or that they were taking attention away from other aspects of their lives.

Levi's eyes became heavy, and he felt his arms loosen around Camden's waist. She snuggled back against him and sighed. It was a happy sound in the quiet hotel suite.

This was all too fast. Too soon. Too perfect.

Yet maybe, just this once, perfection was within his reach.

CAMDEN WOKE IN Levi's arms, her head resting on his arm. The blinds were drawn, but she could tell it was still night outside. Their suite was high enough they wouldn't hear street noise, anyway, but there was a stillness to the room and the occasional faint flashes of light from headlights on the street outside that said middle of the night.

A glance at the clock confirmed it. Just after two. The rest of the dog show would start in about six hours. She should slip away from Levi, get some real sleep so she didn't have bags the size of Oklahoma under her eyes tomorrow.

She couldn't make herself move. Camden wanted just a little while longer like this, a little while longer to pretend that sleeping with Levi Walters hadn't been a mistake. He moved restlessly beside her, his arms coming around her middle. Camden breathed deeply, and the smell of Levi's cologne—woodsy and fresh—settled her in a way that no meditation or mantra before a beauty pageant ever had.

She'd slept with Levi Walters. Because she

wanted to. Because she liked him, all of him. The part that was grouchy with her, and the part that was so kind to his buddies' girlfriends and wives, the part that wanted so much to expand his dairy empire, and the part that respected and loved her grandparents. There were no other words for the way he was with Calvin and Bonita than respect and love.

A man who could be so kind to an elderly couple that had been virtually forgotten by their own family…that was a man who could burrow right under Camden's I Don't Want a Rebound defenses.

That was the kind of man her father had been. The kind of man Grant would never have become.

She should go back to her room. Put a little distance between the two of them before she started thinking really crazy things. Having sex with Levi didn't mean anything, not in the long run. Him taking the land deal with her grandfather off their bargaining table before having sex with her didn't mean anything, either. It probably was a little prostitutey. Probably, she should thank him for saving at least a portion of her virtue.

Stop trying so hard to build up the guilt, Cam. You don't regret sleeping with Levi any more than you regret walking out on your wedding three weeks ago.

Part of her wanted to at least keep attempting to feel some guilt, but a bigger part of her, the part of her that had walked out on Grant, wouldn't allow it.

She'd slept with Levi Walters, and it probably didn't mean to him what it meant to her. That was okay. Sleeping with him was her decision.

She settled against him and let her eyes flutter closed. This was it, the moment she finally broke free of the guilt and recriminations from her childhood. The moment when she started living her life for herself. And what a way to start it.

Camden snuggled Levi's arm close to her chest and slept.

CHAPTER NINE

THE AIR IN the arena didn't seem to move. Levi watched the dog and trainer in the ring work in tandem to herd seven ducks from one side of the training area to the other. The ducks and the dog seemed to be performing an elaborate ballet, with sweeping movements that meandered around the room like a fast-running stream. How the dog kept from nipping at the ducks when one of them tried to make a run for it—and several of the ducks did—was beyond him, but the medium-size black-and-white collie patiently herded the wayward fowl back into line.

When the last duck waddled across the holding area and into the small pen, Levi joined in the clapping and celebration of the other spectators.

"I think those jokes about getting a group of children moving should be changed from herding cats to herding ducks," he said to Camden when things quieted down.

It was Thursday afternoon, a day after they'd

arrived in Tulsa, only about twelve hours since they'd made love, and everything in Levi's life had changed. At least it felt that way.

He'd woken up this morning with Camden still in his arms. Levi never spent the night with women; that was a cardinal rule. Didn't matter if they went to his house, his hotel room or hers, either Levi or the woman left after sex. It made things less complicated. Sex was one thing, a relationship was another, and Levi had never wanted a relationship. But there was something about Camden that made him want more than he'd ever wanted with another woman.

The thought chilled him. He hadn't planned on this, and he didn't know how it would work out. She was just coming out of a long and broken relationship, starting a business, starting her entire life over. Even if she was okay with them continuing what they'd started last night, long-term compatibility wasn't built on great sex. He didn't know her likes or dislikes, her plans for the future. Did she even make plans? Levi shook his head. Of course she made plans. Everybody made plans. It was one of the things that separated humans from animals—the ability to make plans.

"Have you heard anything from Calvin and

Bonita?" he asked when things had quieted in the arena.

Camden shook her head. "Just that they would meet us here later this morning. Grandmom hates the city during Christmas, but she did want to visit a couple of craft stores for the bazaar coming up in a couple of weeks. They probably went there this morning instead of coming to watch the performances."

"Did you want to shop?"

Camden blinked at him. "Why would I want to shop?"

"For the holidays. I wouldn't live anywhere but Slippery Rock, but I'm aware of its shopping limitations. There are only so many things you can buy at Julia's boutique, the coffee shop or the sporting goods store."

"That's why God created online shopping," she said. "I'm covered. Not that I have many people to buy for."

"What do you mean?"

"We don't really do gifts, at least not with my mom and stepdad. Christmas usually means a vacation somewhere tropical. 'Spending time, not money' is what my mom calls it, but Darren—that's my stepfather—usually mumbles something about five stars not coming free. Last year we spent the holidays in those over-the-ocean huts in Bali."

"Sounds warm." The crowd in the arena began to disperse; the next show wouldn't be for another couple of hours. "Do you want to get some lunch while we wait?"

Camden nodded. "Sure." While they climbed the steps to the concourse, she said, "It isn't that I don't appreciate a winter getaway. But one of the things I'm looking forward to in Slippery Rock is a traditional Christmas."

"As long as you don't expect one that's white. We haven't had snow on the ground before late January in a long time." Levi put his hand at the small of her back as they maneuvered through the concourse and into the parking lot. He'd parked the truck several rows back and zipped up his jacket as they walked. The wind had kicked up, putting a chill in the early-afternoon air.

Camden wore another pair of rain boots today, this pair with cartoon owls in every color of the rainbow. The boots should look silly on a grown woman, but somehow Camden pulled off the look. She'd worn jeans and a gray striped sweater with something lacy hanging below the hem. Levi's hand had been itching to explore the lacy whatever-it-was since the moment she walked into the main room in their hotel suite.

Camden pointed to the sky. "That looks like snow."

"More like ice," Levi said, "but I haven't seen an alert come across my phone, so it's probably just a little sleet or freezing rain."

A worried expression flitted across her face as he helped her into the truck. "I'm sure your grandparents are fine. Calvin's a cautious sort."

"Still, I should call them," she said and took her cell from her bag.

By the time he got around the truck, Camden was talking to one of her grandparents on the phone, and she didn't look happy.

"Be safe," she said, frowning as she disconnected the call. Levi pulled the truck onto the street.

"Same diner as yesterday?"

"They left," she said, a note of surprise in her voice. "We've been ditched."

Levi glanced in her direction. "I think we have different definitions of 'ditched,'" he said.

Camden shook her head. "Their text this morning said to go ahead without them and they'd meet us later. But they're already back in Slippery Rock. They left at eight this morning, stopped into Grandmom's craft store and will be at the farm in another few minutes."

"That does seem like ditching."

"You don't seem annoyed by this. Why aren't you Oscar the Grouching them leaving town while we're still here?"

Levi shrugged and pulled into the parking lot of the diner where they'd eaten the night before. He shut off the engine and turned to look at Camden. Her cheeks were pink and flustered, and she turned the phone over and over in her hands.

"Good sex tends to take the grouch out of me," he said, hoping to lighten her mood. He didn't mind that Calvin and Bonita had gone back to the farm without them. He didn't care that they wouldn't have an audience to play to. In fact, not having an audience played into the plan he'd been contemplating since he woke up to the sweet scent of Camden in his hotel bed. "Let's grab lunch, and then we'll figure out how to spend the rest of the day."

The diner was like something out of the 1950s, with black-and-white-tiled floors, Formica-topped tables, and lots of neon lights along the walls. Even the music was 1950s era, running toward Elvis and Johnny Cash and a few girl groups he didn't know the names of.

After the waitress took their orders, Camden took out her phone again. "The forecast just calls for rain, if you want to head back early."

"I had a different idea," he said and smiled when she frowned at him. "What if we stay?"

"The competitions are over. There will be a handful of demonstrations this afternoon, but nothing major. And with my grandparents not here to see the act—"

"What if it isn't an act?"

Camden waved her hand between them. "Of course it's an act. Having sex last night doesn't make this, whatever it is between us, not an act. We're doing this to get Grant out of my life, and so I can casually mention your plans for the—"

Levi cut her off. "Grant isn't here, and I told you last night, I don't need you to talk to Calvin about the land. We have the hotel booked through tomorrow night, we're two consenting adults and I'm asking you to skip dog school this afternoon and spend time with me."

Her brown eyes widened, but she didn't say anything. Her hands, fidgeting with the cell phone, stilled.

"I'm saying, now that we've had sex, I'd like to date you. It's kind of backward, but since our entire relationship so far has been built on schemes, I figure that's okay."

"I don't," she began, but then changed course. "You don't have to say this just because we slept together last night. You barely liked me before the dance on Saturday. We don't have the same interests, the same background." She motioned between them again. "This made sense when it was a plan to make Grant face reality. It doesn't make sense without that."

"Who says people who date have to have all the same interests? We have physical chemistry, you think I'm grouchy, I think you have a few too many pairs of those rain boots. Maybe that's enough. And it sure doesn't have to make sense."

Camden laughed. "Chemistry, annoyance and a shopping addiction are not good reasons to get involved. I just walked out on a wedding to a man with whom I had everything in common."

"My mother was in the Peace Corps and my father was a dairy farmer when they met on vacation. They've been happy together for forty years. You think they had a lot in common?"

"My mother and stepfather have everything in common and barely speak to one another."

"My point."

"Grandmom and Granddad have everything in common, and they've been together almost fifty years."

Levi shrugged. "So sometimes common interests work. The point is, we don't really know that we don't have anything in common."

"Other than that forward pass thing, I know nothing about football. I know even less about dairy farming."

"All I know about stock-dog training is that your dog is an escape artist. That isn't the point. The point is, I like you, Camden Harris. You're not the kind of woman I normally date." The guys' voices echoed in his mind in a chorus of *unavailable*. Camden was the poster child for unavailable, having just broken off a relationship, just come to town, just upended her own life. Probably, he should back off. Give her room to figure out what she wanted out of life.

Yet Levi had no intention of doing that, because after last night, he wanted her to figure out that what she wanted was him.

"This doesn't make sense. I'm not interested in starting up a new relationship. This wasn't part of the plan."

"See? We do have something in common. This wasn't part of my plan, either. Not when we started this trip, not when we went to the holiday dance and not when you suggested we fake date each other to get what we both wanted."

"What if we don't like each other?"

The waitress delivered their meals. Levi took a bite of his burger and considered. He couldn't say that he understood Camden, but not liking her? Infatuation was the only reason he could think of that would have him making multiple trips to check on cattle that were mostly self-sufficient. Her boots were silly, and she'd made a mistake with Khaki Pants, but still there was something about Camden that he liked on a fundamental level.

"What if we do?"

Camden pushed food around her plate with her fork, but she didn't eat.

She cared about Calvin and Bonita, that was evident, despite their sham of a first date. Hell, she even cared about the ex. Wanting to see him move on benefited her, yes, but he'd known a few women in his football days who liked having men on the hook for them, following them around like puppies waiting for a treat. Camden not only wanted her ex to move on, she was adamant that he do so.

Maybe she hadn't changed as much as he

thought from the young girl who used to follow him around the woods of Slippery Rock. The girl who tried to make his streamlined tree fort into a comfortable hideout by bringing pillows from the farmhouse so they would have comfortable places to sit.

"What do you say, Camden? Do you want to have a real first date?"

She nodded her head slowly. "But first, we could just go back to the hotel."

SHE DIDN'T CARE that this was stupid. She already knew that having sex with Levi was like nothing she'd ever experienced. Still, getting involved with him…that was dangerous. Having sex with him again would make it so much harder to go back to being her own woman. To figuring out how to live her life according to her own terms.

Having sex with Levi was definitely wrong. Oh, but his hands on her body, his mouth on hers, felt so incredibly right.

Right now, making it harder for Future Camden wasn't nearly as important as being with Levi in the present. Not when his mouth was doing amazing things to that spot beneath her ear, and not when his hand was at her core.

Most of all, she liked the way she felt with

Levi. Like maybe whatever made Bonita jump off that parade float to lay a hot kiss on Calvin all those years ago could happen to her. That what the two of them had started so many decades ago could happen for her, too. She knew it was stupid; she'd already walked away from one wedding, and this was not the time to start daydreaming—or sex dreaming—about another. But, lord, being in Levi's arms right now felt so close to heaven it was hard to think that maybe this could end somewhere other than with a broken heart or short-term vacation affair.

Oh, how Camden wanted a career that was built on what *she* wanted, on her interests. But she also wanted a life built on those things. Right now, she couldn't see past Levi being part of that life, or at least this one night in that life. She needed to stop thinking and just feel.

Camden wrapped her arms around Levi's neck, reached up on her tiptoes and took his lips with hers. Their clothes lay in disarray all over the sitting area of the hotel suite. They'd kicked off their boots, his sensible and her whimsical, at the front door. His jeans and long-sleeved tee hung haphazardly over the back of the sofa, their jackets were in a pile on the floor, and her sweater and the lacy tank she'd worn under it had landed atop the television set.

He reached under her legs, lifting her against his chest, and began walking down the hall, never taking his mouth from hers. He was too good at this, but she didn't care how many women he'd taken to anonymous hotels all over the United States. All she cared about was having more of him.

When the backs of her legs hit the silky duvet, Camden sank onto the comfortable mattress. Levi rested one knee between her legs as he followed her down, down, until her head rested on a small pillow.

"Camden." He said her name quietly as his hands played with the sensitized skin of her lower abdomen. His gaze caught hers, and for a moment it seemed as if time would stop. She could only look into his chocolate-brown eyes, wondering what he was thinking. Then his mouth descended on hers, and time seemed to speed back up.

His big hands were on her belly, then one hand was over her breast. She grasped the hem of his T-shirt, pulling it over his head. She wanted to see all of him, wanted to feel all of him. A light mat of black chest hair covered his broad chest, tapering down to a V that disappeared beneath his boxer briefs. She teased the back of her hand along the ridges of his abdomen, liking it when his muscles clenched. Camden pushed the boxers over his hips and took his length in her hand, savoring the feel of him, hot and hard in her hand.

"Now that you've got me here, Miss Harris, what is it that you want to do with me?" he asked, grinning at her.

"Everything," she replied and pushed her hands against his shoulders so that he lay on his back. She lay atop him for a while, their legs tangled, chest to chest, pressing little kisses along his collarbone, liking the contrast of their skin tones. Liking even more how his body kept going taut, like a dog's leash when it was on the hunt for something. Levi's hands explored her and she let her fingers walk down, down, through the light smattering of chest hair. Felt his abdomen tense when her hand passed his belly button, and when she wrapped her hand around his length again, he growled. Camden grinned.

"You keep stoking this fire, Cam, you're going to get exactly what you're hoping for," he said as she ran her hand gently along his length and then squeezed.

"That's the plan," she said. "Taking what

we both want, and not worrying about what happens next."

"What does happen next?" he asked, and Camden didn't have an answer, at least not an answer that she cared to think too long or too hard about. Because the only answer that seemed feasible was that this was Tulsa, and when they returned to Slippery Rock, things would go back to the way they'd been, despite their talk in the diner about really dating and not fake dating. An occasional sighting in the fields surrounding the dog school, awkward avoidance when they both showed up at the Slope or ended up in the same line at Mallard's Grocery.

"This," she said and squeezed his length gently in her hand. Levi hissed out a breath. She didn't want the moment to end, that was definite, and she knew it couldn't last, but that didn't mean she had to think too much about it. She just needed a little more Levi to block out the future.

He clasped his hands behind his head. "Okay, then," he said, "call the play."

Camden grinned at him. "Do you always confuse pillow talk with football talk?" she asked, drawing her hand slowly over his hard, velvety length once more. Levi's pupils darkened, and his slow breath whistled as he inhaled.

"I learned a long time ago that football metaphors work in all human situations."

"We'll see about that."

Camden kissed her way down his body, pausing a moment to taste his abs, to run her tongue along the taut ridges there. She wondered what it would take to make him lose that controlled exterior.

She studied him for a moment. His expression was a mask and his breathing carefully steady, but there was something burning in his brown gaze, something that made the fire in her own belly leap in response. Maybe he wasn't so controlled after all.

She put her mouth on his length, just a gentle kiss, and he twitched at the contact. He was holding on to that control, but she was going to make him let it go. She took him into her mouth, and Levi groaned. Keeping her hand taut around him, she began moving up and down his shaft. One of his hands held her head in place for a moment, and then he flipped her onto her back, the move so sudden it took her breath away.

Levi's gaze was fierce, his breathing uneven,

one of his legs insinuated between hers, and his arms on either side of her.

"What was that about?"

"That was about making this last longer than thirty seconds," he said as his hands found her breasts again, the sensation of him against her sensitized breasts magnificent. He tweaked one nipple and then the other, making Camden's toes curl against his muscled leg.

"If you keep doing that…" she warned, a smile on her face.

"I'm going to keep doing this," he said, taking her nipple into her mouth. Camden arched her back. "And this." His fingers found her core, and her belly clenched. He kissed his way to her other nipple. She couldn't take her gaze off him as he worked her body. "And this," he said, and she felt as if her body rested on a taut piano wire, waiting to topple to the ground. Levi thrust two fingers into her wet core.

"Touchdown," she said.

"Told you there was a football metaphor for everything," he said, grinning at her. His mouth left her breast, kissing his way to her belly button, where he paused for a long moment to explore it with his tongue. Camden gave herself over to the sensations darting along her nerve endings.

Levi's tongue dipping into her belly button. His fingers in her core. Her eyes closed. His heat everywhere.

She felt as if she was coming apart, the fire that had been comfortably hot in her belly scorching through her veins now. He made her want things, and the things weren't just sexual. When she was with Levi, she wanted to let go. To not worry about anything except what happened when they were together. Not her work, not his. Not her past, not his. Nothing but what the two of them could do together.

Levi worked his way back up to her breasts and bit her nipple gently. The combination of pain and pleasure sent a wave of wetness between her legs and, lord, the man knew what to do with his hands and his mouth. Camden began to feel wobbly on the leash of desire.

"Levi," she said, his name crossing her lips before she knew what she wanted to say.

"At your service," he said, satisfaction clear in his voice. That cocky expression was back on his face, and when he grinned at her, her stomach flip-flopped.

She tried to hold on to her sanity, tried to think of anything that would slow her body's reaction to Levi, but she could only take in the smell of him, like a hot, summer afternoon, and the feel of him, taut and hard beneath her hands. She wanted more of him, wanted all of him, and she wanted him to have all of her.

She'd never wanted a man to have all of her before, but instead of the thought scaring her back to sanity, it pushed her insane attraction to him up another level.

Levi's mouth closed over her core, replacing his hands, and Camden forgot to breathe for a long moment. She could only feel his tongue against her clit, the suction of his mouth on her. Camden's hands clenched against the silk of the comforter, but she didn't want fabric. She wanted man.

She ran her fingers through his hair, and then everything went boneless for a moment. Her world shattered, bits of Levi seeming disjointed around her. His shoulder here, his pec there. He rested his arms on either side of her head, and that brought him back into focus. That devilish look was back in his eyes. His penis teased against her opening, and just like that, the molten fire he seemed to control in her burned to life. Levi thrust into her, filling her, and Camden thought nothing had ever felt better than that.

Despite the toe-curling orgasm of a moment ago, she was ready to plunge over that ledge with him again. Levi withdrew, and when he thrust back inside her, Camden raised her hips to meet his. She locked her legs around his hips as he plunged inside her once more.

"Levi," she said, his name a whisper against his shoulder. He reached his hand between them, finding that bundle of nerves easily. "More, more," she said, and raked her hands down his back, wanting more of him. Wanting everything.

Levi gave it. He caught her mouth with his, and the wave of her orgasm crested once more, taking her over the edge and toward oblivion.

"Camden," he said, her name a fierce growl from his lips as he thrust in and out, in and out. He grunted his own release a moment later, his body tensed and he collapsed on top of her.

Camden was lost, somewhere between dreaming and waking, listening to Levi's harsh breaths soften and calm. He moved to the side, burying his head in the pillows but leaving an arm across her torso. Their legs remained tangled atop the soft bed, and Camden ran her fingers lightly over his arm.

"I," he began but stopped, drawing her closer to his body. Camden couldn't keep her eyes open. "Didn't expect this," he said after a long moment.

"Me, either," she said, feeling drowsy. They should maybe spend the rest of this trip inside the hotel room, away from everything and everyone that might make her second-guess her decision to sleep with Levi Walters.

"I'm glad we skipped the last part of the dog show."

She didn't care if she ever went to another dog show again. Training Six, rebuilding the school—neither seemed as important at this moment as Levi did. She just wanted to be here, wrapped up in this man. The thought scared her, but the need to stay right here with him won out. Camden's eyes closed, and she let herself drift.

CHAPTER TEN

SUNDAY MORNING AFTER they returned from Tulsa, Levi sat atop one of the training tunnels at the dog school, enjoying watching Camden work.

She signaled Six with the clicker in her hand, and the runt went perfectly still until she offered another signal. She wore the unicorn rain boots again. Levi had decided this had to be her favorite pair. The December air was crisp this morning, as if snow might not be far in their future. Snow on the ground before Christmas. Levi couldn't remember the last time that had happened.

Camden used her clicker again, and the dog took off at a steady pace, weaving around the apparatus on the training course.

He still didn't understand why Camden was working with the dog using what appeared to be seesaws and crawling tunnels and a toddler slide set. She'd said it had to do with Six learning to listen to her commands, and the dog would graduate to working with actual animals in another month or so.

From what Levi had seen with the cattle last week, Six was ready for animal herding now. She signaled the dog, who went down in a crouch and waited, tail still, eyes focused on Camden. When she gave another signal, Six trotted to her side. She gave the dog a treat from her pocket.

"I thought we might walk awhile, do some training off the little course." She used the clicker, and Six trotted to the edge of the training area and waited. "Do you have that presentation to work on? You don't have to wait around here just because we're—you know."

"Sleeping together? I know. I like watching you work."

Camden grinned. "I thought you considered Six a nuisance."

"He is, when he's bothering my cows. Lately he hasn't been bothering them, though."

"I put him in a run with a roof and added a locking mechanism that isn't so easily manipulated."

"He's a smart dog. And I'm happy to walk with you."

They fell in step together, walking in companionable silence across a couple of pastures.

Instead of continuing toward the land Levi rented from Calvin, Camden detoured to another area of the Harris farm. The area was heavily forested and had obviously not been used for quite a while. Six's ears went up when he heard something off in the brush, but Camden used the clicker in her pocket and the dog stayed on the makeshift path.

"Where are we going?" he asked.

"The old railroad tracks. The tree growth and heavy vegetation make great hiding for bunnies, opossums and other small animals. The distraction of their noises makes for interesting training for Six." Camden clicked again when the dog stopped walking to focus on something off to the side of the narrow track.

Levi moved a low-hanging branch out of the way so they could pass. "You could use a trail dozer up here, or at least a chain saw."

"Maybe, but the challenge of this area is the most important thing, at least at this point in Six's training. I was thinking of moving the obstacle course up here, to give the dogs more of a training hike, then the apparatus, then another hike. At least in the beginning stages of their training."

After a long walk under the cover of the trees, they came to a clearing. Six was walking along what appeared to be old train tracks, but this wasn't part of the railroad. That was farther to their south, cutting through the acreage he rented from Calvin. Levi inspected the area with Six.

What had likely once been railroad ties were nearly buried under grass and debris, and what appeared to be an old spike or two was almost completely black from exposure to the elements. Definitely a railroad, but not one he remembered. And Levi made it a point to know everything about his town.

"What is this?"

"It's the spur they used when they were putting the railroad through. Things they didn't use here but that weren't easy to ship on to other areas were trained up here and dumped at the end of the spur." She pointed to a gap in the trees about three hundred yards farther on. "If they'd continued it, the spur would meet up with the part of the tracks that go through Harris and Walters land right through that area."

Huh. He had never known this was here. Of course, most of his boyhood exploration had been closer to the lake side of the ranch. Still, the placement of the spur was interesting. "Let's follow it, see where it goes."

"I just told you where it goes."

"Six looks interested."

The dog had walked to what appeared to be the end of the spur and was looking on toward the gap in the trees as if wondering where it led. Levi thought he knew, but he wanted to make sure. Because if it led where he thought it did, his issues with the bike trail could be put to rest.

"Why didn't you try to make a comeback?" she asked after a moment, and the question surprised Levi.

"After my knee went?"

She nodded.

"Meniscus injuries are challenging, not just in the rehabilitation but in protecting the knee from relapse—"

"The real reason," she said, interrupting the answer he'd given to so many reporters over the years that he knew it by heart.

"I didn't want it."

Camden made a sound of disbelief in her throat. "What American male doesn't want the chance to play professional sports?"

"I'd already been playing, though, remember?" Levi shrugged. They made it through the gap in the trees. Below them, on a slight decline, were the nonorganic cattle. A fence lay across the hilly area, separating the cows and pasture from what would have been a continuation of the railroad spur. It likely would have followed the top of the rise, only dipping down on the far side, where the railroad began cutting north again. This was where the trail should be, high on the hill where hikers and bike riders could look out over the sweeping vista of green pasture and tall, tall pine trees. In the distance, he thought he saw a ray of sunlight dance off the lake.

"Still, you walked away. Didn't you ever look back?"

Levi studied Camden, who in turn studied the distant sky and trees. He had the distinct impression her questions weren't about his walking away from football as much as they were about her walking away from the life she'd been bred to lead. If she were having doubts, if she wanted to go back…

A cold feeling swept through Levi.

He wouldn't hold her here if she wanted to go back. He stayed in Slippery Rock because this was where he belonged. It was the place that called to him every time he crossed the city limits, even if he left for only a day. If this wasn't that place for Camden, it was probably better to know that now than later.

"I've looked back. It helps that I have something solid, a business that means something to people all over this area, to keep me focused on the future."

Camden signaled the dog, and the three of them started walking toward the cows in the pasture below them. "Is it weird that I haven't looked back? I know this is going to sound weird, like I'm looking for trouble where there is none. Maybe I'm too close to Thanksgiving still, but when I have tried to look back, to imagine what might have been, all I feel is relief that I walked away from it. Is that how it is for you?"

The pang that he usually blocked out when anyone brought up football or the might-have-beens struck fast and hard in his gut. If he hadn't been injured, he might be in the middle of a playoff run. He might have a better chance at the Hall of Fame. He would definitely have millions more dollars in his bank account, not that his account was unhealthy in the slightest.

Levi had socked most of his contract money in safe investments, and he'd lived in cheap apartments and driven leased cars while he'd been playing, knowing that he wanted to be comfortable from the moment he retired from football until the moment he died. Living cheaply had its benefits, and he could count those benefits into the tens of millions of dollars.

"I miss football," he said, telling Camden something he hadn't even shared with the guys. "The friendships, the crazy high of a playoff run, the adrenaline rush that comes with winning a big game. When I look back, though, I'm looking at something that was always a means to an end. I belong here, in Slippery Rock, raising my cows. Making safe, healthy products for people I'll never meet."

"I want that kind of connection."

"You'll find it."

She took his hand as they crossed into the pasture with the cattle. Six paused, but when Camden used the clicker, the dog fell in step with them.

"I'm glad you came over today."

"I didn't have any place else to be," he said.

Even if he had, he'd have made an excuse. Because lately, being with Camden was the most important part of Levi's plan.

MONDAY EVENING, CAMDEN sat in the town hall on a hard, metal chair, listening to Thom Hall run down the list of the week's holiday activities. They were bringing in an ice maze that sounded absolutely miserable to Camden. The kids would love the ice stacked up to resemble a frozen version of a hay-bale maze, but Camden thought there wasn't enough coffee, vodka or hot toddies in the world to warm her up after walking through an ice maze that took up all of the area around and inside the grandstand.

Not even Levi, naked and atop her in bed, would warm her if she had to spend more than a minute inside the frigid maze.

Her shoulder brushed his, and the familiar zing of attraction that accompanied even the smallest of touches between them flared to life. She wanted this meeting to be over. Wanted to drive with Levi back to his big farmhouse and climb into his big mahogany-framed bed and forget about ice mazes and Christmas concerts and why, after several nights filled with passionate lovemaking, being with Levi still felt urgent. As if she might combust without the feel of his skin against hers.

She'd never felt this way about anyone, not even her out-of-control teenage crush on Colin Farrell. The crush that had her dreaming of the Hollywood actor every night of her junior year in high school. The dreams she'd had about Colin paled in comparison to the reality of sharing a bed with Levi.

"We could still use a few volunteers at the bazaar next week. Ticket takers, setup and teardown are the most needed," Thom was saying.

"You will regret it more than anything else in your life," Levi whispered in her ear when Camden started to raise her hand.

"I want to help."

"Then man the booth with Bonita, but swear on the baby Jesus in the manger scene under the clock tower that you won't volunteer to be Thom's cleanup crew."

"It can't be that bad." She started to raise her hand again, but Levi clasped her palm in his, stopping her.

"You volunteer and then I have to volunteer, and if I have to deal with Thom's anal approach to sweeping the floor, I might push him in the lake."

Thom dismissed them without anyone volunteering to be on his cleaning crew. The man looked crushed, and Camden decided she would volunteer for cleanup duties when Levi wasn't around to dissuade her. After all, she wanted to become part of Slippery Rock. She wanted what Levi had had all of his life: a sense of community and belonging.

"I need to talk to Thom about something. I'll be right back," Levi said.

Camden grinned. He was going to volunteer to sweep and clean, despite his refusal a few minutes before. "I'll meet you outside by the chestnut vendor," she said and followed the crowd outside. She stopped short when she saw Grant leaning against the hood of another rented sports car in the parking area. His was one of the few cars parked adjacent to the building that the sheriff's office shared with the town hall and the county offices. Residents tended to park closer to the Slope, since most of them wound up there after town hall meetings. Camden had picked up on the routine after that first meeting: listen to Thom, snipe a little about Thom, leave the meeting to get a drink, go home.

Many of the older residents, her grandparents included, skipped the meetings. Tonight, Bonita and Calvin had opted for movie night at the Methodist church off Main Street instead of Thom's upcoming happenings meetings. They were showing the original *Miracle on 34th Street*, one of Bonita's favorite films.

Camden couldn't pretend not to have seen Grant in the parking lot, not when the crowd from the meeting had already dispersed. Camden zipped her coat against the chilly wind and made her way to Grant.

"Camden."

"Grant."

Well, this conversation was off to the races.

"Where's your football farmer?"

"Talking to the mayor. How's Heather?" she asked in a saccharine voice. Not that she cared, but if he was going to be insulting about her choice of boyfriend, she could be insulting about his choice of affair partner.

"I wouldn't know. I've broken things off with her. What I did was wrong, and I'm sorry, Camden. I want you back and—"

"Stop." Camden held up her hands. "I've been nice about things until now, but Grant, you have got to stop acting like we were some kind of fated match. We were friends whose parents were in love with the idea of being in-laws to one another." Camden felt like a broken record. How many times and in how many ways could she tell Grant she didn't want to be married to him? How long until he realized she was right?

She didn't want Grant's gratitude, but she would give just about anything right now for his acceptance that she had made the right decision in walking out.

"Then you leave me no choice." He motioned to the car. The rear door opened, and Camden caught her breath. "Elizabeth made the trip with me."

"You brought my mother?"

Grant nodded. "She is the only one who can talk sense into you when you get in a mood like this."

"A mood like this? How would you know what kind of mood I'm in? We've never talked about moods or what I like or what I think or what I *want*." Camden couldn't believe what she was seeing.

Elizabeth linked her arm with Grant's. She wore a camel coat, four-inch spiked heels and enough makeup for an entire finalist panel at a beauty pageant. Because she'd begun anti-aging treatments for her skin when she was still in college, she looked more like Camden's slightly older sister than her mother. Her expression was icy, but instead of backing down from the hauteur apparent in her expression, Camden stood firm. She was not twelve any longer. She could make her own decisions, and her decision was to walk away from a life that was not only unfulfilling but the opposite of everything she wanted.

When she was walking with Levi yesterday

he'd said something that made Camden think: that he'd always planned on coming back here because the work he did here was important.

Camden had no illusions that the dog school she was rebuilding with Granddad was the same as Levi's organic dairy, but it was a start. The business would become something she could be proud of.

"I don't want to marry you, Grant, and I love you, Mother, but I am not going to be in the pageant business any longer. If you would like the numbers of a few pageant pros who would make great coaches, I'll pass along a few that I know of. But I'm not going back to Kansas City, to Pomp and Circumstance, or to being engaged to Grant Wadsworth." Camden took a breath. "I live here now. I'm training dogs with Granddad, and I have no intention of leaving."

Elizabeth gaped at Camden. She'd drawn her long brown hair into a bun at the nape of her neck, the way she did every time she had an important client to impress. "Sweetheart," she said, and Camden winced at the hated endearment. *Sweetheart* was the way Elizabeth addressed waiters and waitresses and other service professionals she considered subpar.

"I hate that term," Camden said, not caring that she was interrupting what was sure to be a patented Elizabeth Camden Harris Carlson I Have Never Been So Disappointed in You speech. Elizabeth blinked at Camden's simple statement. "My name is Camden. You gave it to me—it shouldn't be too hard to remember. You can call me 'sweetheart,' but don't expect me to answer to it, and no matter what your excuse is for Grant, I'm not going to marry him. I deserve better than him."

Footsteps approached, and before he could touch her, Camden knew Levi had finished with whatever errand he had with Thom.

"I only want what's best for you," her mother said, and Camden could almost hear sincerity in her voice. She knew better than to believe the borderline emotional tone in her mother's voice, though.

"Then trust that I know what is best for me. And what is best for me is being in Slippery Rock with Levi."

Something in Elizabeth's countenance shifted. Her eyes, so similar to Camden's, softened, and she looked around at the Christmas lights, the roasted-chestnuts cart and the boats in the marina decked in fairy lights as if she'd never seen them before. Perhaps she hadn't. Camden could only remember visiting here in the summer months. "Okay," her mother said after a long pause.

Camden wasn't sure she'd heard Elizabeth correctly, and Grant appeared just as shocked. He straightened from his leaning position and said, "But there is the partnership. We have the same interests, the same belief system. We voted the same way in every election since we were eighteen."

"I told you the first time you called that I wasn't some Victorian-era pawn to be married off for a property or income merger."

"But we had nearly perfect scores on that compatibility test."

"Not everything can be measured with a test score or a percentage." Camden linked her arm with Levi's. "Mother, this is Levi Walters. He owns and operates a local organic dairy farm."

Her mother eyed Levi, who never shifted under her critical gaze. Finally, Elizabeth nodded. "Hello, Levi." She unlinked her arm from Grant's. "It's time to go," she said. When Grant protested, Elizabeth looked down her nose at him—an impressive feat, considering Grant was about six inches taller than she.

Grant clenched his jaw mutinously, but he got into the car. Elizabeth stood near the back door for a long moment. "Are you happy?" she asked.

Camden considered her answer carefully, not because she didn't know, but because there were so many things in her life that were making her happy now. Getting to know her grandparents again. Levi. Training Six. She didn't know the partners of Levi's friends or even his friends very well, but they had been welcoming at the dance. Julia, from the pageant circuit, had even wound up here.

Levi, though, stood head and shoulders above every other reason for her happiness.

Levi made her happy.

"I'm happy, Mother."

Elizabeth opened the door of the car. "Maybe we'll see you at New Year's?"

"I'd rather stay here for the holidays, but maybe after the first?"

"We could come to you," Elizabeth said slowly. "It's been a while since I've seen a Slippery Rock Christmas. Or New Year's, even."

"The mayor has planned concerts and live manger scenes and everything else you can imagine through January 5." When Elizabeth looked confused, Camden offered, "The twelfth day of Christmas."

Elizabeth didn't cross the space between

them, but Camden felt closer to her mother now than she had in years. "I'll see if there is a vacancy at the B and B then."

Despite the dim light cast by the overhead light in the car, Camden could see Grant's wooden countenance, annoyance in the set of his shoulders, but he drove away without more of a fuss. Camden turned to Levi.

"That was my mother."

"And the guy who likes to play Pin the Penis."

"His name is Grant."

"I don't care," Levi said. "You want some roasted chestnuts?"

Camden shook her head. "I'd rather have kettle corn or some of that homemade caramel corn at Bud's."

There were no cars driving on Main, so they cut across parking lots, making a beeline for the bait and sandwich shop.

At the popcorn stand outside the entrance to Bud's, they each picked a bag and began munching as they walked through the display that would change from life-size sculptures to real people next week. The sweetness of the caramel was perfect against the slight bit of salt in the treat.

Levi took her hand, and together they walked under the lights hanging from the low tree branches, past the stand with roasted chestnuts and the boats that lit up the marina in Christmas lights. For the first time, Camden didn't care if Grant came back. He could come back a thousand times, and her answer to him would be the same: no. Because no matter what Grant did, he could never be Levi.

CHAPTER ELEVEN

THINGS WERE GOING too well, and it made Camden nervous.

She and Levi had been back from Tulsa for a week and had spent nearly every moment together. They'd gone to more dinners at the Slippery Rock Grill, met his friends for a holiday-themed poker tournament at the Slope and spent every night together.

More than that, he had stood by her when Grant brought her mother to town, but he'd let her fight the battle on her own. Camden liked waking up with Levi in the mornings. Liked even more going to bed with him at night, learning his body.

She sipped her coffee, staring out the big plate-glass window of the Good Cuppa, the local coffee shop. The formerly pink-haired waitress now had teal hair with pink and purple stripes; she also had a new piercing in her eyebrow. Julia slid into the seat across from Camden, iced tea in her cup.

"Sorry I'm late. It's been a crazy day in renovation hell," she said. She looked smart, wearing black pencil pants, a flowing flowered tunic and tortoiseshell glasses perched on her nose. Camden had forgotten Julia was nearsighted; she usually wore contacts. Her outfit made Camden feel underdressed in her plain jeans, navy-striped long-sleeved T-shirt and knee boots. "Aiden found another area of black mold in this closet-size bathroom on the second floor. It looks like a few more walls are coming down before we can move forward."

"More black mold?" She knew Julia was renovating an old Victorian that overlooked Slippery Rock Lake, but Levi was her main source of town information and lately the two of them talked about very little. Mostly their time together was filled with kissing and touching and those sighs that made her toes curl just thinking about them.

"It's to be expected. The house has been vacant for almost fifteen years, and it sits right on the lake. All that moisture isn't great for old houses, even the ones with great bones like mine." She sipped her tea. "It's really good to see you here, Cam, I'd almost forgotten this was the town you talked about in our pageant days. How you were going to come back here, find a farm boy to marry and train a few dogs. Looks like you're living your dream."

"Something like that," she said and pasted a wide smile on her face when the words came out flat. If she could just stop wondering when the other shoe would drop, when things would stop going smoothly with Levi, then everything would be fine. But in her experience, when one area of life started going well, the other fell to crap. It had happened after that first pageant—she'd won the crown, but her father had been killed on the way to the competition, throwing her mother into a tailspin. Camden had sacrificed everything she wanted to pull her mother out of the dark place where she'd been, and it had worked. She went on to win more competitions, but the price was not visiting her beloved grandparents, not working with dogs, not having a life outside of competing in beauty pageants.

"You don't sound so sure." Julia's voice was filled with concern. "Things are going well with Levi, right? I know the two of you just started dating, but you look so adorable together. He's so tall and muscular, the consummate athlete, and you've got that whole tall willowy beauty queen thing going on still. His skin has those dark caramel tones, and you've got all this great, porcelain skin. The rest of us are practically average compared to the two of you."

"You make us sound like some Hollywood it couple," Camden said, uncomfortable at the track this conversation was taking. It didn't bother her that Levi was black and she was white. It bothered her that they still had nothing in common other than the town where they lived and the great sex. She didn't know about his plans for the future; he didn't ask about her plans. They hadn't attended the same schools; she'd been raised in the city and he in the country. Sooner or later those core differences would drive a wedge between them, and Camden had no idea how to bring the conversation to a head.

"This is Slippery Rock, and you're dating one of the Sailor Five, the boys who brought the state football championship home. There's a monument to them in the school courtyard, for crying out loud."

"No way." Camden hadn't made it as far as the schools in her walks around town. To tell the truth, she'd spent more time walking the trails at the farm than she had in town. She'd known about the football championship, of course, thanks to the billboards on either side of town. But the five of them—Aiden, Adam, Levi, Collin and James—were immortalized in a monument?

Julia grinned. "We, Queen Camden, are dating small-town royalty. Football stars are as good as British princes in a small southern town."

"Missouri isn't exactly Georgia or Texas."

Julia waved her hand in the air. "Doesn't matter. Missouri was a border state during the Civil War, remember? Some still consider us a border between the literal North and South, veering slightly more south, especially in the small-town areas."

Camden chuckled. "It's like you studied history or something."

"History major with an art minor. Perfect for a girl who always wanted to properly renovate one of the old Victorians out here."

"And the destination-wedding aspect?"

Julia shrugged. "I never outgrew my love of pretty dresses, mostly. Plus, I'm a sucker for weddings. The dresses and the hair. The shoes."

"The shoes are pretty fantastic." Camden's wedding shoes had had four-inch heels and golden scallops, making them look like something out of a fairy tale. They were the one piece of her wedding outfit that she'd left behind when she'd walked out on Grant. She missed the shoes more than she missed the man.

"Speaking of dresses, the girls are getting together with Savannah at the dress shop this afternoon. She's doing her final fitting before the wedding. You should come."

Camden shook her head. "I don't really know them. I wouldn't want to intrude."

"Are you kidding? You're dating Savannah's brother, Savannah's future husband's best friend. For that matter, all five of them are best friends. Dart-playing demons. Former hell-raisers, at least if you listen to the gossip around town."

"Hell-raisers?" Camden couldn't imagine Saint Levi, as the women had referred to him the night of the dance, raising anything other than the cattle at the dairy.

"It all blew back up when Mara returned to town last summer, but CarlaAnne at the grocery store likes to keep the gossips' tongues wagging. That woman has serious anger issues where Mara Tyler Calhoun is concerned."

"Why?" Camden couldn't resist asking. Mara had seemed like such a nice person that night at the dance, she couldn't imagine anyone disliking the blond-haired woman with the angelic smile.

"Because CarlaAnne's daughter dumped Aiden, breaking his heart just before a big school event. Aiden retaliated by painting the daughter's name and number on the water tower; soon after, she left town and never came back."

"But what does Aiden painting a phone number on the water tower have to do with Mara?"

"Mara's idea—at least, that's the way Carla-Anne tells it. Mara was a kind of ringleader of the guys back in school. They pranked practically everyone in town, not to be mean, but just because they were bored."

Camden couldn't imagine Levi pulling a prank of any kind. He seemed so serious most of the time, and grouchy when he wasn't serious.

"What else did they do?" she couldn't resist asking as they paid their bill. The two of them began walking toward the boutique. Several cars were parked in front of the little store with its pink-and-white-striped awnings. An Elf on the Shelf cavorted in the faux snow–covered window display, and because there were only ten days left before the holiday, Mayor Thom had insisted that local businesses leave their holiday lights on throughout the day.

"Let's see. I only know what Aiden has told me. There was the painting incident. They TP'd several yards and filled the fountain in the town square with Kool-Aid so the water turned lime green. A few of the boys stole a boat one night."

"No."

"They still insist it was a police emergency," Julia said as they pushed through the front door.

Women Camden remembered from the night of the holiday dance focused their attention on her, looking surprised that she'd come to the fitting. Camden backed toward the door, but Julia pulled her forward, and then Savannah, her thinly braided hair pulled back from her face in a long tail, grabbed her hands.

"Are we telling stories on the boys? Because I still say that police emergency had less to do with possible drug runners than it did with impressing those girls from Joplin. Hey, Camden, we didn't know you were coming," she said, pulling Camden to the sofa beside her.

"I don't want to intrude."

"You're not—the more the merrier, and don't think you're going to get out of here just watching me try on the dress. Bud will be here with lunch in a few minutes, and I've been instructed by Merle that we're expected for cocktails at four."

"Merle from the Slippery Slope? The one who grumbles if you order anything but draft beer?" Camden had obviously missed something the handful of times she'd been in the bar. She sat with Savannah on one of the narrow white sofas near the back of the boutique. "He's serving cocktails?"

Racks of clothes filled the front part of the store, mostly designer jeans and cute tops. The back of the store was a wash of jewel-toned or pristine white dresses. One dress, a pretty satin with beading over the bodice and a long train, hung on a rack near a triple mirror setup that would allow the wearer to see herself from all angles. Camden hated triple mirrors—they were so unforgiving. Elizabeth had installed triples in the mansion in Mission Hills when Camden started winning pageants. She'd seen herself from so many ugly angles, it was a wonder Camden could look in mirrors at all anymore.

"He makes an exception for us," Savannah said.

"For his favorite former country singer, you mean," Mara put in.

Savannah shrugged. "I was a good waitress back in the day."

"Merle's just an old softie," said Jenny, the curly-haired woman with the husky voice. "And getting softer every day since he and Juanita outed themselves."

"Wait, Merle and Juanita are dating? I thought they hated each other." Camden had obviously missed a lot of things. Not surprising, since she'd been so focused on Levi.

"For years, although they never told anyone until after the tornado last spring," Julia said. "I wasn't in town then, but I've heard through the grapevine. Van, are you trying on before we eat or after?"

Savannah jumped up from the sofa. "Before. If I put any carbs at all in my stomach before that dress goes on, I'll never get it zipped." The woman slipped behind a Japanese screen. The jeans and top she'd been wearing were slung over the top of the screen, and then she reached for the dress.

When she returned a few moments later, the woman who had looked more like a teenager in her jeans and sweatshirt than the twenty-seven-year-old Camden knew her to be had transformed. The beading on the bodice of the dress reflected light from all over the room, making it appear as if Savannah were glowing. The strapless dress fit her like a second skin, flowing to the floor in waves of soft white satin, leaving only Savannah's toes—with hummingbirds painted on them—showing.

Jenny and Mara put their hands to their faces, tears in their eyes, while Julia walked a slow circle around Savannah, inspecting the fit of the dress.

"You look beautiful," Jenny said once Julia nodded her approval.

"We definitely don't need to take it in. How does it feel on you, Van?" Julia asked.

"Like I'm wearing a dream," she said and twirled before the mirror the way Camden had in her prepageant days. The dress flowed around Savannah's long legs, and when she turned around, Camden saw more of the beading down the side.

All those layers of tulle in her own dress had been overpowering, but the simple beading that flowed from the train to the sweetheart neckline only emphasized Savannah's simple beauty. The dress was perfection.

Savannah's gaze caught Camden's in the mirror. "It really is a beautiful dress," Camden said. Julia fluffed the train, and when she did the beads seemed to dance, and Camden realized the beading wasn't random. The shiny beads were in the shape of a hummingbird, like Savannah wore on her toes, and when Julia fluffed the train again, it was as if the bird floated over Savannah's body. The effect was breathtaking.

This was the kind of dress she would wear if she were ever to get married. A dress that seemed simple but had hidden meaning. Camden had no idea what the hummingbird was about for Savannah, but it obviously meant something. She'd practically covered herself in the small birds.

"It's perfect."

"You think so? It's not too much?"

Camden shook her head. "I don't know you that well, so I don't know your usual taste—"

"Bohemian hippie," Mara offered.

"But you're glowing," Camden finished. "You'll be the prettiest woman in the room."

Savannah twirled again. "Okay, okay, get it off me before Bud walks in, because you know he'll start the phone tree as soon as he sees this dress and then it won't be a surprise to anyone."

Julia joined her behind the screen. Mara and Jenny started talking about someone named

Frankie and a school project, leaving Camden alone with her thoughts.

She didn't want to marry Levi. She didn't want to marry anyone, not right now. So why was she imagining herself in a dress like Savannah's, walking toward Levi in a tux? Camden pulled a throw pillow to her chest and sank back against the cushions. He would look at her the way he'd looked at her that night in the bar, only she would know he was there for her, not just picking up a desperate girl. Or maybe he'd seem a little lost, like those moments after that first night in Tulsa. He'd seemed almost dazed, but his arms had been strong around her middle as he held her to him.

Someone snapped their fingers, and Camden jolted out of the daydream.

"There you are. You disappeared on us for a minute there," Julia said.

A box filled with sandwiches and potato salad sat on the low coffee table before the sofa grouping. Just how long had she been daydreaming about Levi?

"Sorry, I…it's been a weird couple of days."

The four other women exchanged a look, and then Savannah chuckled. "Levi has that effect on women." She frowned. "Not that he brings a lot of women around. The few I've seen, though—" she pointed her index finger at Camden as if circling her "—that same dazed expression."

Levi hadn't dazed her. The two of them hadn't been together long enough for dazing to have happened. This was just…a sex hangover. Lack of sleep or something. She was not falling for Levi Walters. Camden hadn't come to Slippery Rock to fall in love.

Even if she had come back here looking for love, it was too soon to have fallen in love with him. Love didn't strike people down in a heartbeat—it took time. Savannah and the other women picked up their sandwiches, talking about the wedding plans as they ate. Since Camden wasn't part of the wedding, she sank back into the sofa, considering Savannah's statement and the vaguely uneasy feelings she'd been having ever since the trip to Tulsa. She'd fallen right into Levi's bed, had begun fitting her life around seeing him, but did she know much more about him than she had three weeks ago?

She thought of her grandmother's story about jumping off the float to kiss Calvin at that parade. She hadn't exactly jumped off a float, but that kiss at the barn had been pure impulse. The one after it, at the bar, another impulse. Sleeping with him in Tulsa, impulse. And Camden wasn't normally an impulsive person. Her heart stuttered in her chest.

There was nothing in her past she could compare those moments to; no one had ever made her jump into action so quickly, and the clammy feeling in her belly told her those kisses had been more about Levi's nearness than convincing Grant to go back to Kansas City. That didn't have to mean she'd fallen in love with a man she barely knew, though.

Maybe she was just in lust with Levi. The thought was so much more calming than the other option. Because if she was in love with Levi, she was in real trouble. Love, in Camden's limited experience, caused pain harsh enough to break a person.

She couldn't let loving Levi break her.

LEVI AIMED HIS dart at the board, let it fly and rolled his eyes when it hit just left of the board. He couldn't throw a dart for anything lately, and it annoyed the bejesus out of him. Losing at anything bugged Levi. Especially when the loss was due to a lack of focus. Levi never lacked focus. At least, that had been true before Camden blew into town at Thanksgiving.

He was distracted, though, and it had everything to do with Camden Harris. Their fake relationship had quickly turned into a full-blown affair, one that Levi has having trouble keeping in the nice box he usually confined his relationships to. Instead of having dinner with Camden and then carrying on with his life, he found himself daydreaming about her at odd times, wanting to text her to check in during the day. Things a boyfriend would do. Only he wasn't her boyfriend. They were sleeping together but hadn't talked about future plans. Hell, she was less than a month out of an engagement—did she even want a serious relationship?

Levi threw his third dart, which landed on a five spot. He needed to get his game together. James took his spot, aimed and hit the twenty position, putting the red team—James and Aiden—ahead of Levi and Collin, who were playing the blue darts. Adam sat in the corner of the booth, nursing a Coke and texting with Jenny.

He'd finally had hip surgery the week of Thanksgiving and used the excuse that he hadn't been cleared for athletic competitions to sit out their regular Wednesday-night game. Levi thought Adam sitting out had more to do with Jenny, who was at the boutique with

Mara, Savannah and Julia, than it had to do with athletic competition. He started to scratch Adam's service dog, Sheba, behind the ears, but then remembered Adam was the only one who was supposed to handle the retriever. Levi slid into the booth while Collin and Aiden played their round.

"You seem a little off your game," Adam said after a moment. His phone buzzed. He glanced at the readout, then grinned and chuckled.

"How would you know? You've been playing with your phone all night."

"Texting with my wife about your new girlfriend isn't 'playing with my phone.'"

"My new— Wait, what's Camden got to do with Jenny?"

"The four of them have been helping Van with her final gown fitting. Didn't you know?"

The last he'd heard, Camden was having coffee with her friend Julia. She hadn't said a thing about helping Savannah with the wedding plans. For that matter, Camden had only spent a single evening with the other women, the night of the holiday dance. At what point had that dance turned into bonding over wedding finery?

Levi scratched his head. "I just forgot."

"More like you never knew. Don't you know how this works by now? Four of us are either married off or about to be. When wedding fever bites, it takes a chunk out of every single woman within a hundred-mile radius."

"Not Camden. She isn't interested in marriage."

Adam chuckled. "She walked into this very bar three weeks ago wearing a wedding dress. I'd say weddings are somewhere in her consciousness."

Not Camden, not right now, anyway. Not after the way she'd learned about Grant's cheating. Of course, he couldn't really say that he knew Camden, because knowing what turned her body on wasn't the same as knowing what made her mind tick. And he wanted to know what made her tick, Levi realized. Not just sexually, but in all the other ways. So far, he'd settled for only the physical.

Levi threw a few bills on the table. "I have to go."

Adam blinked. "But it's darts night."

No one left darts night early. "I'm off my game. You won't miss me." He escaped the bar before the others could add in their questions or comments and texted Camden from the truck, asking her to meet him at his house when she was free.

It was time the two of them started to really get to know one another.

LEVI STRIPPED OFF his T-shirt, one knee still on the bed. Getting to know Camden outside the bedroom was going to have to wait. He'd had a plan in mind, a good one. It involved him cooking her a meal and not getting distracted with kissing her before it was served. That lasted about five minutes after she walked in his front door wearing skinny jeans, an over-size sweater and those high-heeled knee boots she'd worn to the dance. Was that less than two weeks ago? It seemed like so much more time had passed than the twelve days he quickly counted.

Two weeks of being with Camden, but not getting to know her.

She deserved better than that, and so did he. But right now she was nearly naked on his bed, and that getting-to-know-you session would have to wait.

Camden curled one leg around his, her back against the mahogany of the headboard, looking more inviting than…anything. Levi couldn't remember wanting a woman more than he wanted Camden, and not just for sex. Although he didn't want to delay that part of it any longer than necessary. Her chest rose and fell unevenly as she tried to catch her breath. And after this was done, he already knew he'd want to do it again and again.

Hell, he just might never stop. That thought should've send a jolt of panic through him but it didn't. Because he might know why Camden was back in town, but they hadn't talked about her plans for the future. Was the dog-training thing an impulse? Neither she nor Calvin had added dogs to the kennel yet, although Camden continued to work with Six most mornings. Not wanting to marry Grant didn't necessarily mean she wouldn't want to return to Kansas City—or some other city—in the future.

Levi had no plans to leave Slippery Rock; this was his home. This was where he wanted to be, although the thought of being here without Camden sent a chill through him. As annoying as it was that she opposed his ideas for the bike trail, about adding more tourism, he wouldn't want her to be anywhere else but here, in his bed, with him.

For as long as they both might live.

Levi paused. *As long as they...* Didn't mean anything. With Savannah in full-on wedding-planning mode, James having just married Mara, and Adam recently renewing his vows to Jenny, there was wedding fever in Slippery Rock. It didn't mean Levi was ready to settle down with Camden. Men didn't get that wedding-fever thing Adam had been talking about.

She sucked her bottom lip between her teeth, and the small move brought him back to the bedroom and out of his head. She looked so sweet in the middle of his big bed, surrounded by a thick comforter, wearing nothing more than a few scraps of lace—and who knew that a girl who ran around in rain boots all the damn time would have such…interesting undergarments?

Levi ran the back of his hand over the lace covering one breast, and Camden closed her eyes as she inhaled sharply. Her fists clenched around handfuls of the comforter. He moved closer to her on the bed, buried his hands in her silky hair and turned her face up. Her brown eyes met his, and he couldn't look away. Could only drink in the sight of her, as if he might imprint this night on his brain.

She shifted restlessly on the bed. Ran her bare foot along his denim-encased calf. Screw imprinting. He wanted her, and he was going to have her, and they'd figure the rest out once he'd satisfied the haze of lust that kept short-circuiting his brain.

He took her mouth with his, but instead of the rush of adrenaline he expected, everything seemed to slow. There was only the taste of her on his tongue, only the sweet scent of her perfume in his nostrils as the sun sank slowly outside his window. Her mouth was pliant beneath his, her hands spinning lazy circles on his, which held tightly to her silken head, wanting this kiss to go on forever. Longer than the kiss at the barn. Deeper than the kiss at the Slope.

Need took over. The kiss could go on forever, but sooner or later, the bottom half of him was going to blow. He'd rather be inside her when that happened. To know how it felt to be enveloped in her heat. Levi released her mouth, put his hands on her hips and pulled her down the bed so that she rested against the soft pillows instead of the hard headboard.

"Ooh," Camden squeaked in surprise. "Nice offensive move for the defenseman."

"They don't call linebackers 'defensemen'—that's a hockey term." He pressed kisses along her jaw, settling himself against her. His fingers found her breasts beneath the black lace, and he teased them gently. Camden sucked in a breath.

"Hockey, football. Is there a difference?"

Levi tweaked her nipple a bit harder and Camden squeaked again, not in pain, but surprise. "Because I can't walk away at this moment, I'm going to pretend you didn't just ask if there was a difference between hockey and football."

He kissed his way down her neck, pausing for a moment to play with the pulse at her throat before taking her breast into his mouth. Levi lavished attention on her pink areolae, flattening his tongue against one while his fingers feasted on the other.

"But Sunday, we're totally having a lesson in the differences between football and hockey," he said before moving to her other breast.

"If I tell you a goalie is no different than a field-goal kicker, will you do that tweaking thing again?" she asked, writhing beneath him.

Levi raised up on his elbows, watching her. Camden looped her arms around his neck, trying to pull him back to her. "You're just messing with me."

She blinked. "Did you think for a second a girl who attended an SEC school—even one of the new additions to the conference—wouldn't know at least a minimum about football? You had me on that forward pass thing, and I've never spent more than a quarter at an actual game, but I do know that a touchdown is seven points—"

"Six. It's the field goal that puts it at seven."

"Whatever. And that the quarterback is the most important person on the field."

"Actually, a good linebacker—"

"I'm explaining how much I know about football."

"You're actually explaining how little you know about it but, sure, carry on."

"I also know linebackers are a dime a dozen," she said, referring to his position. A position he'd been damn good at. He caught her gaze with his, and an impish light danced in the brown depths. For a moment, Levi forgot to breathe, he was so mesmerized by the woman in his arms.

"You're going to pay for that," he said after a moment.

"Promise?" The word was barely a whisper, but it seemed to echo around the bedroom. Camden clenched her hands against his head when his mouth found her breast again. Levi kissed his way back to her mouth, capturing her lips with his. She arched her back, pressing her breasts against his chest.

Levi pushed her hands over her head, holding them there while he worked his other hand over her ribs and down her belly, making her muscles jump under his touch. He wanted more. Wanted to feel the smoothness of her skin without the lace between them. In a smooth move, he unhooked the lacy bra, pulling it from her. Her breasts were perfect. Small, but he'd never been a size guy. She had a beauty mark, a tiny freckle or mole, centered on her breastbone, and Levi pressed a kiss to it.

"You're beautiful."

"I'm ordinary."

He twisted a lock of her hair around his index finger as he kissed his way to her rib cage. "There is nothing ordinary about you, Camden Harris. Nothing ordinary at all."

She made a sound of disbelief, but when his mouth reached her hip bone and pressed another kiss there, she stopped talking. He'd have to remember that trick the next time she started going on about the bike trail.

Levi let his fingers venture farther south, to the black lace covering her hips. Camden's breathing slowed as if in anticipation. He paused, one finger under her waistband, and focused his gaze on hers. He studied her for a moment, and then another. Her brown eyes were huge, soft and dewy and filled with wanting.

She wanted him, and the knowledge was a powerful thing.

He'd had women want him before, but never a woman like Camden. The women he'd taken to his hotel rooms in the past were more plastic and less real than the woman beneath him tonight. It was almost as if they hadn't really existed, or as if he had been a different man then. Camden made him want more than just sex. More than the physical, and he'd think deeper about that later. After the sex had cleared his mind so he could figure out what all of this meant.

Levi Walters had never been a relationship guy, not because he didn't want a relationship, but because he'd never met a woman who made him want something that went farther than a few dates.

Camden drew in another breath, and the muscles in her abdomen clenched when he pushed his finger beneath the lace.

He had no idea what a long-term relationship looked like, but he thought, with Camden, he could almost imagine it.

Levi drew tiny circles over the skin at her hip toward her belly button, and then swirled his way to her other hip. Camden made a small sound like a kitten and pulled her lower lip between her teeth. Levi drew another series of circles along her lower belly, entranced by her clenching muscles, at the tension drawing her body tight like the laces on a football.

When her hips bucked, he pulled the damp lace from her, leaving her naked before him. Levi swallowed. Her alabaster skin was so different from his. He pressed a kiss to her hip before working his way over her hip and down her leg, pausing to tease the back of her knee before making his way to her ankle. Camden inhaled, her breathing ragged.

"I know I teased you about punishment for that whole football thing," she said, her voice as ragged as her breathing, "but I don't think I can take much more of this."

Levi began making his way up her other leg, pausing at her knee again. "You'd be surprised what the human body can take," he said.

"You're a bad, bad man, Levi Walters," she said when he pressed a kiss to her center.

"You have no idea, Camden Harris."

Camden lay on the bed, her hands still above her head, although he'd released her wrists several minutes before. Need filled her big brown eyes. He pressed one finger inside her, feeling the heat of her center and wanting more. She closed her eyes and seemed to stop breathing for a long moment. Levi pushed another finger inside her and found her clitoris with his thumb, pressing gently against it.

"God, Levi," she breathed.

Levi flicked against the bundle of nerves again. Withdrew his fingers. Pressed back inside and flicked again.

Camden pressed her hands into the pillows and bit down on her lower lip as her eyes squeezed shut. Levi continued the pattern. Press. Flick. Withdraw. Press. Flick. Withdraw. Until Camden's breathing came in short gasps and her head rolled from side to side on the pillow.

"Levi." She whispered his name as the orgasm came over her. Camden's shoulders stiffened and her hips arched up against his hand, driving his fingers more deeply into her. Pushing his thumb firmly against her body. Her muscles contracted over his joints. Her mouth tightened a fraction, and her fists clenched against the pillows.

She shattered around him. Her hips lowered to the mattress, but still, Levi continued the motions. Press. Flick. Withdraw. Press. Flick. Withdraw.

Levi moved over her, dipped his tongue into her belly button. Her hands reached for him, pulling him up, up her body. Camden's hands found his hips and pressed beneath the denim. She unbuttoned them and pushed the zipper down as his mouth met hers. And then her soft hands were on him, and Levi was lost to her touch.

Pushing his jeans over his hips, Camden freed his length. She circled his erection with her hand, her thumb playing with the little opening at the tip.

He groaned. He needed to keep things under control if he were to make this night special for Camden.

Levi pushed himself off the bed, shucked his jeans and grabbed a condom from the nightstand drawer, but Camden took it from him to slide it down his length. The feel of her hand around him took his breath away, and as she rolled the thin latex over him, Levi thought he might lose it before he got to feel the heaven of Camden surrounding him.

He pushed her back onto the pillows, taking position between her legs. Her hands were soft against his chest, her gaze still filled with need. She wrapped her legs around his waist, pulling him closer to her body.

She was warm, ready for him, and Levi thrust inside her. She caught his mouth in another kiss. He arched and her tongue traced a path from his lower lip over his chin to his collarbone.

He wanted to go slow, wanted to make this last all night, but Camden urged him on, meeting him thrust for thrust. Levi emptied himself into her and collapsed beside her on the bed.

Breathing heavily, he closed his eyes. He'd been right.

Sleeping with Camden had complicated things, and for the first time in his life, he didn't mind the complications.

CHAPTER TWELVE

A FEW DAYS LATER, Camden stood with Calvin in the barnyard as a large truck and trailer drove slowly down the lane. On the way back from Tulsa, Calvin had called the breeder and purchased five new dogs, which were being delivered today.

She hadn't seen Levi yet this morning, and that was unusual. He'd been out of bed when she woke and hadn't been back to the pretty house he'd built only a few months ago. The sun hid behind thick gray clouds today, and Camden shoved her icy hands into the pockets of her coat and hunched her shoulders against the biting wind.

Wherever Levi was, she hoped he was warmer than she was at this moment.

The big truck stopped, and a short man with a large spare tire got out. He held out his hand to Calvin. "Nice to see you, Calvin. Ready to see the dogs? I brought a couple extra, just in case you wanted a few more options."

The three of them went around the big trailer. When the breeder opened the back gate, a cacophony of dog barking echoed into the early-morning air. Camden winced. The dogs were mostly border collies, but there were a couple of Australian cattle dogs in the mix. All of them looked to have good builds, and despite the barking, the dogs seemed even tempered. All good traits in working dogs.

One by one, Calvin led the dogs from the trailer, putting them through a mini workout that would tell him everything he needed to know about the dogs in his school. After each workout, Calvin put the dogs in one of the newly renovated runs. An hour later, the breeder took his truck and trailer back down the drive, and Calvin turned to Camden.

"I guess we're in business."

Camden looked around the barnyard. The dogs were noisily investigating their new home, and even Six seemed excited about the new arrivals. "I guess we are," she said. "Mother was in town the other night, after the meeting. Grant brought her, I suppose to guilt me into going back."

Calvin snorted. "That didn't work."

"No."

"Because of Levi." Calvin started toward the house, and Camden walked with him.

Because of Levi. Because of her. Because of Slippery Rock. Because of all of it, Camden supposed. Inside the house was much quieter than outside.

"They'll calm down. I'll take a couple out on a walk this afternoon. Get them used to the area, used to me." Calvin paused then said, "The two of you are spending a lot of time together."

"I like him." She more than liked him, but Camden wasn't quite ready to admit just how important Levi had become to her over the past few weeks.

"He's a good man."

Bonita came downstairs from her craft room, holding a few handmade bookmarks. "Which do you like better? And how are the new dogs doing?" She asked both questions together, and before Camden could answer either, Calvin broke in.

"Elizabeth was here," Calvin said, and Bonita's mouth dropped open. "Monday night after Thom's meeting."

"She's thinking about visiting, maybe at New Year's." Camden shrugged. "I don't really know what to think about that, but I've decided I'm going to be happy about it."

"You should, honey," Grandmom said. "She's your mother, and she loves you. She loved your father. She never understood either of you, but she does love you. I never doubted that."

Camden had never thought of her mother in terms of love or understanding. Overbearing, yes, broken, definitely. Bonita might be right, though, that Elizabeth's misunderstanding of her father and then of Camden didn't also preclude her loving her family.

Not any more than Camden's inability to fall in love with Grant had precluded her falling in love with Levi. And she did love the handsome farmer. The knowledge scared her almost as much as it made her want to run around the room shouting.

She loved Levi, and she wanted him to love her back.

"I, um, have a couple of errands to run. I'll see you both later," she said.

Hours later, the sun was beginning to set, blazing a brilliant orange in the western sky, and Camden was alone at Levi's home. She'd lit a fire in the fireplace, had peppercorn steaks prepped for the grill and baked potatoes in the warming oven. Levi wasn't home yet, and she wondered where he was.

Camden wandered the big, sparsely decorated room. Pictures of his family, Bennett, Mama Hazel and Savannah, lined the mantel, along with a few action shots of Levi in his football gear. The hardwood floors were polished to a shine, the leather furniture comfortable as well as fashionable. He'd hung long taupe and black curtains at the windows, but she'd never seen the curtains closed. Levi liked natural light.

She checked her watch and yawned. It was barely five o'clock, but Camden could hardly hold her eyes open. She would take a little catnap while she waited for Levi to get back. Settling into the couch, Camden curled her arm under her head and let her eyes drift closed.

It seemed like only a moment later that she jolted awake. But the sky outside the windows was black, so she knew she'd slept. The clock on the mantel chimed the half hour, and she wondered what time it was.

"You're awake," Levi said from the chair next to the couch.

"I was only going to have a catnap. What time is it?"

"A little after eight. Sorry I'm late."

"Catching up on work?"

He nodded. "Dog delivery go well?"

Camden nodded. "Did you eat anything?"

"Not hungry."

"Anything good on TV?"

"I was too entranced by the beautiful woman on my sofa to settle for boring television."

"Dinner is prepped, it'll only take a few minutes—"

Levi leaned across the space separating them. "I already said I'm not hungry. All I want is you."

She wrapped her arms around his neck, pulling his mouth down on hers. The familiar licks of passion burned her belly. This was the man she loved. The realization was still new, but not quite as scary with Levi's mouth on hers, the feel of his body against hers.

He lifted her from the sofa, his arms solid against her back and legs. "We should take this upstairs," he said, and she had no idea how they managed to get from the living room to the master suite without Levi tripping up the stairs or against some piece of furniture, because his mouth never left hers and his pace never faltered.

In the master suite, he set her feet on the floor and cupped her face with his hands. "I missed you today. Came over to Calvin's this afternoon, but you were gone."

"I drove to Mallards for dinner supplies. Peppercorn steaks, loaded baked potatoes, a nice bottle of wine."

"Sounds almost as delicious as you," he said. "What's the occasion?"

Butterflies slammed around in Camden's belly. She loved him, but telling Levi when they'd only been together a couple of weeks? It was probably the worst form of relationship suicide, but she couldn't not tell him. Not when the realization made her feel so very much inside.

"I love you," she said, and Levi froze for a long moment. The butterflies in her belly stopped ricocheting around, and her hands clenched behind his neck. And then his mouth was back on hers, voracious in its plundering, and Camden forgot to be afraid. She'd said what she needed to say. She didn't need to hear the words in return; it was enough to know how she felt.

Levi pulled her hips into his, and she felt his erection hard against her. She took off his long-sleeved black T-shirt then fisted her hands in the light mat of hair on his chest. His frame was hard beneath her hands, his heart thundering in his chest. She flicked her thumb-nail against his nipple, and Levi groaned in her mouth.

Camden had considered wearing a dress to-night, but she'd decided it would make things too formal. As if she were offering herself up or something. So she'd gone with her usual jeans, but opted for a fitted sweater. Levi lifted the garment from her body, and the cool air in the bedroom made her nipples pucker beneath the satin of her bra. He reached between them, lowering the zip of her jeans so he could push them over her hips. Camden kicked them off, her mouth still fused with his. Her hands found his zipper and she released it to push the denim over his narrow hips. Levi picked her up again and deposited her on the bed.

Camden pushed the extra pillows off the side, eager for him to join her.

Levi reached into the nightstand drawer for a condom, and then he was beside her, all six feet five inches of him stretched out, making her feel small, despite the fact that she was five feet seven inches herself.

He pushed a lock of hair behind her ear, and she thought he might say the words, but the moment passed, and she told herself it didn't matter.

For too long she had kept her feelings to herself, but that was the old Camden. The new Camden wasn't afraid of the things she felt. She owned those feelings. Telling Levi she loved him was part of owning them.

When his mouth found hers again, it was gentle, but instead of that dampening the heat between them, the caress stoked the fire hotter. She twisted her leg around his, wanting to hold him here, right here beside her, as long as she could.

She wanted more. More than his mouth on her. More than her hands on his back or tangled in his hair. Camden pushed his jeans and briefs over his hips and was rewarded with the feel of his smooth backside in her hands. That wasn't what she wanted either, though. Reaching between them, she took his length in her hands, squeezing the shaft gently. She liked the feel of him—strong, hard. She ran her thumbnail gently down the vein on the underside, and Levi drew in a breath.

"This is going to be over pretty quick if you keep doing things like that."

She smiled at him. "There's always round two."

"We passed two and then four the other night."

Camden giggled. "I meant two tonight. And you're counting?"

He nibbled her lower lip and allowed his hands to work down her abdomen toward the apex of her. "Counting. Memories seared across my brain. You make the call."

She squeezed again.

"I call touchdown." Levi shifted his body over her and into her in one motion, making Camden gasp. She drew her lower lip between her teeth and curled her toes as he filled her.

"Cam," he said, placing little kisses along her lips and then continuing to the base of her ear.

Camden wrapped her legs around him, urging him farther in, and he began to move. She felt him all around. Over her. Inside her, and she never wanted the feeling to end. Levi sucked her earlobe into his mouth, and Camden clutched at his shoulders. He buried his face in the hollow of her neck, and she wrapped her arms around him. Their bodies seemed to sync as he quickened the pace. Camden's muscles clenched, gathering as he pushed her higher and higher, and then it was as if she were flying. She squeezed her legs around his hips as if to start the whole thing over again and then her body went boneless as Levi charged over his own precipice.

Breathing ragged, Camden sank into the pillows. Levi rolled to the side but brought her with him so that their legs were entwined on the soft bed.

"That's a nice welcome home."

"I was going to say that was a nice wake-up call." She kissed the soft skin above his pec and slid her tongue against his hard nipple. "Was I asleep long?"

"Ten, fifteen minutes. I didn't really count. You looked so cute, asleep on my sofa."

Camden yawned and pillowed her head against his shoulder, her chest to his chest. "We should eat in a little while, and then we could work on that second round," she said sleepily.

He settled his arms around her after pushing a lock of hair behind her ear then kissed her temple. "Sounds like a good plan," he said.

Camden tucked her foot between his legs and threw her arm over his chest. She sighed and allowed her eyes to close.

This was perfect. He was perfect. Fast didn't negate the perfection.

She was in love with Levi Walters.

And she could wait for him to love her back.

LEVI WATCHED CAMDEN sleep for a long time. She looked so peaceful. So content.

And she loved him.

He didn't know what to do with that. No one outside his family had ever said those words to him. He'd never been tempted to say those words to a woman, but saying them in the middle of sex seemed like cheating.

Levi didn't want to cheat Camden—or himself—out of the moment, and so he held her in his arms while she slept, contemplating how this had all happened so fast. She hadn't been back in Slippery Rock for a month yet, and he'd gone from being entranced by her to mistrusting her to being unable *not* to kiss her to being in a pretend relationship that had very quickly turned into a real one. They were still getting to know one another.

Grant of the Khaki Pants was still coming around, although Levi figured that without Camden's mother on Grant's side, that play for reconciliation was likely over.

Maybe it was okay for this to be going so fast. What was it that Mama Hazel had told him? Love happens when you least expect it and so fast you can't believe it. That seemed true in this case.

Levi let his eyes drift shut. He would tell

Camden, but he wanted to make it special, to give her a true memory, as corny as that sounded.

Adam had filled Jenny's backyard with pictures of their life together a few months before.

James had handcuffed himself to Mara in the back of a police cruiser.

Collin had stood beside Savannah when her whole world was crumbling.

He had to figure out what kind of gesture Camden needed, and that would be how he told her he loved her. And in the meantime, he would hold on to her so tightly, she would never feel alone.

CHAPTER THIRTEEN

"Do we know why Thom called this meeting?" Camden asked.

"I have no clue," Julia said. She held up the phone. "I got the same group text everyone else did. 'Mandatory meeting, three p.m.'"

Town hall was once again filled with residents and business owners, but instead of the usual Monday meeting to run down the final preparations before Christmas, Thom had called this meeting on the Sunday before.

Maybe he'd actually managed to get a message to Kris Kringle and the original Santa was coming to Slippery Rock to ring in the holiday. Camden grinned at the thought.

Her first Christmas season in Slippery Rock had been filled with magic, although she had only made it to a handful of events. Levi was the biggest part of that magic. She looked around the room, but he hadn't arrived yet.

At three Thom stood behind the podium and banged the gavel to call the meeting to order.

"People," he said, raising his voice to be heard above the voices. "We have a decision before us that could affect the entire future of Slippery Rock."

That sentence got the room's attention. People stopped chatting and focused on him. Pleased to have their undivided attention, Thom continued. "As you all know, we are hoping to be the final link in the rail trail that will connect from St. Louis through Springfield, then Slippery Rock and on into Oklahoma. If completed, it would be the longest rail trail in the entire country, and it could mean a huge boost of year-round tourism to this town."

"I don't think we're going to see many hikers when the ice storms hit in January," Merle said from the back of the room.

"Of course, we would hope that adventure tourists would not use our trail during inclement weather. However, the trail would be run by the state. We would simply benefit from those spending money on food and supplies while traveling the trail by foot or bicycle."

"We know all of this, Thom," Merle said. "What's the deal with pulling all of us in here on a Sunday afternoon? I had to leave Juanita in charge of the bar, and who knows what kind of drinks she'll start making for the football fans."

"The deal is that we had planned to use only the old railroad route. As you know, much of that land is flat, making it easily traversable. But it has come to our attention that part of the original spur, which was used during the creation of the railroad, is still in existence, and that the area with the spur would add quite the challenging section for either hikers or bikers."

An uneasy feeling crept into Camden's stomach. What were the odds there would be more than one spur along the railroad tracks in Wall County? Probably slim to none. The area had been even more sparsely populated after the Civil War when the railroad went through.

"There's a historical railroad spur? I had no idea," Julia said, making a note on her phone. "This is the kind of thing destination-wedding types love," she whispered.

Camden didn't respond. She didn't care about Julia's destination-wedding business. She didn't care about a more challenging course for those following the trail through Missouri and Oklahoma. What she cared about was the hilly, rocky area around the spur on Calvin's land. An area that would give their dogs great real-world training before they went to working ranches all over the United States.

Levi slipped in through the side door. "What

did I miss?" he asked, reaching for Camden's hand. She pulled away from him.

"Thom wants to vote on putting the rail trail through the spur and not the actual tracks."

"Great idea, don't you think?"

Camden narrowed her eyes at Levi. "No, I don't think. I wanted to use that area for dog training, or do you not remember that conversation?"

Levi blinked as if shocked she hadn't jumped for joy at learning her plans for the dog-school expansion were going up in smoke. "Of course I remember it. We walked through about three acres of similar terrain before reaching the spur, though."

"That isn't the point," she hissed.

Thom turned on a presentation, pointing out the already planned route in yellow. That route cut across Harris land and then hit the northern edge of Walters land, too. Then he flipped the presentation screen and showed the alternate route in red. This time, the trail followed along a larger section of Harris land before dipping into a small corner of the national forest surrounding their land and rejoining the rail trail at the Wall County line.

She'd told Levi just a couple of days ago that she loved him and this was how he responded?

By yanking the proverbial rug out from under her plans for the future?

"As you all know, Levi Walters has been a vocal opponent of the rail trail, fearing too much waste would be left behind, and that hikers or bikers could become lost or hurt. After talking with Levi about this new option, I have been assured he will withdraw his objections to the rail trail. Now, if there are no new objections—" Thom paused for a moment. Camden wanted to raise her hand to object, but she couldn't.

The land belonged to her grandfather, not to her. In her excitement over the new dogs, her plans for the future, over Levi, she hadn't asked Calvin about doing some of the training near the spur. Even if she had, Granddad loved the idea of a hiking trail. How many times had he told her if he weren't so tied to the dog school that he would hike the Appalachian Trail or the Pacific Coast Trail? Having something similar in his backyard—there was no way Calvin Harris would vote against it.

"With no other objections, I'll note that the proposed changes are approved by the town, and submit them to the development crew for their decision." Thom banged the gavel, and Camden flinched. "No other business.

Go enjoy the last Sunday before Christmas," Thom said.

The room buzzed to life, with people talking about the new options for the trail. A few clapped Levi on the back, thanking him for voting with the town. That was the last straw for Camden.

Levi was being celebrated for ruining her business plans.

"I have to go," she said to Julia, who was still making notes on her phone.

"Sure. Call you tomorrow?"

"Maybe," Camden said. She stood, wanting to make a fast run for the door, but there were too many people crowded around the exit.

Levi took her hand. "I thought you would be excited. You're getting the trail."

"And you're getting rid of it," she said. Camden pushed through the crowd until she was outside. She gulped in big breaths of cold December air, wanting to wake up from whatever ugly dream this was. No matter what she did, though, she was still here on the lawn outside town hall. Thom and the rest of the community members were flowing out the doors, talking excitedly about the probability of increased tourism and what it could mean for their businesses.

Levi exited the building, saw her and walked quickly to her side. "I don't know what you think I did wrong, but I was only trying to figure out a way to make the bike trail workable for everyone."

Camden laughed even though she didn't find Levi's words funny. She found them awful. She'd fallen in love with him, she'd told him she loved him. And he had yanked the life she was trying to build for herself away in a second.

"No, you weren't. You were trying to make it workable for you, because you didn't want to deal with tourists hiking or bicycling near your retired, lazy-bones cattle. What did you think, that a hiker was going to be so enamored of those slow-moving cows that they'd pitch their tent right there in your field and never leave?"

"Technically it's your pasture, not mine. And, yeah, I was worried about people who don't know how to handle cattle being too near them, or leaving their trash where the cows can get at it, or where predators like coyotes or wolves could find it *and* the cattle. It will be safer this way, believe me."

"Ha," Camden said and walked away, willing Levi not to follow her. He did.

"'Ha' what?"

"Ha to the thought that you were thinking about the inconvenience of the trail to anyone but yourself. None of the other ranchers—and some of them have Herefords and Angus, which are much more lively beasts—seemed to mind the bike trail crossing their land."

"It was a business decision, Cam. I wasn't trying to hurt you."

"Why is it that when people screw over other people they always say, 'it's business, it's not personal'? It is personal, Levi. I had plans for the area near the spur."

"So you'll move the plans a little closer to the actual training area. Is that such a bad thing?"

Camden threw out her hands. It was as if he were actually trying not to understand her point of view. As if he were intentionally trying to push her away. Fear lashed out at her. That was what this was. His way of backing out of their affair because she'd said she loved him and he didn't love her back. Pain at the realization racked Camden's body. It was bad enough that he didn't love her back, but that he was willing to sandbag her plans… She'd thought Levi was different from Grant. Different from her mother. She'd thought he understood her need to be heard, but he didn't hear her any better than the other people in her life did.

Worse, she thought back to the things she'd told him. He had pushed and accused and pushed some more until she laid her heart and soul bare, but he hadn't laid his own past out for her. Why hadn't he tried harder to return to his career in football? Why was expanding the dairy so damned important to him? She didn't have a clue, not to any of it, because while Levi wanted to know everything about her past, he wasn't willing to share details about his own.

The unfairness of it all struck Camden like a blow.

"I told you about everything. Grant. Heather. My mother. The way I let all of them direct me where they wanted me to be, and I told you I wanted to direct my own life now. Make my own decisions."

"I'm not stopping you from doing that." He cocked his head to the side as if he couldn't understand what she was saying. Camden decided to spell it out for him.

"But you are. You took the one thing I wanted for *me*, for my future, and you handed it over to the state, and for what? So you wouldn't be inconvenienced in the tiniest way. And while I'm telling you all of that, while

I'm trying to figure out how to be the person I want to be, you're in your own little hidey-hole pretending nothing is wrong in your life."

"Nothing is wrong with my life."

"You walked away from a career you loved. You could have kept on with football, but you got injured and you ran away from it. And as for me, you didn't just want to know why I came back to Slippery Rock, you demanded to know the reasons. Was that so you could use those reasons against me? Figure out what makes Camden tick, what makes her angry, what she wants the most? Toy with her a little bit and then take everything away from her? Did you get some kind of warped joy from that?"

"I wasn't toying with you, Cam, and this wasn't a ploy to hurt you. I was only—"

"Protecting your land and sacrificing mine in the process." Camden sighed. He reached for her, but she backed away. If he touched her now she might shatter, and she was not going to break down in front of Levi. She would hold it together, because he didn't deserve the satisfaction of seeing just how badly he'd hurt her. "Just leave me alone, Levi. I can't be around you right now," she said and walked away.

Camden slipped into the front seat of her car

and started driving. She didn't care where she was going as long as it was away from Levi Walters. Another wave of pain hit her heart when she realized how easily he had let her go.

CHAPTER FOURTEEN

TWO DAYS HAD passed since Camden had walked out on him after the town meeting, and Levi still hadn't heard from her. He'd tried calling, but it always went straight to voice mail. Had stopped by the training area when she was usually working, but Camden wasn't there. Even Calvin and Bonita were avoiding him, although they at least were speaking to him. They just weren't speaking much.

He threw a dart at the board on the wall. It hit the bull's-eye. Just figured that when he drove Camden out of his life he'd start playing darts well again. Levi crossed to the board, pulled the three darts from the wall and threw away. Two bull's-eyes and a five. Not bad considering.

The door opened then closed, but Levi kept throwing. He didn't want to talk to anyone, and if he stared at the dartboard hard enough, no one would bother him.

The sound of tennis shoes squeaked against

the hardwood floor, along with the padding of dog feet. Adam. Of course it would be Adam.

"Destroying the dartboard on a Tuesday. Must be some kind of week."

Levi grunted but didn't stop throwing the darts. Gathering them from the board. Throwing again.

Adam would get the hint. After all, it hadn't been that long ago he'd been even more ticked at the world than Levi was at this moment. After being diagnosed with epilepsy from the damage the tornado did to his body, Adam had tried to shut them all out. Friends, family. Jenny. Levi finished his beer and signaled Juanita for another.

From the corner of his eye, he saw Adam take in the two other empties and whistle low. "Definitely not a great start to Levi's week."

Levi threw three more darts, but Adam didn't leave. Levi gathered the darts he'd been throwing along with another set and lined up before the board.

"In case you're wondering, Camden's back at the dog school."

The dart in his hand flew, missed the target and clattered to the ground.

"Good for her," Levi said.

"She's been staying at Julia's."

Levi let another dart fly, and once more the thing clattered to the ground. Levi narrowed his eyes. He just needed to concentrate on the target a little more. He'd get his stroke back. Just like he'd gotten it back after the injury to his knee. Adam seemed to want an answer to his statement. "Okay, good for her," Levi said after a long minute. Where Camden was staying wasn't his concern. He might want to know, but he didn't need to know, not after the way she'd accused him of trying to sabotage her life.

He'd been trying to do something nice for her.

After she told him she loved him, he'd been making himself crazy trying to figure out a way to show her he loved her, too. Adam had done the picture thing, James the handcuffs. The only thing Levi knew Camden wanted, aside from training Six, was for the rail trail to be completed. Having random tourists traipsing across his property, even if it was only an easement to his property, made Levi nervous.

Dairy cattle were some of the gentlest creatures on the planet, but accidents happened every day. What happened if a cow got scared and trampled a hiker? Putting the trail on the spur, an area of land nobody was using, made much more sense. Not only that, but that area would add a challenge element to the Slippery Rock portion of the trail. Win-win.

"Why'd you do it?"

Levi frowned at Adam. "I didn't do anything except push forward a plan that I never wanted in the first place. For her." He threw again, and this time the dart flew true, landing a millimeter outside the bull's-eye. Not bad after the last two throws.

"And you didn't tell her that?"

"She was too busy accusing me of being some kind of cross between her idiot ex, her mother and the chick who pretended to be her bestie for the title of bridesmaid." Levi threw again and again hit the bull's-eye. Who knew darts were therapeutic?

"Maybe you should try again," Adam suggested.

"Maybe you should mind your own business."

"Damn, I thought we'd worked you through this grouch stage after the knee injury."

"I'm not grouchy. I'm trying to play darts."

Although, he had to admit, he wasn't exactly happy. Not about Camden walking out. Not about the way he'd handled it when she told him she loved him. Not about any of it. And now there was nothing he could do about it.

"You want some free advice?"

"Not really."

"You want Camden?"

Levi turned to look at Adam. His best friend, who had come very close to walking out on his family a couple of months before because he didn't want to hurt them. But Adam had stayed.

"Yeah. I want Camden."

"Then you're going to have to tell her."

And with that statement Adam left the bar, and Levi went back to throwing darts. Tell Camden how he felt. To what end? She'd already walked out on him. Already accused him of things he didn't deserve.

Although, come to think of it, maybe he did. She was right that he had made demands on her that he hadn't followed through on from his side of things. Levi had never walked out on a wedding, but he had walked away from a career that was important to him. Because of an injury, but he'd still walked away. When he could have just told Camden how he felt about her, he'd instead come up with an elaborate plan that had blown up in his face. Now he was alone. In a bar. Throwing darts at a wall while trying to convince himself he'd done nothing wrong.

When the truth was, he'd done everything wrong.

How many times had Camden told him she didn't want to be controlled? That she wanted to make decisions based on her personal wants and needs and not those of other people?

He had to show her he wasn't trying to control her with the trail decision; he was merely trying to give her what he believed she wanted.

CAMDEN CLICKED THE mechanism in her pocket, and Six responded by crouching beside one of the tunnel runners, as if waiting for the moment he could pounce on an intruder. She needed the dog to learn to wait there, no matter how long, because there would be times when the animals he herded would not be quick to move.

Something caught Six's attention, and he moved his head. Camden clicked until the dog refocused on her. "Steady," she instructed the dog. "We're waiting."

This time, Camden heard the movement behind them, too. She clicked so Six would stay and turned, expecting to see Grandmom with a thermos of coffee. Camden had taken to having her lunch at the training area since coming back to the dog school after hiding at Julia's for a couple of days.

Hiding hadn't sat well with Camden. Neither had not answering the phone calls that continuously came in, so she'd turned off her phone and no longer carried it with her. Because of that, Bonita would come to the training area every few hours, just to see if Camden needed anything.

Only it wasn't Bonita holding the thermos of coffee. It was Levi. Camden clenched her fist around the clicker, setting off a single click that released Six from his hold. The dog trotted over to Levi, rubbing his head against his leg.

He wore that Carhartt jacket that made his shoulders look so wide. Jeans and boots. The familiar football cap on his head. He looked good. Too good. She hadn't wanted to see him, not until she was over him. However long that might take. She'd been prepared to become a hermit, only leaving the dog school for funerals and weddings, all in an effort to avoid him. Not the most adult of plans, but it beat the alternative, which was leaving Slippery Rock so she wouldn't be faced with the colossal mistake she'd made by falling for Levi Walters.

She might not have the man she loved, but

she had found herself here, in a tiny map dot of a town that threw a monthlong celebration of Christmas and New Year's.

"Hello, Levi," she said, proud that her voice was steady.

"Bonita said you might need this," he said, holding out the thermos. Camden took it and set it down quickly on the seesaw apparatus. The usually cool metal was warm from Levi's hands, and she couldn't feel his heat, not right now.

"Don't pet the dog," she said when Levi reached toward Six's ears. His hand stilled, and the dog whined. Damn it, the poor thing only wanted a little head scratch. She shook her head and Levi scratched, and the dog sighed happily. "What do you want, Levi?"

He reached into the pocket of his coat. "I was hoping to have better news." He handed her the sheet of paper from the trail designers, accepting the new layout of the trail. "I asked Thom if he could stop it, put the trail back along the actual route instead of the spur, but the designer won't budge."

"Great. Thanks for the good news."

She turned away from him but didn't hear him leaving. So she turned back around. "What? You want to check up on me, see if I'm handling the disappointment of loving you well? Make sure I'm not a puddle of goo because you don't love me back?"

"I do love you."

That stopped Camden cold. "Don't." She didn't want him to say that just to make her feel better. Although stomping all over his heart the way he'd stomped on hers wasn't the worst idea in the world.

"I love you. I think it happened somewhere between seeing you in that wedding dress in the bar and that first kiss outside the barn. But I didn't realize I loved you until after you said you loved me. But we were in the middle of making love, and I didn't want you to think I was confusing sex with love, so I didn't say it back. Then I thought maybe you needed a grand gesture—"

Camden didn't want to believe him, but his brown gaze was focused and clear. "And you thought putting the trail through the spur would show me that you loved me?"

Levi shrugged. "I knew you were in favor of the trail, that you had good memories of the trail up north. I wanted to give you a trail here. The original route would have mostly bypassed Harris Land. The spur puts part of it directly on your land."

"You mean my grandfather's land."

"I mean your family's land. It'll be yours someday, legally, but it's already in your blood. It's a part of you." Levi twisted his mouth. "I'll admit, moving the trail to the spur meant less work for me, but mostly, it was about giving the trail to you. To walk, to use with the dogs."

"You…you wanted to give me a trail?" It was too crazy, too weird, too unlike Levi. He couldn't have believed that approving a rail trail to run directly through the area she wanted to use for training would show her how much he loved her.

She didn't need a grand gesture. She only needed him.

"I've never been in love with someone before. I love my family, my friends. But I've never let a woman get that close to me. Not because I was afraid or had been hurt, but because I like to plan. I planned my way to the football scholarship and then to a draft choice. I planned how I'd expand the dairy. The knee injury, that was unplanned, and it moved up my timetable, and I've been so conscious of that change that I started overcompensating in other areas. I thought if I told you how I felt on my terms it would be easier to control the feelings."

Camden shook her head. "I've never been in love before, either, but even I know you don't get to control feelings like love."

"I guess I'm a slow learner." He took another piece of paper from his pocket and handed it to her. Camden opened it and found a map.

There was an X marking an area with training tunnels and other apparatus. Levi pointed at the X. "That's where we are now." He pointed to another X. "That's the land I've been renting from Calvin." There was another X, just past the rented land.

"What's that?"

"That's about ten acres of completely worthless land. It's too rocky and steep for the older cows to be safe there, and it would take too much money to make it habitable for them. So it's just sitting there. Useless, at least to a dairy farmer."

Camden swallowed, and focused her gaze on him. "Levi—"

"I was thinking that I needed a grand gesture to show you how much I love you, and it occurred to me, over a game of darts, that maybe what I needed to show you was how much I believe in you." He handed her a third piece of paper. "It's yours, Camden. You can use those acres for your on-the-job training sessions with the dogs, if you choose to. I figure since you don't mind hiking all the way out to the spur, you won't mind hiking past a few head of cattle."

"You don't have to give me ten acres of your property to prove a point."

"I know." His fingers traced over her chin, and it was all Camden could do not to press her lips into his palm "Consider it an early Christmas present. I love you, Camden. I want you to build this dog school to be whatever you want it to be. I want you to stay in Slippery Rock. I want you to be with me."

Her heart beat rapidly in her chest. She wanted to be with him, to build up the school, to make her grandparents proud. To stay in Slippery Rock. Mostly, though, she wanted Levi. "I didn't get you anything."

"You already gave me the most important gift in the world."

"What's that?"

"Your heart," he said.

Camden looked at Levi and knew there were tears in her eyes. "I do love you, Levi Walters."

"And I do love you, Camden Harris," he said as flakes of snow began falling from the gray sky. Levi grinned.

Camden put her arms around Levi's neck.

"Snow before Christmas. You said that never happens in Slippery Rock."

Levi gathered her in his arms and kissed her. "It's a season for miracles," he said.

* * * * *

Get 2 Free Books,

Plus 2 Free Gifts —

just for trying the Reader Service!

HRLP17R3

Get 2 Free Books,
Plus 2 Free Gifts—

just for trying the Reader Service!

Get 2 Free Books,
Plus 2 Free Gifts—
just for trying the
Reader Service!

READERSERVICE.COM

Manage your account online!

- Review your order history
- Manage your payments
- Update your address

> *We've designed the*
> *Reader Service website*
> *just for you.*

Enjoy all the features!

- Discover new series available to you, and read excerpts from any series.
- Respond to mailings and special monthly offers.
- Browse the Bonus Bucks catalog and online-only exculsives.
- Share your feedback.

Visit us at:

ReaderService.com